USA TODAY BESTSELLING AUTHOR

Dale Mayer

Tomas's TRIALS

HEROES FOR HIRE

TOMAS'S TRIALS: HEROES FOR HIRE, BOOK 27
Beverly Dale Mayer
Valley Publishing Ltd.

ISBN-13: 978-1-773365-60-2
Print Edition

Books in This Series:

Levi's Legend: Heroes for Hire, Book 1

Stone's Surrender: Heroes for Hire, Book 2

Merk's Mistake: Heroes for Hire, Book 3

Rhodes's Reward: Heroes for Hire, Book 4

Flynn's Firecracker: Heroes for Hire, Book 5

Logan's Light: Heroes for Hire, Book 6

Harrison's Heart: Heroes for Hire, Book 7

Saul's Sweetheart: Heroes for Hire, Book 8

Dakota's Delight: Heroes for Hire, Book 9

Michael's Mercy: Heroes for Hire, Book 10

Tyson's Treasure: Heroes for Hire, Book 11

Jace's Jewel: Heroes for Hire, Book 12

Rory's Rose: Heroes for Hire, Book 13

Brandon's Bliss: Heroes for Hire, Book 14

Liam's Lily: Heroes for Hire, Book 15

North's Nikki: Heroes for Hire, Book 16

Anders's Angel: Heroes for Hire, Book 17

Reyes's Raina: Heroes for Hire, Book 18

Dezi's Diamond: Heroes for Hire, Book 19

Vince's Vixen: Heroes for Hire, Book 20

Ice's Icing: Heroes for Hire, Book 21

Johan's Joy: Heroes for Hire, Book 22

Galen's Gemma: Heroes for Hire, Book 23

Zack's Zest: Heroes for Hire, Book 24

Bonaparte's Belle: Heroes for Hire, Book 25

Noah's Nemesis: Heroes for Hire, Book 26

Tomas's Trials: Heroes for Hire, Book 27

Carson's Choice: Heroes for Hire, Book 28

Dante's Decision: Heroes for Hire, Book 29

Steven's Solace: Heroes for Hire, Book 30

Boxed Sets and Bundles
https://geni.us/Bundlepage

About This Book

Tomas is excited about this new direction in his life. Working for Levi allows him to use his vast array of skills in new and varied ways. He doesn't expect to be sent undercover in a supremacy group, loaded with weapons. Yet what he finds is much more complicated than that.

Amber had joined the group to help get her friend away from the members, only to find out her friend is dead, and no one will talk about it. The group is in the middle of a coup from within, as the leader barely maintains control. It's a dangerous place to be, but she is not leaving without answers. Needing help, she contacts an old friend. Tomas isn't what she expects.

Still, as long as he will help her do what she needs to do—before she gets into further trouble—he is fine with her. Except it doesn't take long for both of them to realize that the danger is escalating to the point where it is possible that neither of them will leave the compound—at least not alive.

Sign up to be notified of all Dale's releases here!
https://geni.us/DaleNews

Prologue

B ACK AT LEGENDARY Security HQ, Levi walked into the massive dining room. "What do you think about this guy?" he asked Ice, dropping a file in front of her.

She flipped it open, looked at it. "Tomas. I brought up his name last year."

"Why didn't we go with him then?"

"Just after I talked to him, he got hurt."

"What's his status now?"

"Let me see." She pulled out her phone and called him. "Tomas, how are you doing?" A strong male voice came through her cell, and she turned on Speaker.

"I'm doing well," he replied. "How are you?"

"I'm doing fine, and Levi's on here with me. We're looking for some more men."

"Oh, hell. I figured I would be out of the running for good after last time."

"What happened?" Levi interjected.

TOMAS STARED AT the phone. "I was shot on a mission. A revenge scenario," he explained.

"Fully recovered?"

"No. Well, as recovered as I'll be," he noted, not pulling any punches. "I'll always walk with a bit of a limp."

"Anything else?"

"Isn't that enough?"

"Nope," Levi stated. "If it's just a limp, I'm good with that. Are you still a weapons specialist?"

"For anything I've had a chance to work on, yes," he agreed, "but I've been out of touch for the last six—make that eight—months."

"That's fine," Levi replied. "We're looking for somebody to take over. One of our people who handles some ops for us is pregnant."

"Pregnant?" Tomas shook his head at that. "You have a female field agent there?"

"Several actually, but Kai is pregnant, so we're changing her duties temporarily, so we've got her in charge of the arsenal for a bit."

"Makes sense to me. Is this a full-time or part-time gig for me?" he asked. "I never expected to take over for someone on maternity leave."

Levi burst out laughing. "You should be honored in this case, if you get the opportunity."

"So, what do I need to do? Try out or something?"

"Not so sure about that, but we do have a job opening. If you want to come on as a spare," Levi offered, "we'll see how it works out."

"I can do that," Tomas replied.

"Are you on any medication?" Ice asked.

"Nope, I came off the last of them a couple weeks ago."

"And what were they for?"

"Blood thinners. I was having clotting issues early on."

"Interesting," she murmured. "But, as long as you're healthy enough, and you think you're ready to give it a go, we're more than ready to give you a shot."

"Perfect. What's the job?"

Levi and Ice both hesitated, then Levi looked over at her, shrugged, and said, "We might as well tell him."

"Tell me what?" Tomas asked curiously. "I don't like going into things without knowing at least a little about what I'm dealing with."

"That's fair," Ice agreed. "We have news of a militia group that's collecting weapons and possibly women."

"Where?"

"Just outside of Houston here," Levi noted. "We don't get too many local jobs, and we have a lot of people who want to do this one. So, while we do have men available, we just thought it might be an opportunity to see how you handle things."

"If you say so," he stated, "I'm totally up for it."

"Whereabouts are you right now?"

"Dallas," he replied, "so I can be in Houston in just a few hours."

"Good. I'll set you up at a hotel with an alias to check in."

"A hotel?"

"Yep, you'll be joining the group as a friend of a woman who's already inside. Amber contacted us a couple days ago. She wanted in to help free her friend from it, but that friend is now dead, so Amber's looking for help. Not just to get herself out but to burn the group to the ground."

"Ah, undercover then. That's perfect. You got a story for me?"

"Yep, I do." Levi chuckled. "It's a doozy. If you're in, I'll send you the details in a minute."

"I am definitely in," Tomas replied, "particularly for bringing down something like this."

"Absolutely. Way too much of this shit happening in town right now."

"Send me the details. I'm packing already." And, with that, Tomas hung up, a broad smile on his face.

When Ice had called him before his injury, he'd been thrilled. Only two months out of the navy, he was at loose ends, figuring out what to do next, when she had contacted him. But, sure as hell, he'd been called back in because somebody had a grudge to settle, and Tomas had ended up in the middle and got shot. Now, here he was with the potential for a second chance. He felt good about that, particularly in this case.

He smiled a happy smile. Who the hell knew where this job would take him? Wherever that may be, he was more than ready for the journey. He'd had his fill of the last several months of nothing but rehab and physical therapy and just wanted back in the action. As he walked around his small apartment, his to-go bag in his hand, he took one final look.

If things worked out, he may never live here again.

And, with that thought, he walked out with a huge smile on his face.

Chapter 1

TOMAS SWIPED THE card key and stepped into his hotel room. It was empty, as expected. He quickly locked it behind him, dropped his bag, and sent a text to Levi. **I'm in.**

Levi's thumbs-up was a quick acknowledgment, followed by an incoming text. **Company coming your way in two minutes.**

Knowing this intel came from Levi, Tomas expected two minutes to be right on schedule. He stood in the middle of the room, mentally listening for the sound of footsteps coming in his direction.

Sure enough, within two minutes, a knock came on the door.

He quickly stepped behind the door and pulled it open. In walked Saul and Dezi, both men Tomas knew. He looked down the hallway, then closed the door behind them. He smiled. "Now these are faces that I haven't seen in a very long time."

They greeted each other, as always. Tomas had met these men in the line of duty and had served with them on multiple occasions. He was even happier to see them now. "Damn," Tomas muttered. "It's really good to see you guys."

"Same," Saul agreed, looking at him. "So how much experience do you have with the prepper world?"

"Not a whole lot." He shrugged. "And yet in a way, …

far too much."

"You'll have to explain that one," Dezi stated calmly, as he looked around the small room and sauntered over to sit in the single chair beside the only bed. "We'll need to know everything about whatever experience you do have."

"Any prepper experience I have," he explained, "comes from an older brother who got involved with a really heavy militia group." He winced. "He never joined the navy, like we did, and had no interest in anything to do with the government. Therefore, I was quite surprised that he ended up in civilian militia, until I realized it branched into all kinds of anti-movements."

"Like?"

"Anti-government, anti-authority, anti-everything it seems. It made more sense as I heard more about the group. It was right up his alley, and I knew he was hooked."

"Yeah, a lot of those are out there, aren't they?" Saul nodded.

"Too many, honestly," Tomas murmured.

"So what is your brother up to now?"

"He's dead," Tomas noted quietly. "Things got a little ugly at one of their meetings, and the cops came in heavy. Somebody started shooting, and the group returned fire, and the gunfight was on. He ended up taking a bullet, which nicked an artery, and he didn't make it."

"Wow," Dezi replied, fascinated. "You could definitely be the right person for the job then."

"It depends." Tomas frowned.

"On what?"

"On what you have in mind."

"Tell us everything you can. First, would you be recognized?"

Tomas sighed wearily. "I don't know anybody in those groups. My brother's death does give me some backstory and maybe a little bit of an edge on anybody who doesn't have any experience or knowledge of groups like these at all. I definitely had a lot of back-and-forth with my brother, as I tried to convince him to get the hell out. He wasn't having it though." His voice took on a note of sorrow, mixed with anger.

"He wanted nothing to do with the government or paying his damn taxes, but that was just the start of it. He definitely wouldn't serve his country," he murmured. "Honestly, my father really struggled with Torres's choices. Then, after my brother died, things just got worse. It certainly was harder for my father to deal with his loss because it was such a senseless death," he added quietly. "I mean, not that any death is ever good or makes sense, but, in this case, it just didn't need to happen. He didn't need to be involved with those people at all."

"No," Dezi murmured softly. "I agree with you there. Too often that's exactly what does happen though. You really try hard to keep everything normal. However, when one of the family goes off like that …"

"What are you even supposed to do?" Tomas asked, his voice riddled with memories.

"Sometimes you can't do anything," Dezi replied.

"It broke my mother's heart. And my dad took it really hard. I mean, losing a child isn't easy at any time, but in a deal like this? … Just makes it all the uglier."

"Did you have any contact with the group after that?"

"No, none at all," he confirmed. "Are we thinking it's the same group?"

"No, I don't think so. My guess is that Ice has already

run into this intel and has taken a deep look into what group your brother was in and where that was, so I would think that connection would be a long shot at this point."

"You've certainly got my attention," Tomas noted. "Can you fill me in a bit?"

"In this case," Dezi began, "Amber joined the group, hoping to get her friend out, but found out the friend was already dead by the time she was let in. Details are sketchy at this point, but what we do know is that Amber can't get out."

"So is she the one who contacted Levi and Ice?"

"Yes, some of her message was unclear. We're not sure, but maybe she can't get out safely, or maybe she thinks her friend was shot by somebody within the group. Either way, our job is to get her out."

"So you suspect the friend was murdered then," Tomas remarked quietly.

At that, Dezi nodded. "Yes. So it's not just Amber we're after. We're also trying to figure out just how far and wide the rot inside this group has gone."

Tomas stared at them, as he slowly sank onto the side of the bed. "That's interesting." He paused. "You know what? That angle never once occurred to me. I knew that my brother's life was in danger, but I never considered the idea of betrayal coming from within his own group."

Saul pointed out, "We're in an odd scenario here where it seems like a possibility. Who knows? Maybe something like that is what happened to your brother too, although the truth would be hard to find now."

"Wow." Tomas gave his head a shake and returned his attention to them. "It's too late for my brother but not for Amber," he stated. "If they are anything like my brother's group, I'm pretty sure something's seriously wrong with them. Anytime I talked to him, he seemed pretty strongly affected by the groupthink and was always spouting off about how the US needed to go back to the way it was and how he was part of a crew strong enough to make it happen." Tomas shook his head. "You know—that cult brainwashed stuff."

"We do, but, at the same time," Saul asked, "did he say anything specific that would give us something to go on or an angle to pursue?"

"Not that I know of, or maybe I just haven't thought of it much," he admitted. "Honestly we didn't know anything much about it until he was killed and only then what the cops told us. Supposedly he died in the middle of a gunfight, and he was on the wrong team, more or less. Obviously they didn't say it in those words, but the cops did ask us back then if we had any information about his associates. I wasn't even in the country at the time," he murmured. "So I had no answers for them."

"No, of course not. When you came back, did you look into it?" Dezi asked. "Sorry, I know this is painful and not the thing you want to be dealing with right now, but you must have had some inkling."

"I did. Absolutely." He got lost in his thoughts for a moment. "But I also knew that he was either bad news or somehow caught up in trouble all the time. I don't have any illusions about my brother, so let me make that clear. If anybody was looking for trouble and looking to get himself into something likely to blow up in his face, that would be Torres. Regarding the group and the cause, he was a die-hard believer, and it seemed almost a religion, cultish to me. I don't think he was a leader type, so always the follower."

Tomas stopped, then thought about it and shook his head. "No, I can't see him as a leader in the group at all. I see him as somebody who got caught up in it as a fervent follower. He's been dead a few years …" He stopped for a moment, making mental calculations, then added, "Four years, I guess. I lost track of time in the service and later with my injury and rehab, but I think it's been four years. So, not all that long. It just seems a lot longer."

"It also seems like a long time because you've been superbusy dealing with your own life."

"Absolutely." He nodded. "It feels strange to even think about it that way, but …" He shrugged. "My parents buried him, and we moved on."

"What else can you do?" Saul asked. "You carry on because that's what you've been left with."

Tomas smiled at them. "Exactly. Accept the facts. Move on. That's all there is to do with my brother's death."

At that, both men nodded. Just then the door burst open, and a tall lean woman with a long auburn braid stepped inside, closing the door quickly behind her. Saul opened his arms, and she raced into them.

"Oh my God," she murmured, "I'm so glad to see you."

Saul chuckled and turned to introduce her. "Tomas, this is Amber." Saul pointed his finger back and forth by way of introduction. "Amber Billings. An old friend."

Tomas looked at her in surprise. "I thought you couldn't get out." He walked over to shake her hand, with a welcoming smile.

She looked at him carefully. "Believe me. I'm definitely *not* out, and, if I want my life back, it'll take a whole lot more than slipping free of the noose," she noted. "As it is, I have to be back before someone notices that I'm missing."

She handed something to Saul, and her gaze shifted to Tomas. "We'll talk later. I don't know you."

"I don't know you either," Tomas repeated calmly.

She studied him, and then a narrow cunning look appeared in her gaze. "So I dropped the hint that I might want to bring in new blood. A friend. A special friend."

"Why would you do that?" Saul asked her.

"Because I'm getting some heat from some of the guys," she replied calmly. "I needed an excuse to keep them at bay, … like away from me."

"Like arm's distance away? Like physical touching distance?" Tomas asked curiously.

"Something like that," she murmured. She looked at the other men and continued. "The guys all have a code, but unfortunately some of these men tend to be on the raunchy side. In many ways, they are like a biker gang, and some believe women should be locked up and held tight. Otherwise the women are pretty free for anyone to use."

"I can certainly be your special friend, if you need me to be," Tomas stated, surprising them all, his mind racing at what she was dealing with.

It was apparently something she hadn't anticipated either, and she laughed. "You must be prepped to fight for me." She stared at him, smiling broadly.

"Interesting." He wondered what he had gotten himself into.

"Some of these guys are pretty … rough." She stopped to collect herself, then continued. "Let's just say I'm willing to take all the help I can get in order to get out."

"Why is it that you're going back if you're not comfortable?" Tomas asked, confused.

"Because someone else is still on the inside, so I need to

be there," she murmured. "And I know Saul and Dezi don't understand that, and they don't like that I'm going back, but, until you can get all the women out safely—those who want to leave, me included—I have to be there. That's non-negotiable." She had already made up her mind, and there was no way out of it. "It's just the way it needs to be."

"So, Amber," Tomas said, yet looking at Saul, who smiled and shrugged, "is this other person willing to be there?" He needed to ensure they were talking about a rescue, rather than a kidnapping.

"No," she confirmed. "She wants out, but getting her out, and everyone else, will be tricky."

"*Everyone else*? Great," Tomas noted. "I always like a challenge."

"My kind of man." She flashed him a smile. "When you see me, and I throw my arms around you and give you a big smacking kiss," she explained, "know that things have gotten a little bit uglier, and I needed the excuse to go a little further."

"Got it." Tomas nodded, and, with that, she was gone. "Wow. She's intense." Surprised and confused, he turned and looked at the others. "Interesting life you guys have."

"She and my wife are friends." Saul shrugged. "She's good people. I'm not terribly happy that she went into this on her own or that she keeps ignoring our warnings and going back."

Tomas snorted at that. "That's not exactly a surprise," he murmured. "Most people don't respond well to orders, and my sense is that she is a freaking force of nature. You know? Like a thunderbolt."

Saul chuckled and nodded. "But everybody needs to listen to sage experienced advice sometimes," he added. "It might keep them alive."

"I hear you there. So who is this other person she wants to get out so badly?"

"We're trying to track down information on her now," Dezi shared. "But we don't really have anything much to go on so far." Saul remained silent, lost in his thoughts.

Tomas knew too well that scenario could be deadly. Things tended to go sideways when you didn't have enough intel. He worried about that, but not a whole lot he could say. As he looked around, he asked, "What is your take on this then? Are you guys in or out?"

"I've been in already. I came from one of their other bands," Dezi explained, with an eye roll. "Saul is keeping an eye on the outside."

"Good enough."

"So let's get our stories straight. You and I are friends." Dezi pointed at Tomas, then turned toward Saul. "And you, I don't see."

Saul chuckled. "Exactly."

"Simple, I like it." Tomas laughed too.

Then Saul added, "I'll head out back to avoid anyone. Plus, I need to send in some reports and pick up a few supplies. I'll see you on the ground." And, with that, he just walked out. Tomas wasn't surprised, as many people in this line of work weren't big on formalities; their focus was purely business.

Tomas waited until the door closed, before he turned and looked at Dezi and asked, "And what is my relationship with you?"

"We're friends," he repeated, adding, "from the same division that I'm from."

"Has anybody checked into your background?"

"They sure have," he said cheerfully. "You can bet that, when it comes to these things, we set them up perfectly."

"I'm sure you did. The story has to be solid with guys like this. They are always suspicious as hell."

"That's also why Amber has to watch her every step. She' pretty stubborn and won't leave until she gets her answers."

"That's not good."

"Nope, it sure isn't, but she's a little more obstinate than most," he stated, with half a smile.

"Got it. Okay, so what's our plan of action?"

And Dezi laid out the plan as he had it. "Remember. We're just gathering information, while trying to get Amber out, collecting as much evidence as we can for the cops," he reminded Tomas. "We're not there to take down the group or to start World War III."

"Sounds like they're already pretty edgy about starting a war to begin with," he murmured.

"I think they're dying to start it, and I'm pretty sure that's what the girlfriend's murder was about. It also sounds like maybe it's similar to what your brother went through, but that group of men wanted to be warriors, and, of course, … the ultimate warrior is the one who takes a life."

"Sure, but a real warrior isn't just somebody who takes lives," Tomas protested. "It should be somebody who understands the value of life and only takes one when there's no other way."

At that, Dezi looked at him and nodded appreciatively. "Glad to hear you say that," he noted, "because, in this place, sometimes people don't know the difference. Now you need to understand these people. Stop thinking about yourself as a warrior and be the spy this time."

THE WHOLE PURPOSE of getting free of her guard was to see who Tomas was. Having accomplished that, Amber also knew that absolutely no way could she stay gone much longer. She returned to the mall, breathless, bolted downstairs, taking the steps two at a time, until she slipped into the ladies' room. She needed to go badly and then stepped out, all in record time. As she did, her handler, as she liked to call him, stepped out and glared at her.

"Will you stop taking so damn long?" Brutus spat.

"Hey, when Mother Nature calls," she snapped, with a shrug, "what am I supposed to do?"

The fact of the matter was, he didn't give a shit. He'd prefer it if Mother Nature didn't call at all. Then he could keep her under watch all the time. She wasn't exactly sure how she'd become somebody who had to be under guard all the time, but somehow she had.

It was also a very strange feeling, having somebody always looking after her—or spying on her. It might be because of her dead friend Annette or because Amber was a single female. It was hard to know. Annette had supposedly died under natural circumstances, but Amber had yet to see any proof of that.

In Amber's mind, no doubt this group had done this a time or two before, and it really made Amber mad to think of somebody like Annette falling in with this group. Early on, she may have had a chance to get out, but she'd stayed too long. Nobody had been there for Annette, and that was something that Amber would always regret.

Annette had written her a letter, saying that she was in deep trouble. Amber had come running but had been too late. And that was the only reason she was still with this group. She wanted to make sure that these assholes paid, but, to do that, she needed to get as much information as she could. And now she needed to help the other women, as needed.

To help her, she'd called Saul, and Saul had a perfect solution, or at least she hoped it was. Only time would tell. She quickly hustled to keep up with her guard, Brutus. The name was most apt. The males all had a chance to change their names when initiated. They picked the names that they liked and wanted to be associated with.

So Brutus was it. He was rough, uncivilized, and didn't give a shit about anyone or anything. He loved his guns a little too much for her comfort. He even slept with them. He liked his booze about the same.

He'd held one of his *pretty beauties*, as he so lovingly called his handguns, against her throat multiple times, reminding her who was boss in this dynamic. But, so far, he hadn't crossed the line, and she wasn't sure why, but that's what bothered her the most. It was like walking a double-edged sword, and she didn't know when she would fall and be cut in half.

She'd always expected this shit to blow up in her face; she just didn't know when. She could only hope that she would survive whatever the hell was coming her way, but the more help she could get on her side, the better her chances were.

And having Saul out there was a huge help. She almost never got a chance to get into town. The group bought all their supplies in bulk, and usually one of the guys did the errands. But today was a different story, and she'd asked, pleaded really, just for a chance to get out. And having done that had given her a chance to meet up with Saul and to get a visual on Tomas.

She couldn't let Annette down. Not now. The fact that Peaches was desperately trying to get out herself was another hard reality. These women didn't have anywhere to go and nobody to help them, and that made it almost impossible for them to leave.

When Amber was cuffed a little heavily on the side of her head, she cried out and turned to glare at Brutus.

Brutus glared back. "Come on! I called you twice." He shook his head. "Remind me why the hell we even have women in the group?"

As a woman hater, that made him even more dangerous.

He just wanted an excuse to pop one on her head or to smack her. At the same time, she'd already figured out that he wasn't interested in her sexually, and she was damn grateful for that. But it also made him something of an anomaly in the world of wannabe-warriors and frustrated men. It was like he didn't want any women around, unless he could beat on them. She was sure that the world would be a much better place without him.

Chapter 2

W HEN AMBER EXITED the vehicle at the compound, she quickly helped unload the groceries. The protocol was clear: pick up and carry them into the kitchen. As she walked inside, her gaze quickly flickered to Peaches. Her anguished eyes flared with relief, as soon as she saw Amber.

Amber quickly dropped the bag of groceries she was carrying on the counter.

"How was town?" Mary asked her curiously. Mary was always upbeat and totally okay with anything that went on in this place. It's almost like she didn't have a brain in her head. But she did, and anybody who misjudged her would surely pay the price.

"Busy," Amber replied. "The traffic was a mess."

"Houston traffic is the worst. One of the reasons I won't go into town anymore," she said calmly. "Who the hell needs that?"

Amber nodded. "Still, it was nice just to get out for a moment."

"I don't know about that." Mary studied Amber carefully. "I wouldn't have thought getting out was anything you'd enjoy. Why would you?"

She turned in surprise. "Just a change." She shrugged. "Nothing wrong with that."

"No, nothing wrong with that," Mary repeated, but an

odd note filled her voice.

Enough to remind Amber that she could never discount this woman, the head guy's wife or girlfriend or whatever. She was dangerous and difficult at the best of times. And, at the worst of the times, she was totally amiable, which made it easy to forget that she had another side. Sometimes Amber worried that the damn woman had a split-personality disorder.

Under everyone's watchful eye, Amber quickly put away the groceries, knowing the chance of ever being accepted in a place like this was nonexistent. While that was a good thing, as far as she was concerned, it also made her job to get more info more difficult, more complex, with too many moving pieces.

When she had put up all the food, she walked over to the coffeepot and poured herself one.

"Now you can help Peaches with the potatoes," Mary stated calmly.

Maybe *calmly* and in a decent tone of voice but it meant *Do it, and do it now.*

Amber nodded, walked over, picked up a paring knife, and got to work. She didn't say anything to Peaches but casually asked Mary, "How were things while we were gone?"

"Peaceful as always," she replied. "That's the nice part of coming back to a refuge."

"Exactly," Amber murmured.

And, with that, Mary walked to the other room.

Peaches kicked Amber ever-so-slightly, as if warning her of something she had missed. She looked at her friend and raised an eyebrow. Peaches just gave her a quick head shake.

Amber realized that maybe things hadn't gone quite as smoothly as Mary had described. Amber frowned at that but kept quiet. She was pretty darn sure that these guys and gals, with their extra paranoid personalities, had every room bugged.

So Amber spoke as if everything were normal. "We caught a couple sales today. I picked up a few extra bananas. I wasn't sure if banana breads were wanted," she added, carrying out a quiet conversation, until Mary walked back in again.

They had done a pretty good job on the potatoes. As she looked around, Amber asked, "What else can I do?"

Mary looked at her in surprise. "We need a dessert."

She picked up the bananas, and she asked eagerly, "How about a banana bread?"

Mary smiled, a first real smile at that. "Sure, that sounds great."

With that feedback, Amber mixed up ingredients for the banana bread. She knew that the only way to get along in this place was to work her ass off.

It truly seemed like the only thing appreciated around here was working yourself to death. Multiple houses were here on the acreage, and not everybody came to this communal area, but those who did were expected to be fed. Mary always made sure that they were.

Something was so very strange about the way this society functioned, and Amber had never gotten any explanation on the policies this group was founded upon. The only way to succeed here was to fake it till you make it, and that was all Amber could sort out.

Mary added, "Make sure you do lots."

"Sure," Amber replied, with a casual shrug, because to show any refusal or argument would get her smacked. "Banana bread is always good to eat the next day."

"There won't be any leftovers," Mary stated. "Got a couple new guys coming in tonight," she murmured.

"Sounds fun. We haven't had anyone new around in a while."

"Don't assume anything. We keep to ourselves as a rule. New people aren't always welcome."

Amber looked at her in surprise. "And here I thought you were the social one."

"I'd prefer we stick to ourselves and keep everyone else out, but always somebody from another group wants to join us and see how we run things," she muttered. "And that's what's happening tonight. So I certainly won't be socializing with them," she snapped. "They should learn from others."

That isolation mentality was something Amber had seen before with others here, but, at the same time, she presumed the visitors would be Dezi and his friend Tomas coming in. "Hey, new blood is always fun," she said, with a casual note.

"You say that now," Mary muttered. "I'd just rather not have any new blood. We have more than enough people for us to deal with now. The bigger you get, the more problems come up."

"I guess," Amber agreed, with an unconcerned shrug. "But it's also fun to get to know other people. I hadn't realized I was as social as I am, until I got here."

"Yet you're keeping all the men at arm's length," Mary stated, as she eyed Amber intently.

"And I told you why too," she said cheerfully.

"No point in saving yourself for somebody who'll never show," Mary snorted. "And it's pretty damn lonely if you're sleeping by yourself at night."

"I'm fine." Amber knew that Mary's insistence was getting louder and more obnoxious as time went on. At some point, Amber understood that she must come up with a better excuse. Since she didn't have a whole lot of choice as to her timing of these things, it would be now or never. "Besides I haven't even heard from him in a while, but, the last time I did, he was planning a surprise for me."

"He better not just show up here out of the blue," Mary replied. "You know the men don't take to that very well."

"Not surprising," Amber agreed. "I don't know what he's up to." And she really didn't, but she truly hoped that this Tomas guy could handle himself. Otherwise they were all in deep shit.

She just barely got the banana bread pans in the oven before Mary called everybody for dinner. As Amber walked out to the other room, she was surprised at how fast the time had gone by. It was already going on six.

As the men gathered, one guy walked over and slung an arm around her neck and said, "See? I told you to stick around with us. You'll always do well here."

She smiled, slipped out from under his arm, and scolded him, "And I told you not to hang on to me like that."

He gave a raucous laugh. "One of these days you won't be playing quite so hard to get."

She rolled her eyes at him and quickly moved out of his reach. That would be the day that she ran into the woods, looking for Saul to get her ass out of here. But no way she could tell these guys about that. As she quickly took her seat, she noted more chairs were around the table.

Her gaze quickly swept the room, and then she saw the men, standing off to the corner. She gasped because, sure enough, there was Dezi, with Tomas right beside him. She bounded to her feet and raced toward them.

When he caught sight of her, a grin lit his face. He

opened his arms, and she bolted right into them.

As they closed around her, he whispered, "Looks like good timing."

"The best," she murmured quietly, as she hugged him close. There was a deafening silence for a few moments, then immediately everyone started talking around them. While she tried to step back, he kept his arms wrapped around her and kissed her. A kiss that was hard, fast, and incredibly possessive.

As much as it caught her off guard, it also gave her confidence that he knew what this scenario was like, and maybe, just maybe, they would get out of this alive.

She stepped back, then turned and looked at Dezi and grinned. "I didn't know you were bringing him," she said in delight.

"No, it was meant to be a surprise." He chuckled. He looked at the table, then rubbed his stomach. "It smells like we made it just in time for dinner."

"Of course." Amber quickly motioned toward the table. But they had garnered a lot of interest, which was expected, because she had drawn a lot of attention as a single female. Unwanted attention. Yet that didn't matter to these guys. She would need to do an awful lot to get that calmed down because this stake-a-claim-for-the-single-gal frenzy wouldn't end anytime soon.

She quickly pulled out a chair beside hers and parked Tomas at her side. She picked up the platters and started moving them quickly around the table. It was a jovial atmosphere, as people asked questions, and Mary even looked over at Amber with a bright smile. "So he was real."

"He always was," she stated, with a beaming smile, trying to make it obvious to everyone that she was thrilled. But she also knew that some of these guys weren't so happy. They looked over at Tomas, having noticed a limp as he walked across the room.

She wondered about that too, not sure how that would help her chances. She knew too well that anybody who was even one percent less physically dominating in a place like this would end up in trouble. She thought about it for a quick moment, then dismissed it. She couldn't deal with it all right now, so she'd deal with what she could, and hopefully they would find another way around the rest. And, regardless of his limp, he looked like he could hold his own. He was big, like Dezi, but harder-looking, like Saul.

He didn't look like the kind who couldn't hold his own, but, at the same time, Amber didn't know what he was really like because she hadn't had the chance to get to know him yet. When she looked over at him, she leaned forward and whispered, "Glad to have you here."

He turned his head, caught her quickly, and gave her a gentle kiss. "Glad to be here," he murmured, as if trying to put everybody's mind at ease.

She also knew this relationship would likely start problems.

Wolf laughed. "Interesting timing for you to show up. We thought it would take a flip of a coin to get her laid."

At that, Dezi stared at Wolf, looking quite threatening. "Seriously?"

Wolf shrugged, with a look. "Hey, you know people take their women pretty serious here, and she's been unattached for quite a while."

"Does it look to you like I'm unattached?" Amber snapped. "I told you that I had somebody. You just weren't listening."

"We were listening, but, without anybody physically here, nobody would give a shit." Wolf smirked. "Single women don't stay single for long."

She shrugged. "I wasn't single," she replied bluntly. "Believe me. I'm happy Tomas is here too. After this many months apart, I am really glad to see you." She turned to look at Tomas. "It's been brutal."

Wolf turned toward Tomas suspiciously. "Why the hell did you leave her alone for so long?"

"Didn't intend on that," Tomas replied, "but sometimes family stuff has to be dealt with. I wanted her to come with me, but it wasn't to be."

"Yeah, and how's the family now?" Cal asked belligerently. "Maybe you should take a hike and go back and deal with them again."

At that, one of the other men laughed, then called him out. "Hey, Cal, you had your chance, and she wasn't willing to be with you. Maybe you should just butt out."

Cal shot him an ugly look. "You butt out, Steel. I don't even know who this guy is. How come you guys just let him into our group like this?"

"What did you say?" Steel shot Cal a scathing look and asked, "Are you doubting my judgment?"

All of a sudden, silence fell over the room. Cal shrugged. "Just saying. I don't know anything about this guy. For all I know, he's some spy or something."

"A spy?" Steel shot Cal a hard look. "That kind of projection just means you have something to hide."

"You know what? ... We don't discuss any business crap like this out in the open," Tomas snapped, with a hard look at Cal, and then turned to face Steel, the leader it seemed, "unless that's different here than it is back at my place."

"No, that's exactly how it is here." Steel was super pissed, and it showed. "Knock it off now, Cal!"

"Fine. Whatever then," Cal muttered.

"No *whatever* here." Steel glared at him. "Unless you want to have a little talk with me later."

"No, it's fine," Cal agreed quickly, swallowing a mouthful, as if to keep himself quiet and to not respond to the antagonism.

Still, it was obvious Cal wasn't happy, and that this discussion wasn't over yet.

Amber settled at Tomas's side and whispered, "Well, that's a great start."

"Not really," he murmured. Then he spied a currant on her plate. Stabbing it, he quickly popped it into his mouth.

She looked at him, her jaw-dropping act making him chuckle. "Nice," she teased, "really nice."

"Hey," he replied, "you didn't use to mind it at all."

"I still don't," she admitted. "It was just funny to have you do that." Then she reached over and hugged him tightly. "It's really good to see you."

"All right, knock it off, you two," one of the women said, adding an eye roll. "I get that you're happy to see him but enough already."

And, with that, Amber subsided, chuckling. "Got it."

As a tool to convince people that they really cared and missed each other, it seemed to be effective. She settled in her chair, then smiled at Tomas and proceeded to eat the rest of her dinner.

She couldn't help but think that this would be interesting.

DINNER WAS PRETTY much how Tomas had expected. A little jarring, with those few shots lobbed, as the men assessed him. Amber kept up with a bumbling commentary beside him, and he sensed the unrest in her movements.

He wasn't sure if anything had happened since he'd seen her at the hotel or not, but she was definitely nervous right now. She should have just stayed in town while she could. Maybe that would have made a difference, but, then again, if she was trying to help somebody else she obviously cared for, that attachment could get her killed, and that just wasn't an option.

It was funny that he already had a good idea of who Amber was. Even though he didn't know her, he definitely knew her type. And they were the ones looking out for the underdogs of the world. He casually glanced around at all the others, trying to pick up on the innuendos of who had gelled together, who stuck with who, and picking up on the body tells. There would be little time to get out if things went sideways, so he needed to know as much as he could. His first priority was the exit doors.

It was easy to see that several of the women were quite adjusted in their own happy-place, talking cheerfully, apparently without a care in the world. But some of the women were silent, too silent for him, and a few looked like they were frigging statues. Nobody was talking to him now. That made things a little bit awkward.

As he watched the room, one of the guys who had caused the ruckus—when Tomas had kissed their supposed prized possession—got up and left without another word.

As soon as he did, the atmosphere relaxed slightly. It was almost like that guy was the fucking executioner. Someone who did his job, then removed the body, so it was all good now.

One of the guys laughed, then looked over at Tomas. "You watch out for that one," he stated. "Cal's been after her for a long time."

"*Nah*, he hasn't been a bother at all." Amber laughed.

He just looked at her, then shook his head. "You know he is."

She shrugged. "I never gave him any reason to think I was interested."

"Guys like that don't need a reason, honey." His voice slurred at *honey*. He finished his meal and headed out too.

Tomas looked over at her. "Problems?"

"Nope," she replied, trying for a bright smile. "Just somebody showing a whole lot more interest than I could dissuade him from."

At that, Tomas raised an eyebrow, knowing he was playing a set part. "Did he hurt you?"

"No, it didn't come to that," she stated, jumping in to try to make him feel better. "He was just persistent."

At that, Tomas turned and stared at the doorway through which the guy had gone because Tomas knew everybody else was watching him. "I can have a talk with him, when he comes back again," he said, as he looked at her. "And you stay away from him."

"Obviously," she noted. And then she tucked up close to him again and asked, "Did I tell you how happy I am to see you?"

"You did," he said, with a bright smile. "And I'm glad to hear it. Sounds like I wasn't a moment too soon."

"No," she agreed, "you weren't. And I'm still happy to see you."

He chuckled. "Good! Nutcase then. … We cannot

count him as a problem."

"No, I don't think so," she replied lightly but with a forced joviality in her tone. Then she whispered to him, "I'm not sure."

He nodded and swept a look around, just to see how everybody else was reacting to their interactions.

They were all seemingly just paying attention to what was going on but not in a way that concerned him, more like interest in seeing what he would do. He suspected he would have a fight on his hands the minute he let down his guard.

Something that he would do well to remember, though letting down his guard wasn't exactly an option. Not in a place like this. Too many people were always a little too eager to jump in and to take what he was leaving behind.

In this case it would be Amber.

It wasn't the same as most biker gangs, but definitely a code was here. She could say no, and most of the guys would respect that, but always one or two didn't give a shit what she said. It sounded like Tomas had literally shown up at the perfect time for her.

With that in mind, he quickly finished his meal, then looked over at her and asked, "So where are we staying?"

"If you had told me that you were coming," she said, with an eye roll, "I could have made things better."

"Doesn't matter anymore. It's all good," he replied.

"Of course it is, and we'll make the most of it. I do need to help with the dishes though," she added.

That note of anxiety in her voice made him wonder. He nodded. "I can give you a hand."

At that, she shook her head. "*Great.* Nobody would let me live that down."

He just smiled and carried the dishes into the kitchen,

then very quickly they made short work of the dishes. Several other women walked around and helped out.

Finally one of them nudged her gently. "Leave it. Go, go on, and be with him. You haven't seen him in forever."

"I know." Amber gave her friend a grateful look. "Thanks, Peaches." As she quickly stepped away from the kitchen, she grabbed Tomas's arm. "Come on! Let's go."

"I'm not sure where we're going."

"To our place," she murmured.

He hid his startled surprise at that. "Sounds good to me." He called out, "Good night," to the others, as they exited the kitchen.

Just out the connecting doorway, they passed Dezi, still in the dining room, who grinned from ear to ear.

"Good night," Dezi said, with a smile. "Talk to you in the morning."

Tomas nodded and let Amber lead him. As soon as they were outside, she kept pushing him forward. "I'm going. I'm going," he said, laughing. "Are we in that much of a hurry?"

"Maybe not," she replied, but then he realized that she really didn't feel comfortable with what was going on—or at least being around all these people.

When they made it farther away, she relaxed and whispered, "I'll show you where you're sleeping first." At a distance from the prying eyes, she stopped, looked up at him, and added, "We do have to keep up pretenses."

He shrugged and nodded. "I just need a place to lay my head."

She led him into what looked like a basement suite of one of the houses. "This is mine," she murmured.

"Good," he noted. "It looks decent."

"It is," she agreed. "This house is where Peaches lives,

and they've given me this space."

"Nice." He asked, "So you and Peaches? Everything okay there?"

"Well, yes and no," she replied, in an almost nonexistent whisper, coming close to him to avoid the potential for eavesdropping. "She's the one trying to get out."

At that, he went still and thought about it. "Interesting."

Amber nodded. "Peaches has been here a long time."

Tomas noted something familiar in her eyes that he had also seen in Peaches's gaze.

"I'm not exactly sure how she'll handle things, when she gets out of here, but she's looking to get out. She just doesn't have the financial means and has no friends on the outside. At least, not like I have Saul and Dezi and now you."

"And she has a partner?"

"She did, but he was killed," Amber murmured. "She's still adjusting to life as a single woman, and they won't let her be that way for much longer."

"She doesn't have a choice?" he asked, his voice taking on a hard tone.

"She does in a way. As long as she makes a choice that everyone around her approves of, she'll be okay, but she doesn't want anyone. She wants to get out before someone forces another relationship on her."

"I can understand that," he murmured. "*Nice* people, yet nicer digs here."

"Very close-knit too. You need to know that these guys are tight. They are very strongly united in what they think is right and wrong," she murmured. "Most of them are good and just looking for a place to belong. They want to live alone and off the grid, away from everybody."

"And yet they still want everything that society has to

offer, I presume."

"Yep, you better believe it, but still, I don't have a gripe with many of them, and a few of them are tolerable," she nodded. "But there are others, … and I'll give you some names." She took a deep breath before continuing again. "A few of them are bad news, and they prance around like they own you," she murmured. "Those are the ones you need to stay clear of," she warned Tomas.

"Those are the few who will be gunning for me after this," he noted. "I assume they'll test me."

"Probably," she murmured, "and all I can tell you is that most of them are not very fair. They say they have this code that they live by, but honestly it seems like whoever is the strongest can decide whatever rules they choose."

"A lot of people in this world live that way," he noted, with a smile. "And no need to worry. I get that the limp may be a concern, but I'm still plenty capable, physically speaking."

She hesitated, then nodded. "Thank you, I did wonder," she confessed. "Sorry."

"It's all right," he said, "consider it though. I'll be fighting for your safety after all. And Peaches too." He smiled. "You have every reason to be worried."

"Not really." She shrugged. "If you're part of Levi's team, I'm fully prepared to believe you can do everything you need to do."

"Good, because I can." If his tone seemed short, maybe she would forgive him. He was struggling with enough self-doubt in some areas of his life to begin with, but he knew that this was something he could handle. Guys were the same no matter where they were, and always somebody would push it. He'd had to prove himself time and time again, so all of this wouldn't be any different.

"I really can't guarantee that they won't jump you in the dark," she noted apologetically.

"Got it," he replied. "*Really* nice people."

"No, not really. I do like some things about them, but there's an awful lot about them that I don't," she murmured. "And the fact that I can't trust them is a big one."

"But, looking at it from their point of view," he added, "they can't trust you either."

She nodded, giving him an odd look. "Exactly, and, because of that, it's hard to make friends."

"Yeah, it absolutely would be. I think, … hopefully you won't be here long enough to worry about it."

"God, I hope not," she replied, "but it's really disconcerting not knowing what's coming."

"So how do you plan to get your friend out?"

"I don't know. They don't really want to let her leave."

"Interesting, and why is that?"

"I don't know," she said. "I think because she's alone."

"Are they afraid she'll leave?"

"Possibly," she guessed. "I mean, why wouldn't she? It's not as if this is home for her anymore, not without a partner."

"Could part of it be that they don't have many women and that they want to keep what they've got?" he asked, checking her face for visible clues.

"That's quite possible," she admitted. "I hate to think that they would force her to stay, but, when she did try to talk to them about leaving, she got a flat-out response. 'No, and don't even think about it or talk about it ever again.' She wasn't leaving because that's just the way it was here. She is part of the group, and they would keep her safe and keep her to themselves as part of the group, … whether she liked it or not."

"In that case, it sounds more like she's a prisoner, and that's a problem," he murmured.

"It absolutely is a problem," Amber agreed, "and Peaches is also terrified to leave or to even bring it up again."

"Right, so it looks like we've got a couple things to deal with. One, she doesn't have the confidence to make that decision on her own and to step out and to make it look real. I also get the sense that, two, we've got some dealings going on, where somebody specific doesn't want to let her go."

"I think the somebody who doesn't want to let her go is the one who wants to keep her for himself, and, if he can force that to happen, she'll never get out."

"Of course," Tomas agreed, "and she'll be stuck yet again. What was her marriage like?"

"It was terrible," Amber replied. "He got into this group without her knowledge or agreement. One day she came home from work, and the house had been cleaned out, and he said he was taking her for a ride, and they moved into this place. She didn't like it here and didn't really want to stay, but she didn't have a whole lot of recourse at that point."

"Interesting," he murmured. "So how did the guy die?"

"Nobody really talks about it."

"What does she say?"

"She's not talking either. Don't forget. We're always under surveillance, and it's never something that you can trust. There is never an opportunity to talk without somebody listening in."

"That's a problem," he murmured again.

"Not quite what you expected, *hmm*?" she asked him.

"Preppers are one thing," he noted, "but this sounds

much more like a cult."

"It is. I agree." She smiled, with a nod. "The thing is, don't ever underestimate these guys."

"But every cult has a leader," he asked, looking at her intently. "Who is leading this one?"

"He keeps a low profile, but, as far as I can tell, … Baxter."

Tomas hadn't met him yet, but he thought he recognized the name. "I might have heard that name," he noted. "Baxter, *huh?*"

"Yes," she nodded. "Baxter is the only name I know. I've met him a couple times, but he doesn't really have anything to do with me."

"And maybe that's a good thing," Tomas said.

"Absolutely. I have more than enough to deal with on my own," she muttered.

"Yeah, I agree with that." He nodded. "So we'll do what we can, and we'll get this cleaned up."

"I don't think any of it'll be easy," she admitted, with a heavy feeling in her chest. "Honestly, some guys are on the fringe here who seem to be looking for an explosion to happen."

"Yeah. When these guys don't get an outlet for all that hate and violence," he explained, "what happens is they create their own explosions within the groups. Often groups like this don't stay together, simply because they don't have enough of a physical outlet to blow off steam."

"That could be what's happening here." She shrugged. "I really don't know, but it's unnerving."

"It is," he noted. "An awful lot of testosterone is here."

She nodded. "Too much."

He smiled, as he looked over at her. "Considering you're

responsible for bringing more in, thunderbolt—"

She looked at him in surprise, then smiled at him calling her *thunderbolt*. She had been expecting it in a way. She had been called *hardheaded* and *stubborn* before, so she didn't take offense. *Thunderbolt* was a nickname she liked. "Yeah," she agreed, "I guess I am responsible for some of it, but let's hope that it's your testosterone that'll focus on the job and get me out of here, before it all goes to shit."

"You and your friend."

"Yes," she agreed, "and before it all goes south."

"Are you expecting it to go south?"

"I've never expected it," she noted, "but, with some of these guys around here, I'm not exactly sure."

"And what have you seen that you feel is problematic?"

"Outside of stockpiling weapons, which I know is perfectly legal in Texas," she noted, "I haven't seen too much in the way of illegal dealings here. But I do know that some people here I am somewhat close to, like Peaches, and others to a degree, they won't talk about what happened to my friend Annette or to Peaches's husband. They won't talk about what's troubling them. They are too afraid. It's unnerving to say the least."

He nodded at that. "Do you know where they're buried?"

"No." She frowned. "Not exactly. But I know it's somewhere on the other side of the property."

"Are we allowed to go pay our respects?"

She stopped, looked at him in surprise, and replied, "You know what? I'm not sure. But that would be a good thing to find out."

"It would be a *really* good thing to find out," he agreed. "And it would give us a chance to figure out just what leeway we have or don't have."

"Count on having none," she noted calmly. "And you'll be prepared for the answer that they'll give you."

"Right." He nodded. "Sounds like a fun place."

"If you're part of the team and if you're somebody they're willing to keep, then absolutely," she replied. "But, other than that, not so much."

"What about the women?" he asked. "The other women?"

"Some of them you have to watch like a hawk," she admitted, "because they appear to be completely innocent and, you know, fragile and sweet. Like they may even be trying to get out of here," she added. "But then you hear them talk behind your back, and you realize that they're all just part of the same nightmare."

"Sounds like you've been having fun," he teased.

"Hell no," she stated quietly. "Just so much is going on here that I feel like there's more than can really be explained."

"Okay," he said. "That's all good. We can sort it out one step at a time."

Looking up at him, she added, "I'm warning you specifically about Mary. She's Baxter's partner. She's … she's somebody you must steer clear of. More so because you'll think you never have to watch Mary. Or you might have. But she is deep. I'm pretty convinced that she plays both sides, then takes everything back to Baxter. You'll see him occasionally, but he does like to stick to himself. He's rarely even at dinner."

"It adds to the mystery," he noted, with a nod.

"If that's what it is, then yeah," she agreed. "Yet seems we already have enough mystery in this place though." She shivered in the cool air, even though they were inside.

"What about heat?" he asked, looking around. "Do you have any?"

"I do, but then I pay for it," she muttered. "Everybody has to contribute in places like this, and, since I'm not paying rent because, you know, … how can you earn any money in a place like this? So I just help out," she added. "I don't feel like I should add to the problems."

"Does Peaches live alone upstairs?"

Amber nodded. "It was given to her and her husband when they moved in, but, in the group's eyes, she doesn't have any right to stay here all alone."

"Ah, so then the property itself is a problem too?"

"Exactly," she said, with a nod. "In a case like this, I think that property becomes a bigger problem than most of us realize."

"If you realize just what these people are like," he replied, "it does make sense."

"Maybe it makes sense to you, but, for me, it doesn't make any sense at all," she admitted, with a half smile. "A lot is going on here that isn't comfortable, and I would just as soon get out of it all."

"And the only problem you're concerned about is—"

"Peaches," she stated. "Plus, I would like to know what happened to my friend Annette."

"In order to get one out, we might not get the other set of answers."

"We just need as much information as we can uncover right now," she replied, "because, when I get out, I'm not coming back in."

Tomas believed her, evidenced by that resolute sense within her that she was coming to the edge of whatever it was she had committed to doing here. "Hold tight," he murmured. "Just a little longer to give me a chance to see what I can find."

"You can't find anything," she declared. "That's the problem. Whatever was to be found is not down here. Maybe at Baxter's but not here." With that, she picked up a napkin and quickly drew a map of the houses. "That's all I know," she stated.

"When did you last see Baxter?" he asked, and she frowned, as she thought about it.

"Quite a while ago."

"Any idea if he's even still alive?"

She stared at him in surprise. "I assume so, of course, but I guess I don't have any reason to believe one way or the other."

"Okay," Tomas said, "and what about his number two?"

"That would be Brutus, I guess," she replied, a shadow crossing her face, immediately dimming her features. "He's the guy who took me to town. I begged and pleaded for a chance to get out, so I could meet up and see you. I knew what was happening in town, and he allowed me to tag along, but I'm pretty sure it was more because he is trying to get me for himself. But he's a cagey one so I'm not sure."

"Is that the guy who was trouble at the dinner table earlier?"

"No, that was a different one, Cal. Brutus wasn't there tonight. I don't know where he was. Maybe he's finding out more about you."

"Maybe." Tomas shrugged. "I'll individually *interact* with all of them at some point, so that is inevitable."

"Maybe," she murmured, "but remember. A lot of firepower is here, and plenty of people don't have a problem using it. Particularly if they get to use it illegally."

"And is Brutus one of those?"

"I'd definitely say Brutus is gun-happy." She nodded. "He likes to flaunt all his firearms. Yet I've never seen him fire any of them. I can only tell you what I've seen, but it seems to me that a couple guys are quite happy talking about killing for the sake of killing, and Brutus is one of them."

"Good enough," Tomas noted. "When I have a chance to meet with the real leaders, Baxter and Brutus, you need to point out each before either surprises us."

"Yeah. Of course I will let you know."

At that, a heavy banging came on her front door. She gasped and stepped closer to him. In a low voice, he asked her, "Is this a normal thing?"

She shook her head. "No, never. Honestly, I've made it a point of coming to my room every night, right after doing the dishes, and locking myself in," she replied, looking terrified. "I don't answer the door, and I don't bring anybody over. Not ever."

"So, what do you think this is then?" he asked, as he walked to the door.

"I don't know. But I can tell you that it's not good."

He smiled at her. "Maybe we should open the door and find out for ourselves then."

She immediately shook her head. "That's a bad idea."

"Sure, but we don't have a whole lot of choice."

And, with that, he opened the door.

Chapter 3

AMBER BARGED UP to the front door, now open, and plastered a smile on her face when she saw Brutus, clearly angry and red in the face. "Hey, Brutus. What's the matter?"

"He's the matter," Brutus snapped, looking at Tomas. "What the hell happened?"

She looked at him in surprise. "What?" she asked, with what sounded like genuine shock. At least she hoped it sounded genuine. "What are you talking about? You know how long I've been waiting to see him. Why are you even bothering us right now?" she asked, stepping closer to Tomas.

Brutus looked at her in disgust. "I figured you were just lying."

"Lying about what?" she asked, staring at him in shock. "About his existence?"

"Yeah," Brutus said. "And I didn't know until just now. I had dinner at my place tonight, so I didn't meet your mystery man."

"Believe me. They were all bugging me about Tomas. I'm sorry if his appearance was a surprise," she noted. "Obviously it was a surprise for me too and a welcome one at that," she said, with a smile. "I've been waiting for him for months."

"I just didn't believe that boyfriend line," Brutus repeated, growing impatient.

Amber tried to calm her nerves. "Let me introduce you two now." She then quickly made the introductions.

Tomas nodded and reached out to shake his hand. Brutus looked at him in disgust. "Office type, *huh?*"

"Definitely not the office type. And, hey, sorry to arrive unannounced."

"Yeah, sure you are," he said, with a hard look at Tomas. Then, without another word, he turned and walked away.

She wasn't even sure what to say about that, but, as soon as she shut the door, she turned to Tomas. "Now that's *not* normal," she murmured. "In fact, this makes me even more worried."

"He obviously thinks that you should be his," Tomas stated.

"I never gave him any reason to think I would be in favor of that. In fact, he's not been one of the grabby ones," she muttered in a low voice. "He's always given me the creeps because I never really knew where he stood on that issue. Honestly, I thought he might be gay, which, in this group, is not something he'd want outed. But he's the one who took me to town. So maybe that was part of his motivation."

"Understood, but, judging by the way he looked at you just now, he considered you his," Tomas murmured. "So that'll be a problem."

"I don't want it to be a problem," she muttered. "I don't want any of this to be a problem. I'll try again to calm him down. We sure don't need his ugly self on our asses all the time."

"Maybe not, but you've stepped into something that's

ugly regardless."

"What you're saying is that I stepped into something that's uglier than I had any idea of before," she corrected. "I don't think that Annette and the guy Peaches was with are the only two people these guys have killed."

"Probably not," Tomas agreed. "Once they get a taste for that kind of thing, it's pretty hard for them to stop."

She nodded slowly. "At the same time, it's just pretty unnerving."

He smiled, then wrapped an arm around her shoulders. "Hold on tight," he said. "The ride could get a little rough, but we'll make it to the other side, okay?"

She looked over at him, smiled. "I wish I knew that for sure."

He nodded. "You came here for a reason, so, if you want me to get you out now," he stated, "I'll get you out. Just say the word. I have no idea what excuse I'll give them, but I'll come up with something."

She immediately shook her head. "No, we can't leave Peaches behind. That woman's been through enough."

"You want to elaborate?"

"No, I don't," she replied. "I just know that her husband was very abusive, and everybody here knows it. She's pretty damn sure that, if she hooks up with any of these men, it will be more of the same, and that's the last thing she wants."

"When you've already experienced being a punching bag, you don't want to go back for round two," he murmured.

"Exactly," she agreed, looking at him in surprise. "You do understand."

"Of course I do," he stated, looking at her. "I've never quite understood why women stay in the first place, but I know that they do. Maybe getting her out of here will her set up with enough of a life that she can live in peace beyond this."

"That's my hope," she agreed quietly. "But I know she's also terrified. I don't think she sleeps at night."

"Anybody bothering her?"

"No, that's outside the code," she replied. "I mean, if she were to complain, then I'm sure somebody would step in and say something."

"Maybe, but who would she complain to?"

"That's part of the problem," she murmured. "Mary is always watching, but I'm not sure exactly what side Mary is on anymore."

"I think Mary will be on Mary's side, and, if she's partnered with the big boss, then you can bet that she's providing information to him constantly, letting him know exactly how things are down here," he murmured. "It's just interesting that he keeps himself apart. And, like I said earlier, I just think that's part of the mystery. The mystique that is required to keep people believing in him and this place."

"So how would you do it?"

"Stay out of sight, have my various spies watch for any dissent in the group, and, when there's a problem, come down on them, raise complete hell. Then clean it up, lay down the law, and fade back into the shadows."

She smiled. "Exactly. You know how they think."

"Oh, I do," he agreed. "The question is whether Baxter himself understands just how badly things will go to hell down here."

"I think he's also getting older, and he may be unwell. I don't know if …" She hesitated. "I would say *cranky*, but I don't know. I think he's not … I mean, I don't know if he's as bad as the rest of them." She fumbled on the last sentence, lost in her racing thoughts.

"He might be the one making the rules," Tomas noted calmly. "He could be the one who's running it all from the shadows, and maybe there is a chance that he gave the order to kill Peaches's husband. He might even have pulled the trigger himself," Tomas added, looking at her calmly. "You cannot trust anybody in a scenario like this."

"Got it," she replied, then relaxed ever-so-slightly. "You know what? I'm really glad you're here."

"AND NOT A moment too soon from the looks of many things." He didn't like any of what he had heard so far. The sooner he got Amber out of here, the better.

"No, I think you're right," she agreed, shuddering. "I didn't realize how much getting into town would stress me out."

"There are other ways to make it to a meeting," he murmured.

"You don't understand," she argued. "I'm not allowed any electronics—although Saul hooked me up. It's a sexist thing here, where none of the women have phones, computers. Maybe Mary does. Anyway I feel like I'm being watched all the time."

His gaze sharpened. "And do you still think that?"

She frowned and then nodded. "I don't know how else to explain it."

"Anybody in particular?"

She shook her head. "No, not really. It's just, just … everybody, I guess."

"Good enough," he replied gently. "How about getting some rest, and we'll have a go at this tomorrow."

She added, "There may not be a tomorrow, you know? I don't like it either, but we don't have time to wait."

"Understood," he agreed. "I need to meet up with either Saul or Dezi."

"Or not," she said, shuddering from the cold or her fear, Tomas wasn't sure. "I'm not kidding. These guys are watching, and you meeting with Saul or Dezi right under their noses is sure to land you in trouble."

"Did anything happen earlier today?" he asked. "You seem to be really spooked."

"I am, and I don't know why," she replied. "I feel like I'm watching my *P*s and *Q*s, yet, every time I turn around, somebody there has their gaze on me."

"They probably are watching you closely." He nodded. "Particularly once you start talking about leaving, then everybody else just seems to know that you're doing shady stuff on the side."

"That's how it feels—like they know I'm up to something," she murmured. "And it's really unnerving me."

"Then first things first," he stated. "I will make contact with my guys and set up what we need to do tonight, and, if there really is no time, then we go out tonight and take care of business."

"But if you get caught?" she asked, hating the shiver that racked her body.

"Then so do you." He stopped, looked at her with a frown, and then nodded. "That we can't have."

"I really would appreciate not getting in any more trouble than I am already in," she noted. "Only so much any of us can handle of that."

"You're already at the end of your rope," he noted, smiling at her gently. "I get it. So let me discuss it with the guys, and we'll have an idea of what we can do."

"I don't think we'll even have that option," she muttered, "but go. Go talk to Dezi. At least he's somebody they have more or less cleared here."

Just then came another knock on the door. She immediately sat back and stared at the door, like it was a viper. He looked at her, smiled, then added, "Take it easy."

"What was that weird knock?"

"That is Dezi." Tomas walked over to the door and let in his friend.

Chapter 4

AMBER SMILED AS Dezi slipped inside. "Hey," she greeted him, pushing her tousled hair off her face. "Any news?"

"Not yet," he replied, "but I am hearing some rumblings from other members."

She nodded. "There is a tension. I'm not sure what it's all about."

"Agreed," he murmured. "Saul is out there, keeping an eye on everything, noting some activity in the back forty."

"I'm not surprised," she murmured, "but I have no clue what they're doing."

"And you're not close enough to the group to find out?" Dezi asked her.

She shook her head. "No, not at all. They're very close-knit when it comes to that type of thing. I'm not sure that even three-quarters of the men have any idea just what is going on here."

Dezi nodded. "Which is an interesting conundrum for most of them. They're equally involved, but it's almost like they have given up any right or reason to argue or to even be in the need-to-know category."

"Agreed," she murmured. She looked around, feeling a shiver as if someone had just walked over her grave. She shuddered. "I think we need to get out of here as soon as possible," she stated. "I just don't know how to make it happen."

"Neither do I at the moment," Dezi noted, "but we're talking. I've already communicated with Saul, without anybody catching us. However, somebody followed me here."

"I'm sure they *are* following you," she confirmed, with a smile. "All the time, as in all the damn time."

He nodded. "That's what it felt like. Not a lot of trust around here, is there?"

"None," she stated, "and, considering that potentially murderers are involved, I think it's even worse."

"Which makes sense," he agreed. Then he looked over at Tomas. "Feel like taking a walk?"

"Absolutely," Tomas replied. "Where are we going?'"

"Let's get out in the bright lights and see what's happening," he suggested.

"Are you sure that is safe?" she asked in horror.

"Probably not," Dezi said cheerfully. "But they'll have to stand up and stop us in order to tell us that we can't go somewhere, and that will require some explanation."

"That's … true," she hesitantly agreed.

"Stepping out boldly is probably our best bet at this moment," Tomas noted.

"Sounds like a suicide mission," she murmured. "What the hell am I supposed to do, if you guys get shot and buried out back?"

"You run," Dezi stated, staring at her intently. "And I mean that. You travel light, packing only essentials, and you slip out in the middle of the night."

"Have you seen the fence and the gates?" she asked, staring at him.

He nodded. "Don't worry. Saul will be there to help you."

"Unless he's taken too."

Dezi smiled. "If Levi doesn't hear from us at regular intervals, that will bring down a wave of people here, who will take care of it. These guys have no idea what they're up against."

"No," she replied quietly, "but I think a shooting event like that is something that many of them are anxiously looking forward to."

"I get that impression too," Dezi agreed calmly, "but we're not newbies at this."

She shivered again, then wrapped her arms around her chest. "And I get that. I just wish it was already over."

"Is there any way for you to visit Peaches?"

She shook her head. "No way. Even though we share the same house, me in the basement and her on the ground floor, we're not to talk in private. We're asked to stay inside after dark, and it's a very unforgiving rule here."

"Interesting. I wonder what they are trying to keep you from seeing."

"Everything, I imagine," she guessed. "I don't know if they're running guns, running drugs, booze, whatever. Or maybe they're just trying to be little boys with their own secret clubs. I really don't know."

"Good enough," Dezi replied, then he looked over at Tomas. "You ready?"

"Absolutely."

When the two men stepped out into the night, she sat inside for the longest time, trying to figure out what she was supposed to do with her time because that's not exactly how she had hoped her evening would go. Then again, she didn't have any plans, and the guys needed to do some recon. So, what could she have expected?

Still, it would be nice if she had answers. They hadn't told her to stay inside, and they hadn't told her to keep the doors locked, but she did both regardless. She didn't want anything connected to her, if there was any way to avoid it. Not that she was just looking after herself. As much as she just wanted to stay clear of any supposed rules, it was probably stupid to even consider it because, with Tomas here as her fiancé, the connection between them would be seen as far too strong for anybody else to ignore.

When a knock came on the door about an hour later, she frowned, not sure what she should do. When it came again, she checked her watch and realized it was only 8:30 p.m., so she hardly had any reason not to answer it. So, brushing her hair back, she walked over to the door and opened it up. It was Mary. Amber smiled. "Hey, what's up?" she asked.

Mary frowned at her. "I was hoping to talk to Tomas."

"He's gone for a walk," she said, with a random wave of her hand. "He and Dezi had some stuff to talk over," she added, with an eye roll.

Mary just smiled. "Oh, that's unfortunate. Any idea where they went?"

She shrugged her shoulders. "Nowhere in particular, as far as I know," she said cheerfully.

Mary took a step back, then looked around the basement curiously, as if not quite sure that she should believe Amber, then nodded. "When he comes back, tell him that Baxter wants to see him."

"Wow," she said, "of course. I'm sure he will be thrilled. He was talking about it earlier."

"Both he and Dezi need to be there, so let them know."

"That's pretty special then?" she asked cheerfully, "I'm sure the guys will be happy to come meet him."

Mary gave her a nod and then cast a searching glance around. "As soon as they're back."

She nodded and went to close the door, when Mary reached out a hand and asked, "You're not mixed up in anything stupid, are you?"

She stared at Mary, her jaw dropping. "Mixed up in what?" she asked in surprise. And she realized she was lucky because the question did surprise her.

Mary nodded, as if satisfied with that answer, and added, "Just a thought." She turned and then quickly disappeared around the corner of the house.

It was dark, and Amber stood in the doorway, watching as Mary left, walking toward the house she shared with Baxter.

Amber wasn't sure what was going on right now, but something was, and it was enough to make her reconsider her plans. The sooner they got out of here, the better. But she also had to find out what had happened to Annette.

That investigation was getting to be a goal that was becoming harder and harder to achieve. She needed time and resources to do it right. Frowning, she closed the door and stepped back ever-so-slightly. Almost immediately her phone buzzed.

She checked it to see the text message. Tomas was checking up on her, so she quickly responded with a text about Mary coming for a strange visit and that Baxter wanted to see him and Dezi.

He sent an acknowledgment. **We'll be back soon.**

She frowned at that. **You may want to go to Baxter's**

first.

When no response came to that, she sat back and wondered just what she was supposed to do here. Was there any way to get control of the situation? She couldn't see how they could manage to wriggle out of this one and get her and Peaches out safely too. Or at least have the guys put her on alert that there would be an attempt to escape here soon enough. It could be just a strong-arm move on their part that would get her out of here because of the sheer possession-crazy rule the group worked off of when it came to Peaches and Amber. It could also mean that Tomas would be challenged for her.

That scared the crap out of her.

What if he lost?

If it were Saul and if maybe it were a fair fight, she'd worry less. But she didn't know this Tomas guy at all. And that was a little bit concerning—to put all her trust in the one and then find out that she might have backed the wrong horse. Of course she felt bad even thinking about it that way, but, with so much at stake, she and Peaches didn't have a whole lot of options.

But Amber was still hesitant to be spooked too early. If chaos happened, it would be a case of *grab her and run.* And she could only help them when Peaches was willing to come. Still, nagging in the back of her mind, Amber was worried that when crunch time came, Peaches might back out. Not that it would be a surprise, given everything Peaches had gone through already, but it would be difficult to come back and get her later.

Once they left—without Peaches—her life would be even harder. And maybe the gang wouldn't care. … Maybe if Peaches chose nobody to replace her husband, … maybe they wouldn't force it, and they would just let her go on, without giving a rat's ass. Maybe they would let her be.

In a mess of *maybe*s, Amber was not so sure. She doubted that would happen. Enough men were around who wanted Peaches. Plus, she was afraid of something happening, and it was inevitable. It would happen with or without her consent, and she didn't have a choice in the matter.

Not something Amber wanted to think about, but something hard to ignore. These men had more of that thought process instilled in them than anybody she'd ever seen before.

They were all of the opinion that this was their clan, their group, and it would be hard for anybody else to come in, and, when they were allowed to come in, they would be part of the same chaos.

Maybe Tomas would do just fine.

He was certainly someone Saul trusted, and Tomas seemed to know how to blend in. But, at the same time, it was unnerving watching it all happen and not knowing what her role in this was. *If* there was a role in this for her.

There had to be some way for her to move forward. But was she prepared to forget about what happened to Annette?

Well, *that* she didn't know. And, for that matter, also what happened to Peaches's husband. Peaches wasn't exactly talking, and that was a disturbing thought too. Amber didn't want to think badly of her new friend, but it was hard when evidence pointed to something nefarious going on, yet Peaches not saying anything. Amber understood that her friend was terrified to talk here. Peaches had no way of knowing where any words she spoke would go.

It would be nice to know for sure on which side Peaches would fall.

Amber could only hope Peaches chose the side of right, no matter how scared she might be. However, Amber also knew that, when things broke, they often broke to the left. With that thought in mind, she tried to settle down to wait. The men should be here soon. They texted they were coming straight back but maybe not.

When they didn't return in an hour, Amber started to worry. When they didn't return in two hours, she was pacing rapidly, and her feet were starting to hurt. By the time it was well past her bedtime, she had about decided to head out. She knew she would do something to find out what was going on. She was just getting ready to step outside, when she got a text saying they were on their way.

As soon as they got close to the door, she heard them. She waited to make sure that it was just them, figuring Tomas could pick a lock, and, as soon as the door opened, and Tomas stepped in, with a smile on his face, she burst into a run, and he opened his arms to enclose her securely, shutting the door firmly with his foot.

He whispered against her hair, "We're fine."

"You're fine?" she repeated. "What took you so long? Couldn't you have told me?"

"No. Not in this instance."

"Why not?" She frowned at him. Now that the worry was over, she wanted to rail at Tomas and to scream for making her worry like that. But, at the same time, she wasn't even sure what he was supposed to have done differently. She took a deep breath, stepped back, and stated, "You need to explain."

He smiled, locking the door again, while she looked out a window into the dark night, then asked, "Is Dezi okay?"

"Yes, he left me at the door. He's heading off to his place

now."

"Fine." She rubbed her forehead. "Did you guys meet up with Baxter?"

He nodded. "We did," he replied, his tone hard. "He had a few choice questions for us."

She frowned. "What was the problem?"

"He had some suspicions," Tomas replied.

She nodded. "That's not a huge surprise," she murmured. "He's been running this place for a very long time."

"Turns out you were right. He's also not in the best of health, although he did his best to hide it."

She looked at him in surprise. "What do you mean?"

"Something's going on with him physically," Tomas noted, "and I think he's trying to hang on to his position by not letting anybody know."

"And yet," she added, "everybody here is supposed to be helping each other out."

"I suspect, at this point, it won't work out that way."

"It's not like a true gang scenario."

"No, but it's very much like a cult," he reminded her. "And everybody who is here, Baxter wants to keep here. He doesn't want to expand the group because he'll have trouble trying to keep everybody under his control."

"That makes a weird kind of sense," she said, slowly nodding. "So what about you guys?"

"We're allowed to visit, not to stay," he stated simply.

"Oh, well. I guess that makes sense too, particularly if he's struggling to hang on to whatever's going on here."

"Yes, and he didn't talk about anything other than the fact that the area was closed to future members for the time being, but, when they decide to open it, he's promised ..." Tomas stated, with a wry smile, "that they'll let us know."

"If you're still around and if you're still interested?" she noted, with a nod.

"Exactly. I think, in the meantime, they'll do a thorough check on us, at least as much as they can. I don't know how computer savvy they are or what investigative skills they have," he added calmly, "but they'll do their best."

"Of course they will." She shook her head, wrapped her arms around her chest, and paced again. "I want out," she stated abruptly. "It feels really ugly right now."

"Anytime you want," he said. "I'm not sure if you're classified as being part of the group or not. Yet you're still here, so there's a good chance that you are. Also, and I hate to say it out loud, but you're female, so I don't think Baxter or Brutus or any other male here would consider you much of a challenge."

She snorted at that. "They all look at women that way," she stated, "so I don't know that it's anything different when speaking about me."

"Probably not," Tomas agreed, with a gentle smile. "But since you're the one who raised the alarm with us, Baxter is doing himself a disservice by discounting the women who are here."

"In a big way." She nodded. "At the same time, I also know for sure now that Mary is keeping tabs on everybody. When she came tonight, I was not at all sure what was going on."

"Just a *friendly visit*," he noted cheerfully. And then he stopped, looked at her, and added, with a dark overtone, "Nothing to worry about."

"Right!" she said, clearly worried. "Did you guys figure out what was going on outside tonight?"

"No, but Saul is on it," he stated, with a smile. "So we

give him a chance to do his work too."

She groaned. "What does that mean? We just go through the days and wait? Is that it?"

"We've been given three days for a visitation by Baxter, and, after that, we were asked to leave."

She immediately frowned. "That won't give us much time to do anything," she stated cautiously.

"Nope, it doesn't," he agreed, "so we'll work fast."

She collapsed onto the living room chair and stared at him wordlessly.

He smiled. "It'll be fine."

"I don't have your confidence," she mumbled. "This place is starting to freak me out."

"Part of that is because you know that you can't walk around freely, and, as soon as someone can't walk freely, their suspicions get aroused."

"And because I know what happened to Annette and because I don't know what's happening with Peaches."

"And do you have any idea what happened to Peaches's husband?"

"No," she murmured. "Neither does Peaches, and I think that's the part that really got to her."

"Do you think it's guilt keeping her here or something else? Like fear, most probably."

She stared at him in surprise and then shrugged. "You know what? I have no idea. I think she wanted out as soon as she got in and couldn't find a way to get out because of her husband. Now she wants out before she gets assigned to somebody else."

"*Assigned?* That's enough reason to get out pretty damn fast then," he said, with a raised eyebrow.

"That was my take on it, but I think either she's scared

to walk away from where her husband was—you know, like abandoning him—or she's just scared she won't get out."

"Either are valid points," he noted, an odd look crossing his face. "Grief does weird things to people."

"And I'm not even sure if she's grieving," Amber added. "I think we're back to that whole *feeling guilty* scenario."

"Which is also interesting, when you realize she was abused by her husband. Yet I guess that is part of the abuse cycle too," Tomas noted. "Regardless, an awful lot is going on here that they're not letting us know about."

"Because you're not part of the inner circle," she explained, with a nod.

"Then point me to someone who is."

"Brutus." She winced. "The guy who took me into town and who is *sweet on me*," she added, with a grim smile, "but he scares the crap out of me."

"And we don't want you too close to him," he noted.

"I try never to be alone with him, not ever. When I went to town, it wasn't just the two of us, there were more. But he's the one who won the argument to let me go into town, and I think it was a concession on his part. He was putting himself on the line over it and could have gotten into trouble, but he was willing to do that for me. It worked at the time, but it also says that there are some shifts in the hierarchy even now and that the ranks are moving. He has quite a bit of the say around here and has the firepower to back him up."

"Speaking of ranks and firepower," Tomas began, "any idea where they keep all the weapons?"

She shook her head. "I know an armory is here, and it's in one of two buildings," she noted. "The other one, I'm not sure what it is. I thought it was a target range, but it would be inside, so I guess not. There's also a shooting gallery."

"It could be in that building with a target range in the back or something," he murmured.

She nodded. "I haven't been to either of those places, so I don't really know what they are or how that works."

"Got it, and it's enough info for now." Tomas slyly moved the curtains and stared out the side of the window for a long moment. He turned, looked at her, and asked, "Will you sleep tonight?"

She looked at him in surprise. "Yes, I think so. Why?"

"Because I'm leaving again," he replied. "I need to check out some of the areas that Saul can't access."

"Well, shit," she said, staring at the door. "That's not what I want to hear."

"I'm sure it's not, but it is important."

"Of course it is," she replied and raised her palms. "All of this is important."

"Exactly," he agreed smoothly. "And we do need to fig-ure out who is a threat, who can be trusted, and what is really going on."

"Nobody can be trusted," she stated flat-out. "You can't trust anybody here, and, as I said, Mary is at the top of that list."

"Which is also interesting because she is either trying to keep the power hierarchy intact or to keep it as fluid as she can. Maybe she is trying to help Baxter maintain control, or she's in on it with somebody else and is planning on sending Baxter packing."

"Ouch. I hadn't really considered her as somebody who would betray Baxter. Yet, in a situation like this, I really don't know."

"And that's good enough for now, and all we can do.

We just speculate, then gather information to test out our theories as fast as we can," he noted. "Mary's got to do whatever she thinks she needs to do to stay safe. In a place like this, there might not be a whole lot she can do." He seemed to be sympathizing with her.

"What kind of a world is it," Amber replied, "when you know a woman like that isn't even safe to stay with her husband and wait out his years."

"The one they created for themselves. It's all based on power, and whoever has power has to keep it," Tomas explained. "For them, any loss of power is a loss of face, and conversely, any loss of face is the loss of power. It is simply the law of the jungle. If you're not physically fit and strong, you're done." Tomas paused. "Believe me. Your friend Baxter, he knows it all too well."

"No friend of mine," she argued. "I had a 'meeting' with him when I first arrived and had come looking for Annette. When he told me the sob story about how she died and how they had buried her with great honor, I wasn't even sure what to say. I was so shocked. He immediately said I could stay, but I think it was more so I would calm down and not see anything suspicious about being here."

"And no doctor is here or any death certificate for proof?"

"No, they don't do that here," she replied, with an angry voice. "They don't deal with the establishment if they can get away with it. He obviously didn't think anybody would care or even know about Annette, so my arrival was an unhappy surprise for everyone."

"She probably had to say that she had no friends when she arrived, or at least that she would keep them in the dark," he noted.

"Not only that," she agreed, "I'm pretty sure she signed over whatever money she had."

He winced at that. "Now *that* is very cultish," he noted, "and then the question becomes, how much money did she have?"

"I have no idea. I might have asked her, but, when I arrived, she was already dead, probably because they got her to sign whatever document they needed." She stared at the window with disgust. "It makes me sick to my stomach even thinking about it."

"And that," he noted, "would give us a motive for her murder."

She shuddered. "I don't like the way you think."

"I'm not surprised," he said calmly, "but it doesn't change the fact that, if they took her out, and I'm not saying they did, but there had to be a reason. Betrayal and money are two of the biggest."

She slowly sucked in her breath and then nodded. "No, you're right," she replied, thinking hard and fast. "Annette did have money."

"A lot?"

She frowned at that. "I don't know what *a lot* even means," she stated, "but I would say that she definitely had more than a hundred grand. And, for a place like this, maybe that's quite a large sum."

"Do you know anything about Peaches's husband?"

"As in how and why he died?"

"Either or anything at all," he added. "At this point, we need to know who all the players are and why things are happening that are this out of control."

"I don't know very much about Peaches's scenario, but, if they had money, why wouldn't Peaches get it?"

"For one thing, the husband was the kind to not allow her to have it. Or maybe he didn't know that it wouldn't go to her when he died. For another thing, maybe it is sitting somewhere, and the gang needs her cooperation to get it but hasn't quite figured out how to do that yet. Maybe they're hoping that somebody will woo it out of her."

Amber stared at him in horror. "Or force her to give it up."

"Quite possible," he agreed, with a quick nod. "I mean, they won't let that kind of money walk, will they?"

"So they'll never let her go then."

"Depends on how much money there is."

Amber frowned at that. "I wonder how to find that out," she murmured.

"We already have an investigation ongoing. Levi's handling that," he replied. "He'll find out if there's property owned or bank accounts and that sort of thing." He stared at her and added, "If most of it went to the compound, it would stay with the compound in their bank accounts, but that could also be why they're trying to be gentle with her, hoping for an easy transition. And then, if it looks like it won't go easy, … well, it'll go hard on Peaches because these guys won't do it any other way."

TOMAS HATED TO leave Amber alone, knowing that she was so unnerved by the whole thing, but having put something into motion, she also needed to hold steady a little bit longer, while they figured out just what the hell was going on. No doubt in his mind that something *was* going on.

He just wasn't sure what. The thought of Annette having been killed for her wealth or property was also a disturbing concept. It seemed like it would have been better for them to have found somebody for her to partner up with and to get the assets that way. It ended up still the same, but it didn't involve killing her. And killing her was a risky thing to have done in haste. There had to be a reason, and, as he thought about it, he figured the better reason was that she might have been wanting to leave.

With that thought in mind, he turned his attention to the dead man. What were the chances that Peaches's husband was looking to leave and to take Annette with him? That would have been very risky on their part but also quite possible, depending on their states of mind. Tomas frowned at that concept, and, as he met up with Dezi, Tomas quickly brought him up to speed.

Dezi considered that point. "It would be pretty shitty if they were killing people for their assets."

"Yeah, but we've seen it happen time and time again," Tomas noted, "like old people dying and the caregiver not telling anybody, so the checks keep coming, then deciding to help the next one because they could use even more money." Tomas shook his head. "You know that's a potential problem no matter where we are."

"Yeah, it seems like it's always about money and greed in the end." Dezi frowned.

"Power too," Tomas added. "And we're definitely up against power here. Based on what Amber has said, Peaches's husband was an asshole and treated her like crap."

"So what are the chances that he had changed his ways?"

"Not much," Tomas declared. "A place like this would certainly suit him."

"It would, but what if you wanted him to help with a takeover? What if he was involved in a takeover, knowing that the boss was getting weaker and not capable of holding things together, but in the end the attempt failed?"

"That would certainly get him killed and deep-sixed in the back forty," Tomas agreed. "Particularly as a warning to keep the others in line, now that you mention it."

"But what would Annette have to do with that?"

"Maybe she knew too much or maybe she was in the wrong place at the wrong time, where the failed coup somehow got her killed too." Tomas nodded slowly, as he thought about it.

"It sucks, but it makes sense," Dezi stated.

"It does, and I really hate that because these guys will only have so much tolerance for Peaches and Amber too, before they both get paired up with somebody else, whether the women like it or not. And since they both seem to be aware of that, it makes even more sense. I think Amber knows how deep she is in this now and is just hoping to get out in time, yet won't leave without Peaches."

Dezi was quiet for a moment. "Maybe. I'm wondering about Peaches's assets. Or the husband's anyway. And maybe there's a problem because they can't declare him dead exactly, so maybe they're trying to find a way around that. Baxter may want to keep Peaches close, until they figure out how to get the assets secured for themselves."

"Man, this is a mess. I just love how people start to act when money's involved." Tomas shook his head.

"When you think about it, it's all the same damn thing again and again. It's really shitty."

"It is, but at least it gives us a potential motive that makes sense," Tomas added.

"Agreed," Dezi noted. "I just wonder how far they would take it."

"As far as they can because they're already in for a penny, which means they'll be in for a pound."

"And, once those pounds start adding up, there's no going back. Nothing like free money to make people act out of character."

"*If* it is out of character," Dezi murmured, as they slipped through the trees. "Maybe this is exactly what they wanted in the first place, and they just hadn't gotten that far yet."

At that, an odd sound rippled up ahead. The two of them split up and went around the trees, looking to see what was going on. With Dezi heading left, Tomas took the right-hand path and slipped through the trees. He came upon a scene that had him almost giving away his position.

A truck was unloading weapons and not just a few but a lot of them. As in cases and cases. And not only was there heavy artillery but semiautomatic and automatic rifles, from what Tomas could see, but he wasn't close enough to get a good look.

With his phone, he quickly took as many photos as he could and then caught sight of somebody on the far side, sliding down a hill. It was Dezi, which scared Tomas, because these guys might spot Dezi too. Acting quickly to create a distraction, Tomas tossed a rock, and it scuttled down the hillside.

Several of the men frowned, then looked around, until one of the guys ordered, "Go check it out. We won't take any chances at this point."

"We should have postponed it, when we knew we had the two other guys here."

"Who the hell let those guys come here in the first place?" one of the drivers asked angrily. "You know that's not part of the deal."

"Hey, the boss okayed it."

"Yeah?" He didn't say anything else, though his tone of disgust was evident.

And Tomas could definitely understand why. It wasn't what anyone would consider a sensible answer to be, given the craziness going on. But, at the same time, it was interesting that the boss chose to keep the gun delivery as scheduled, and Tomas could see how disgruntled everybody here felt about it. And that was fine with Tomas because anything that caused any disparity among this group would be good for Tomas and his group. And, with that, he sent yet another rock scrambling a little lower.

"I think it must be a deer," he heard one of the men say.

"Nothing's up there. But, hey, if it's a deer, we can put it in the freezer," he snapped. "We could always use a bit more meat."

At that, the other guy disappeared, knowing it was dicey and hardly the time to take anybody out. Tomas quickly jumped his way up into the leaves above, without making a sound. His leg screamed a little bit in protest, but nothing that truly hurt him. And that was good because it was one of the things that he didn't really have any way of testing, until he was out in field conditions.

He was pretty damn sure he was back to fighting form, but convincing other people was a different story. The good news was that it looked like everything functioned just fine, and Levi was to be commended for his trust in Tomas.

With any luck, they could get the hell out of here and figure out how to stop this band of merry men. Bringing in law enforcement was not the answer. These guys would be incredibly uncooperative, and, if Tomas didn't have a dead body, there wouldn't be anything that the local authorities could do anyhow.

Finding the bodies now was a different story, and, as he studied the area around him, he pondered the layout. Acres and acres were here, and they would have had to bury the bodies deep to stop the wild animals from digging them up, and they did have heavy equipment here, presumably for building and planting fields, which would make the job that much easier.

Keeping that in mind, he climbed a tree to better study the area, looking for a break in the trees and where the brush had been removed to form a pathway. There was one a little farther off to the right, where Dezi had disappeared, but it wasn't on tap for tonight. Still, Tomas marked the location in his mind to check out later.

When Dezi appeared at the base of his tree, Tomas slowly lowered himself and said, "Time to go."

Dezi nodded. "Yeah, time to go," he murmured. "Past time."

And with that, the two men snuck back to home base. They were almost to Peaches's house, where Amber was staying in the basement suite, when they heard a ruckus on the front porch.

Peaches cried out, "No, I told you that already. I don't want to."

"I don't care if you want to or not," one of the men said, his voice rough. "You need to choose, and you need to choose now."

"I don't want to," she said, crying now. "Just leave me alone."

A tussle followed that looked to not be going Peaches's way, when Dezi looked at Tomas. He just gave him the thumbs-up.

Dezi disappeared, and Tomas knew that he must make it look like he had just arrived. He quickly slipped around to the basement suite, then came out to the front in order to make sure that they saw him there, as if he had just been woken up.

"Hey, what's going on?" he asked, pretending to be rubbing the sleep from his eyes.

"None of your fucking business," the guy yelled at him. "Get back down to where you belong."

Tomas stared at the man, feeling the same old anger rise, and he could not let that go unanswered. No one was talking to him like that. "Not if you're manhandling this woman," he stated. "A woman doesn't cry out like that for nothing."

"Yeah, sure they do," he snapped, with a sneer. "They always cry out. Sometimes it's good. Sometimes it's not so good. This one just needs to be reminded about a few facts in life." He shot Peaches a hard glance. Then he lifted his hand to her, pointing. "I'll be back tomorrow night. Make sure you give me the right answer then." With that, he disappeared.

Tomas had barely taken two steps toward Peaches, when Amber burst from the basement suite and raced to her friend. "Are you okay?" She wrapped her arms around the other woman.

Peaches wept in her arms. "Russ wants me to marry him," she murmured. "But I don't want to. I don't want anything to do with him. He scares me. I can't live like that anymore," she cried out, shivering in Amber's arms.

"*Shhhh*, it's okay. It's okay," Amber said. After a look around, she added, "Better keep your voice down."

But it seemed like Peaches was too far gone. Amber

quickly ushered her inside, stopping in the living room, and Tomas followed. "She shouldn't marry him if she doesn't want to," Amber stated, glaring at him.

He nodded. "Sure, I get it, but you know that things here run differently."

"It's not fair," Peaches whispered. "It's not fair, and I don't want to."

"Then what will you do about it?" he asked because he hadn't had a chance to get this woman's measure. He didn't know whether she was serious or not.

She looked around fearfully.

"It's okay," Amber said. "You can trust him."

She shook her head. "No, you can't trust anybody here." She gave him a shattered look. "I need to rest."

"And then what?" he asked, looking at her. "Will you give in tomorrow night?"

"No," she said, as she looked to Amber, and then her shoulders sagged. "I have to get out."

"I need to ask you a couple questions," Tomas stated forcefully. "What happened to your husband?"

She hesitantly looked over at him. "I don't know. They just told me that he died, when they were out on a training mission. They wouldn't let me see his body or the belongings he had on him."

"So, you don't know for sure that he's dead?"

She stared at him in surprise. "Oh, I'm sure he's dead. I never got the impression that he wasn't, and believe me. If he wasn't, he would be right here, raising hell."

He nodded. "Was he a troublemaker?"

She frowned and then shrugged. "Yes, I would say so. It was his way or the highway. He was one of the early adopters of this lifestyle but didn't want to give it 100 percent until a few years ago. Then suddenly he was all in. I don't know what the inducement was, but, once they got his attention, he jumped in with both feet, whether I liked it or not."

"Were you happy with that?"

She stared at him in surprise again and then slowly shook her head. "No, I wasn't happy about it at all. I'd have done a lot to get away from him, but I didn't kill him."

"I didn't suggest that you did," he stated calmly. "All I'm trying to figure out is what they might have done."

"I don't know," she said, and her voice dropped to a faint whisper. "But his death left me in a really ugly spot."

"But you were in an ugly spot beforehand, weren't you?"

Her eyes darted over in a quick glance at Amber. "Did you tell him?"

"I did," Amber stated calmly. "Your husband was a miserable bastard who beat you, and I don't want to see you hooking up with somebody else, who'll just do the same thing."

The older woman ran her hand lightly up and down her arm. "No, I don't think I could take it anymore."

"And you shouldn't have to," she said immediately. "But getting out is a different story."

"I know. I don't have any idea how to leave," she replied, looking around frantically. She stopped and sagged into the only chair in the place. "Sometimes I think the only way out is to die."

"Don't do that," Tomas said immediately. "Please don't do anything rash. We're working on it."

Peaches stared at him. "You're not working fast enough," she replied quietly. "If he comes back tomorrow night, there'll be hell to pay if I don't give him the answer he wants."

"Then come and stay with me," Amber suggested.

She stared at her in surprise. "You don't understand. They want my house. They want everything."

"Of course they do," Amber agreed.

"I'm wondering if that isn't why your husband was killed," Tomas added.

She stared at him in shock, then slowly nodded her head. "You know what? Maybe that's why they keep asking me to sign some paperwork, but I won't do it."

"So now they are trying to get a husband for you instead," he noted, "who will then have rights and can make you do all kinds of stuff."

She shuddered. "Mostly I just give in because the pain isn't worth it."

"Exactly," he noted quietly. "So, did you and your husband have any money?"

"We sold everything to come here. This house was ours right from the beginning, but I don't know that there's any title to it. It's something that I've been thinking about, now that I'm wondering if there is any way to get free and clear," she's whispered. "I don't know that I can start all over again."

"You might not have a choice," Tomas noted. "But, at least, if you do get free and clear, you have a chance to start over, to be truly free. That has got to be better than staying here and slowly dying under a man's fist every day."

She shuddered at his words. "I can't do that again." She looked around frantically. "I can't. … I can't."

Chapter 5

AMBER GAVE TOMAS a quelling lock. She understood what he was trying to do, but, at this point, Peaches was too freaked out to handle much more.

He nodded at Amber, then walked into the kitchen and put on the teapot. Peaches might calm down with just Amber at her side, not a man hovering over her.

Amber and Peaches sat together quietly, talking in low whispers, when he walked back out again.

"I don't know what I'm supposed to do," Peaches moaned. "I don't know how to get out of this. I think they'll just force me into another marriage, whether it's legal or not. It won't matter because I'll never get away."

"If you want to get away," Tomas said immediately, "I can pick you up and drive you out of here right now. They won't stop me."

She looked at him in surprise. "I think you're wrong there. I'm pretty sure that, in your day, you were probably big and menacing, but I'm afraid since your injury," she added, with an apologetic look, "they've sized you up as weak and as somebody they can take out easily."

"They can size me up any way they want to," he stated, crossing his arms over his chest and leaning against the doorjamb. "That gives me a hidden advantage."

She shook her head. "They'll kill you."

"Is that what they did to your husband?"

She looked at him. "I'm afraid so, but I don't know why. Was any money involved? Or maybe he wanted to leave? I don't really think so," she said, "but he was acting *off* the last few weeks before his death."

"*Off* how?"

She frowned. "Honestly, if we were anywhere else, I would have suspected an affair."

At that, Amber froze. "It's still possible here, isn't it?"

"Only with a single woman. Anybody else would be asking to get herself killed," she stated bitterly.

Amber shifted uncomfortably. "Generally there aren't single women here, although there was …" She stopped, her voice dropping to a low tone, before it petered out.

Peaches look at her in surprise. "You're thinking about your Annette?"

Amber nodded. "God," she said, "I don't know."

"The stupid thing is, I would have welcomed him having an affair. I would have welcomed him leaving, if he wouldn't end up leaving me here. I didn't want to come here in the first place, and I sure as hell don't want to stay. But him dying like he did has left me in a terrible position," Then she shook her head. "I see no easy answer to getting out of here."

"There won't be an *easy* answer," he stated, "but we can certainly make it happen. Tell me about your financial situation and your husband's. What might they know about that?"

"It's quite possible that they know a lot, and it's also possible …" She stopped and looked at him. "I don't really know what's going on, but I know that a big chunk of money was put into our bank account about two months before he died."

"When you say a big chunk, what does that mean?"

"One hundred thousand dollars," she stated.

"What? And you don't know where it came from?" Amber asked, staring at her in shock.

"No, and see? That's the problem," she murmured. "Nobody understands what it's like. I had no idea where it came from. I didn't even know it hit the bank, until I heard him gloating about it one night. When I asked him about it, he just told me to shut the fuck up," she murmured. "So I did because, if I didn't, I would have gotten a fist in the jaw."

"Right," he replied. "So, what's your best guess for where the money came from?"

She stared at him. "Honestly, I would think they're doing something illegal here, like maybe buying or selling something, but I don't know what."

"Like what? Do you think your husband may have dealt in drugs?"

"I wouldn't have thought so," she said, "but honestly, I don't think he was bothered by things. He had no morals, no code."

"Right," he murmured, studying her. "What about guns?"

"Oh, he would definitely buy and sell guns if he thought he could get away with it," she replied, with an airy wave of her hand. "He had absolutely zero tolerance for any government interference. I don't think he ever paid income tax, and, as far as he was concerned, politicians should just be shot right from the get-go."

"That's a handy way to look at life, isn't it?"

"Handy for him," she muttered. "Not so much for the rest of us."

He nodded. "So, given your best guess out of all those options, which one do you think he would have been involved in?"

"Guns," she stated instantly. "And I know there was talk about it, but I don't know what they would sell to make that kind of money."

"Depends on what they are growing in the back."

She stared at him. "I mean, what do I know?" she said. "I didn't even know what he was up to before he died. I just know that he's dead. I didn't want to be here in the first place, and now I don't know how the hell to get out."

"We'll help you with that," Tomas repeated. "But we also must ensure that we do it in a safe way."

"You think?" she huffed. "Is that even possible?"

"Is your name on his bank account?"

"Yes. At least I think so. He handled all the money."

"And do you know how to check it online?"

"Not really." She frowned. "He wouldn't let me close to the computer. He was always sitting off to the side, so I never saw anything. I know I've had several guys ask me if they could have his computer because, in their minds, I'm not computer-savvy enough to use it."

At that, Amber walked over and asked Peaches, "May I take a look at it and maybe log on?"

Peaches looked at her friend in surprise and said, "Sure, if you know how to, and maybe you can make sure any of that stuff is safe?" She turned her back on Amber and told Tomas, "If I could get out of here, I could live my life on that money. That would be great too."

"I'm not sure how that works," he said cautiously.

She stared at him and then nodded. "Oh, right, illegal guns and all that."

"Depends on what he was up to," Tomas murmured.

"*And* if he was killed for it." Peaches winced. "I mean, … I hate to make a big deal about him dying because a huge part of me is damn glad he's dead and gone, but I know that is wrong of me."

"Yet you can't help the way you feel when you were battered by him, so don't be too hard on yourself," Amber added.

Peaches groaned. "He did have some family at one time. But I know he told them all to get a life and to leave him alone. I never met any of them."

"Did he leave a will?"

"If he did, I never saw it," she replied, with a shrug. "I am his legal wife, so I don't know if that makes a difference."

"It might," Tomas noted. "At least the bank accounts that he had his name on would automatically become yours, I would think."

"I don't know if he had other bank accounts," she replied. "He was supposed to go in and do a bunch of paperwork, but he was killed first."

"Interesting," he murmured. At that, he turned and looked over at Amber. She was staring down at the laptop in surprise.

"So how much money do you think you have?" Amber asked Peaches.

"Can you see it?" Peaches asked, sitting up straight.

"Yeah, he's got auto-log-ins here. I just went to his history and checked."

"I didn't know you could do that," she admitted, staring at Amber.

"He really kept you away from technology, didn't he?" Tomas confirmed.

"Yeah, he wouldn't even let me have a phone," she added. "And it wasn't worth getting beaten up for something that I didn't know how to use anyway." She paused. "Any computer I was ever near was years and years ago, and I'm sure they've all changed by now."

"They've changed a bit, but they aren't that hard," Amber shared, as she looked at Peaches with a big smile. "I could teach you. It is easy enough to navigate a lot of this."

"That would be good," she replied, "at least it would be, if we ever got out of here."

Amber suddenly shook. She held her breath as she said, "Come over here and take a look at your bank balance."

Peaches walked over to look at the screen and stared at it for a solid minute, her jaw dropped in shock. "Oh my God," she whispered, "is that half a million dollars?"

"Yeah, it sure is. So now you know why they're rather desperate to make sure you don't leave. All the next guy has to do is get ahold of this laptop, and you're in trouble."

"Can they take all this money?" Peaches asked.

"Well, with a fist, I think they could quite easily do just that," Tomas answered. "What do you think?"

She shuddered. "Oh my God." She sat down again. "They asked me about the laptop, but I just didn't say anything. I had it in the closet. Russ and I had an argument about it earlier, and I just … I didn't even know what to say to him, so I just said that I hadn't seen it and that my husband had it with him when he died."

"Which is another reason why people are very interested in what's going on here right now," Tomas stated. "Have you had anybody search the place?"

She stared at him. "I have no idea. How would I know that?"

He nodded again. "I suppose in your case it would be hard. Anybody ever question you about being here still with this group?"

"Everybody," she stated adamantly. "They're all bugging me to choose another partner. But I don't want another partner. I just want to be left alone."

"I don't know that being left alone is something any of us can do for you right now," Tomas admitted. "We'd have to get you out of here first."

"And that's not likely to happen," she muttered, as she stared again at the laptop. "Oh my God! How did he get that kind of money?"

"You had a house, and you sold it, right?" Tomas asked her.

Peaches nodded. "Yes, but I don't know what Tristan sold it for."

"What was the address?" he asked. Once she replied with that info, he quickly moved through various websites on his phone and then shared, "The house was sold for $262,000."

She stared at him in complete shock. "Wow."

Amber went through the history of the bank account, and she added, "It's all here. So a lot of this is legally yours, the proceeds from the house that you sold. But a lot of other money is here, and these guys want it. Some of it must have come from whatever they're doing, and, in their own minds, they probably think it's justifiable that they keep it."

"Of course they would," Peaches snapped. "Everything here is done without a woman's permission."

"I don't think so," Amber retorted, fired up and choosing her words carefully. "I think a lot of women are complicit, and whatever is going on here, at least some of them are active participants."

"In your case," Tomas suggested, "I think he brought you along because he didn't know what else to do with you to keep that money, and maybe it gave him a way in the door because he was bringing in a woman."

"I just don't know," Peaches replied, with a weary shrug.

"He may have even thought he could use their help to get rid of you." Tomas shrugged.

She winced at that. "God," she said. "You know what? That is more likely than not. I did ask him to leave me alone, but I don't know why he didn't do it then."

"Because, once you went to the bank," Tomas theorized, "you might have discovered the truth much earlier than now. You may have taken some money, and he didn't want you to know about any of it. He kept you away from it as long as he could, and, by bringing you here, he made sure that you weren't a problem. But the minute you knew something, or he couldn't get to town and change something, then you would become the problem. It's easy to make problems go away in a place like this."

"There's also a chance," Peaches added, "that he was having an affair like you suggested." She looked over at Amber, with an apologetic face. "Maybe with Annette."

"Did you remember something specific?" he asked.

"Just that he always acted weird around her, as if he were going out of his way to act different."

"Which is often a sign of something going on," Amber murmured.

"It is pointless to speculate about it now though. Just tell me how I get out of here," Peaches told Tomas. "I was thinking I wouldn't find another way to live, but surely, with that kind of money sitting in the bank, I could find a way. Please." She looked at the two hopefully. "Could I buy a nice little house somewhere and maybe find a simple job?"

"I'm sure you could," Amber said warmly.

"First things first though, we've got to get out. And in order to do that and to ensure they don't come after you," Tomas explained, "we'll solve some of these problems, and we need information on those issues badly."

"How? The minute you do that, they will know something is up, and they'll try to take us out," Amber noted calmly.

Peaches stared at her in horror. "Just leave it. Let me get out of here and just leave all this."

"It'll still take a little time," he warned. "And it's not just your husband who died. Remember that Annette died too."

"I know. I know," Peaches replied, raising both hands. "But seeing this now, … seeing that there is a chance I can get out of this place and have some sort of a real life," she murmured, "I just … I don't even want to take the chance of staying around. I just want to go."

"I get it," he stated. "When Russ comes tomorrow night, tell him that you want three days."

"What?" Peaches wasn't expecting that.

"Three days to think about it, and then you'll decide."

She stared at him. "I don't want to still be here in three days, if that's what you're trying to tell me."

"You won't be," he replied calmly. "But it will give you some time to adjust and to collect yourself and to give me time to map out the escape plan."

"Yeah, time that they will not allow me to ignore."

"Maybe," he agreed, "but we need a few days. Whatever they are doing here could be taking other people's lives," he explained. "We can't take that chance."

She shuddered, then closed her eyes and nodded. "Fine,

but three days? … That's it. If you can't get me out of here by then, I'll get myself out." She stared down at the laptop. "And I need to hide this."

"Nope," he argued, "you just need to change the password." And, with that, and all three of them knowing exactly what the password was, in case there was a problem, they changed it.

"So now nobody else could get into the bank account?" Peaches asked them.

"No," Amber confirmed. "If anybody tries to log in using the history, they won't be able to. I've cleared it all, and, no, it's not saved," she added. "So, you need to remember what that password is and to never write it down anywhere," she ordered. "I've got a printscreen capture that I've sent to my phone, with all your account numbers."

At that, Peaches looked at Amber gratefully. "My God," Peaches admitted, "I'm just now realizing how absolutely blind I was to everything." She shook her head. "I don't even understand how he could do all this or even know to do all this." She sighed. "It's just too unbelievable."

"When people want to be assholes," Tomas said, "they always find a way."

At that, she snorted. "That's the truth." Then she smiled. "I'm just grateful that you guys aren't."

"Nope, we're here to help," Amber told her friend. "But you don't dare act any differently for the next few days."

She nodded. "No, I won't. And, if I am, maybe they'll take it as me thinking about which one of these guys I want," she said, with a shudder.

"Maybe," Tomas replied. "But you don't want anybody to assume anything, so stick to yourself, and no happy expressions. You are beaming right now, so fix that and make it seem like you're struggling to deal with whatever is happening in your life—because you are."

"Then we'll see what we can do to get us all out of here," Amber added.

"Got it," Peaches confirmed. "Three days. That's it then," she said, with a worried look. "Please don't let me down."

At that, Amber reached out and gave her a quick hug. "We won't. Now try to get some sleep."

With that, they took their leave and headed back to the basement. As they walked into her living space, Amber whispered to Tomas, "Do you think she's … I mean, can we trust her?"

He shook his head. "No, we sure can't. It's not that I think she'll betray us, but I think she'll be incapable of keeping this to herself."

"I was afraid of that," Amber said, "and that'll be a problem."

"Not only is that a problem but it's a big one," he noted, "but I needed some way to get her to stay calm."

"Oh, I get it." Amber rubbed her temples. "But this is like her first ray of hope since she arrived here, and I can see how it'll have an effect on her."

"Of course," he replied gently. "And we'll do everything we can to get her out safely, but just doing everything we can won't necessarily be the answer."

She wanted to know what that was, but she understood. "That's fine. I need to crash now. Tomorrow will be a tough day, and I'm still expected to help here."

"This is indelicate, and I hate to bring it up, but … you'll also be expected to look a little ragged."

She stared at him for a moment. "Why is that?"

"Because I'm in town," he replied, with a wry look. "They'll assume you didn't get much sleep tonight."

She blushed at that. "Oh, Jesus. I didn't even think about that, but you're right. These guys will be looking for signs that this is a real relationship, won't they?"

He nodded. "They will. And not that I'm against making it look real for the sake of the guys," he teased, with a big grin, "but we both need some rest." He looked around the room and offered, "I should sleep on the couch."

"I wouldn't," she stated. "If anybody had any inkling that you were sleeping on the couch, that would make our story very unworkable, and it will be hell to explain."

"So what do you want to do then?" he asked.

"We can share the bed," she replied. "It's not an issue for me, and honestly, I'm so exhausted that it really won't stop me from sleeping."

"Okay," he agreed. "You get ready for bed. I'll come in after a bit."

She nodded. "What will you do?"

"I need to check in with Levi," he said. "I need to pass on information gathered here, and we need Ice's help. I want them to take a hard look at Tristan's bank accounts."

She nodded. "What? Are you thinking he has more than one?"

"I do," he said, looking at her. "Don't you?"

She frowned, then nodded. "You're probably right. But she won't access anything her name isn't on without a death certificate."

"No, and that'll get ugly at some point in time," he noted. "But that's not today's worry."

And, with that, she nodded and headed off to bed.

RUNNING SOME WATER and a radio to make some background noise, so hopefully Peaches couldn't hear his phone conversation, he called Levi and caught him up on the news, knowing that it would get passed on to Dezi and Saul. It felt right. Tomas was enjoying this work, at least for the moment. When Levi asked him for an action plan, he told him the little bit they had set up.

"Finding the graves would be helpful," he replied thoughtfully.

"If the police were to come in," Tomas noted, "cadaver dogs would take care of that in no time. Yet, without a body, I'm not sure we'll do what we need to in the end," Tomas admitted.

"I can talk to some local cops here and see," Levi replied.

"Good," Tomas said, "but make sure nobody is connected to this place. I'm thinking they have a pretty widespread network, including cops on their payroll."

"You really think they're running guns?"

"I know they are. I saw them with a delivery. I'm just not sure yet how they are paying for them."

"And maybe that's all they're doing. Maybe they're bringing in product and reselling at a higher market price."

"Maybe, but they're taking an awful lot of risk for that," Tomas said. "This wasn't just one dozen guns. This was a huge delivery of weapons and ammo."

"Guys have done risky stuff for even just the hope of more money."

"I hear you, and I don't know exactly what they're up to," Tomas admitted. "All I can tell you is that this kind of shit is definitely going on here right now."

"Fascinating," Levi murmured. "Just understanding what motivates people and how they go about doing what they do? This shit always makes me interested in mankind."

"Yeah, well, these guys are a little more depraved than that, with their sexist attitudes toward women. Pretty sure they're after Peaches's bank account and don't particularly care how they get it."

"What would be interesting," Levi added, "would be finding out if any of these other members had other spouses they may have gotten rid of."

"Ouch." Tomas cringed. "Sorry, but I guess you're right though. It would be interesting to know because how else are they collecting money to buy any guns or to even purchase food for all of them?"

"I wonder if they are marrying up?" Levi muttered. "It seems like you know what I'm talking about. Everybody's had at least one spouse before."

"All except for Baxter potentially."

"We haven't got a last name on him," Levi noted, "but we do have somebody named Baxter who's a troublemaker, including a record for running around with guns, also selling them—but doing deals that make everybody quite wary. I bet he's on the FBI's watch list," he guessed. "So, if this happens to be that Baxter," he added, "we'll get whatever it takes to tear apart that place."

"You'll need it too," Tomas agreed, "but, if you don't take them by surprise, you'll meet more firepower here than anybody can deal with. It will become another Waco."

"Yeah, unfortunately that happens way too often. Any way of finding out if it's the right Baxter?"

"Yeah, I got a picture," Tomas replied. "I took it while I was there today."

"He let you?"

"No, but I have an interesting little app on my phone,"

he explained. "So I just have my phone in my hand and click a button, once it's at the right angle. No fuss and all is good. It doesn't bring the camera on screen, and there is no flash."

"That sounds like a pretty good deal," Levi noted, "and also very handy in situations like this."

"Right, so I'm sending the photo to you."

Levi waited, as he checked his phone. "It's here," he confirmed. "I'm forwarding it on to the tech team. They can dig deeper."

"Okay, I'll get back to you later," Tomas said, and they terminated the call.

Putting away his phone, and making sure things were secure for the night, he looked around to see if Amber was in bed, and she was. After his usual short nightly clean-up ritual, he quickly joined her in bed. It was late, and he had no energy left. Wishing he could have a shower, he promised himself one in the morning and crawled into bed beside her.

When she shifted his way, he murmured, "It's just me. Go back to sleep."

"Okay," she said, yawning. "I was waiting for you to come in anyway."

"Why is that? I hope my call didn't disturb you," he asked curiously.

"No, I heard your voice but not your words. I don't know why but it just feels safer somehow with you here," she replied. And, with that, she rolled over, only to scooch back ever-so-slightly toward him, and then fell asleep.

He took in a whiff of her exotic perfume and relaxed himself. Soon he too found a way to sleep.

The next morning started off with a heavy pounding on the door. He rolled over to find the side of his bed empty and a muffled voice at the door.

"Yes! Of course I'll come," he heard her murmur to someone.

When the door closed, he got up, walked over, and asked Amber, "What's going on?"

"It's Peaches," she whispered.

He bolted upright. "What's the matter?" he asked warily.

"They can't wake her up," she said, sending him a worried look. "I'm going over to give them a hand."

"Why you?" he asked suspiciously.

She stopped, looked at him in surprise, and replied, "I don't know. They asked for me. Everybody here pitches in on emergency situations."

"Oh, I get that," he noted. "I think I'll come with you." She frowned, and he shook his head. "No, after the conversation last night, hell no."

She nodded and said, "I didn't hear anybody upstairs."

"No, neither did I," he noted. "My biggest concern was that her place is bugged."

She stared at him in shock. "Oh my God, that didn't even cross my mind. I should have thought of that. Now what?"

"If that turns out to be true, we're all in trouble." And, with that said, he quickly dressed and was at the door with her in five minutes. As they ran upstairs, several people were gathered in a cluster in Peaches's bedroom.

"What's going on?" Amber cried out, as she walked in.

"I came over to talk to her this morning," Mary stated, "but she didn't answer the door. When I let myself in, I found her on the bed, … unresponsive. I'm trying to run some tests on her now."

"Are you a doctor?" Tomas asked in surprise, and she stared at him sharply.

"No," she snapped. "We don't do doctors here."

And, with a growing sense of suspicion, he asked, "So then what? How do you know what's wrong with her?" He tried to remain calm and detached, as much as he could manage in this absurd situation.

"Doesn't matter. She knows the rules, as well as I do. We look after our own here." She shot him a hard look. "And, if you'll cause any trouble, you can get the fuck out." Her face was beet red, with all kinds of emotions. She looked worried sick.

He shook his head. "I've become quite fond of her," Tomas stated. "I'll be staying."

"I don't think so," she stated, with a snort. "You can take that attitude outside now!"

"Not unless I see that she's improving." His tone was hard and low, forcefully getting the words out.

She stared at him in surprise and looked over at Amber, who sat beside Peaches, her hand on her forehead, and a horrified expression on her face.

"If you'll stay here with lover boy," Mary snapped, "I'm leaving."

"That's fine. Ignore him. He's new, and he will improve," she stated, looking over at Mary. "Was she exactly like this when you found her?"

She nodded. "Exactly like that. You know how depressed she's been," she began, "so you make your own inferences." And, with that, Mary stormed out.

Another woman crept forward. "Do you really think she's dying?"

"I hope not," Amber replied, as she looked over at her. "But I don't know yet. All right, so let's take few steps at a time and not get ahead of ourselves. Do you know anything?" She looked around at the people, hoping someone had a clue.

Betty looked at Amber and called out, "I have a first aid kit."

"And I've got basic first aid training," Amber said, with a shrug, but she looked over at Tomas and smiled. She nodded in his direction and added, "He's got a lot more."

"Oh good," Betty replied, turning to look at him in relief.

"I sure hope so," Amber noted. "Give us a few minutes to check her over and see what we can do."

At that, the others nodded and quickly exited the house.

"What the hell?" Tomas asked in rage and beyond disbelief. "So somebody comes up sick like that, and they just live or die on their own?"

"Yeah, more or less," Amber confirmed.

"I also don't trust Mary," he stated. But he was already over at Amber's side. "Help me turn her over," he said.

"Why?" Amber asked, as they flipped Peaches onto her stomach.

"I'll see if I can make her throw up."

She looked at him in surprise.

"That doesn't necessarily mean there are drugs in her system," he explained, "but, if anything is, then we need to make sure we get them out, if we can."

"Do you really think she tried to commit suicide?" He shot her a knowing look, and she shrugged. "I don't, but, yeah, that's what I mean about Mary. I don't trust anything about her."

Then he sniffed the air. "I'm smelling something else too." He sniffed once more. "It smells like chloroform in here."

She stared at him in shock. "But then why would Mary contact me?"

"I'm not sure, but I think it's important we get whatever's in Peaches's stomach out *now*. Chloroform is a different issue altogether."

With that, he pulled Peaches onto his knees with a trash can underneath, and he shoved two fingers down her throat. Almost immediately she bucked in his arms and upchucked.

He did it several more times, until he was satisfied that her stomach was empty, and then eased her back onto the bed. "My God," Amber said and sighed. "I see pills here."

"Yeah, and I highly suspect that the pills would take time to take effect. I'm also guessing that Mary's the one who forced Peaches to take them. Who knows how she did it though."

"You think she was forced to take them?" Amber cried out in a low whisper.

He nodded. "I do. I mean, if she didn't like something or smelled a trap, maybe it made her anxious so she reverted to being docile." He stooped over to point out the contents in the trash can. "All this, and there's still no way to know anything for sure, but the room isn't right."

"Where did you see pills?" she asked pointedly.

He pointed to the night table, where there was a little saucer with a bunch of empty pill packets. "Oh, that makes more sense," Amber said.

"Mary may have made Peaches drink it forcibly," he suggested.

"Maybe," she added. "And maybe Peaches said she wasn't feeling good this morning, meaning she couldn't stop smiling, and then Mary came over and gave her something." She stopped to think it through. "But that would also imply that Mary was trying to kill her. Or at least knock her out," she said fearfully.

"Whichever was more convenient for them."

At that, Peaches gave a low groan, and she slowly opened her eyes. When she saw the two of them, she shattered into tears. "What happened?" she whispered, softly crying.

"What happened to you is a very good question," he said. "I'm hoping you can answer that."

She stared at him. "I don't know," she replied, clutching at her throat with one hand, her other arm wrapped around her stomach. "My throat, it hurts."

"Yeah, I made you throw up," he explained calmly, "and, according to everybody else, you tried to commit suicide."

She stared at him in shock, and she frowned. Her eyebrows pulled closer, and she looked around to make sure they were alone, then she whispered, "I didn't. I was just upset."

"After what we found last night?" Tomas asked her. She nodded, and he looked at her thoughtfully. "That was my take on it too," he agreed, lost in his own head. "Did you see Mary this morning?"

She nodded. "I wasn't sure that I could act normal with her, and she's very perceptive, so I told her that I wasn't feeling good, and I couldn't do the morning shift. She came back and gave me a tisane tea."

"Well, guess what? … That was a bad idea." Amber shook her head. "Whatever these pills were, and whether they were part of the tisane or not, you were unconscious when we got here. Supposedly Mary couldn't wake you, which is when she came down and got us."

Peaches stared at Amber and then stared at the empty

pill packs. With her hands at a throat, she whispered, "What the hell?"

"Yeah," he agreed. "*What the hell* is about right. We need to get you some medical help."

"They won't let me," she stated. "They won't let anybody."

"That's just too damn bad," Tomas said, with a hard smile. "They'll have a fight on their hands if they try to stop me." And, with that, he got up, then scooped Peaches in his arms and carried her outside to his vehicle. He put her in the passenger side, and, with a hard look over at Amber, he said, "I'll be back in a little bit." He fired up the truck and took off like a bat out of hell.

Several people came running after he left.

"What happened?"

"What's going on?"

"Where's he going?"

"How is she?"

The voices were a cacophony of shock, anger, and curiosity, all as one.

"I think he'll get her medical help," Amber said.

"But it's not allowed."

"Apparently it is now," she replied in a dry tone. "Good luck trying to tell him that he can't do it. By the way, she was awake and said that she didn't take those pills."

The women looked at her in shock.

"But then …" One woman tried to say something and suddenly stopped dead in her tracks.

"Yeah. That's what I thought too," Amber agreed, then turned to go to her basement suite, shaking her head. She went straight to her room and got dressed properly. This day would be shit, and it was a little warmer too. She would have some pretty uncomfortable questions to answer, and, sure enough, by the time she walked into the kitchen, trying to appear as normal as possible, Mary glared at her.

"No medical help. That's the rule."

"Considering that it was quite possible you'd end up with a dead body here and lots of questions to answer, it seemed like the most prudent thing to do."

"Even after we said no?" she growled.

"Maybe, but what was I supposed to do? Let a friend die?"

"She chose it herself, and she was conscious when he took her out of there," Mary snapped.

"Mary, Peaches said that she didn't take any pills."

"Well, of course she would say that," she spat in disgust. "How many people admit to trying to commit suicide? Now go report to Baxter," she ordered, her voice ringing with authority.

Amber stared at her. "So I do something good for a friend who's unconscious and quite possibly dying," she said slowly, "and now I'm in trouble?"

"You know the rules."

"Even if somebody is in deep trouble?" she asked in complete bewilderment. She had a good idea what was happening, but to even think that something like that was possible seemed incredulous. She looked over at the two pregnant women. "And what about the pregnancies?"

Mary snorted. "Women have been giving birth for centuries without the need of a doctor," she sneered. "Nobody here needs medical attention for something like that."

Such a noticeable scorn was in her voice that Amber was literally shocked. "Wow." She looked over at the other two women again, who were definitely listening to this conversation, but carefully kept their heads down. "Meaning, a problem is here, and you think it's me?"

"There's no problem," Mary snapped. "It's just obvious that you don't have the personality that we need here."

"You mean that of someone who chose to look after a friend," she stated calmly. "One who obviously needed medical help—lying there helpless and dying this morning. Why did you call on me if you thought she didn't need help?"

"I wasn't expecting you to do what you did," she snapped, sneering. "But obviously it's a good thing I did contact you, so now we know."

"Know what?" she asked, pressing forward, even though she knew it was best to just shut up … yesterday.

"Oh, don't you worry," Mary said, with a hard laugh. "You'll find out soon enough." At that, she looked over at the other two women and told them, "Go about your work."

The other women immediately got up and left.

When both women were out of earshot, Amber crossed her arms and stared at Mary, exasperated. "I don't get it," she said. "How is this even a place worthy of living here if you don't look after your own people in an emergency?"

"We look after them just fine." Mary nodded, looking behind her, and Amber was alarmed at hearing a sound behind her. "These two will escort you to Baxter." And, with that, Mary turned away, as if to say Amber was dismissed.

Unsettled, and with an icy finger of fear clutching at her heart, Amber knew she might very well be led to her death. Her insides were cold, as she walked toward the leader's house.

The two gunmen led her up to Mary and Baxter's house, then motioned her to go inside. As she stepped up onto the deck, Baxter called to her from the other side. "What did you do?" He sounded vexed but not angry.

"I was helping a friend," she stated. "It was obvious that she needed her stomach pumped, or she could die. She needed help, so how could that be wrong?"

For a long moment, he looked at her. His hard eyes were calculating, as if looking into her soul. Then he sighed. "In a normal circumstance it probably wouldn't come to this," he said, and, as she tried to get closer to him, he held up a hand. "Stay there."

She frowned, but she stayed where he asked. Something was going on here that she didn't quite understand and wasn't even sure she would ever get a chance to. This place was a ticking time bomb, with so many innuendos and undercurrents that made no sense. "I don't understand," she admitted, and there was no need to even feign the bewilderment. "I thought I was helping."

"Of course you did," he replied, "and, in many cases, that's what it would look like."

"*Would look like?*" she repeated, holding up her hands. "So what does it look like now? Mary is really angry with me."

"Yes," he agreed, with a ring of authority, more so than Mary. "She has a very strict sense of right and wrong."

"How can helping a friend *not die* be wrong?" she asked, almost crying, her tears nearly ready to spill, hoping it helped her be seen as a victim, not a spy.

"In this case we all know that Peaches has been very distraught lately," he noted. "So it's that much more of a problem."

"It's not a problem if she gets help," Amber murmured. "It's not a problem if it's the people who are supposed to be her friends. Let her see that you care. We all do."

He looked at her sharply. "And it's nice that you worry about her," he noted, "but it would have been best if you hadn't interfered."

"Baxter, I don't understand that," she said. "I really don't. I was scared. … It never occurred to me that … that I was doing something wrong." Tears spilled down her face, and the words came out sounding choked and hysterical. Her anger was tamed, and she needed to look remorseful.

"No," he agreed, "and I understand that."

She stared at him, trying to see through the shadows on the deck. "So, what am I supposed to do? I mean, we have pregnant women here. Are they supposed to die in child-birth, if something goes wrong?"

"Well, let's hope it doesn't come to that," he stated. "We didn't always use to be quite so black-and-white about things. And I do trust Mary to keep everybody safe. To keep you all safe."

"Mary? … I thought she looked like she had given up. Like she would have been happy to let Peaches die."

"Was she dying?" he asked, with a note of finality in his voice. "Even if she was, it was by her own choice."

"She certainly didn't like being pressured to marry somebody," Amber shared, knowing she really shouldn't be bringing it up.

"Who was pressuring her?"

"I think it was Russ," she murmured.

"*Hmm*," he murmured, his voice soft as he contemplated. "I'll have a talk with him."

"It wouldn't be good …" She suddenly stopped, realizing her mistake. "I mean, if a woman has to commit suicide to get away from him, definitely something is wrong there."

He let out a short bark of laughter. "Isn't that the truth." He was laughing hard now. It took him sometime to collect his bearings. "Anyway," he said, "I'll talk to Mary. Obviously you didn't have any idea what was expected."

"No, I didn't," she agreed, "and I … I'm really struggling now to understand how this is supposedly a good thing for anyone."

"Of course," he said. "Those who have been here for a long time understand, but, when you bring in new people, it gets complicated. They're new, young, hotheaded, and they don't understand our system."

"I'm sorry. I should have known, and apparently I messed it up," she said, with their arms wide. "And still I feel like I would do it again to help anybody in trouble. I care for the people here. This is the only family I have."

He nodded, and his voice was soft when he said, "Yes, of course you would." He paused for a moment. "I'll think about this. Go back to your house and stay there."

She stepped back. "Have I really done something terribly wrong?"

"By the rules that we have set, yes," he stated, looking at her keenly. "I do understand why you did it, but there still must be consequences." When he said the word *consequences*, his voice hardened.

She gasped. "My God." Her whole body shook, and, as much as she wanted to shut up, she still asked, "Like what?"

"I'm not sure yet," he admitted. "Again, I have to think about it. Now go on back to your house and stay there until you're contacted."

She nodded slowly. "And what about my fiancé?"

"He won't be allowed back on the property," he told her flatly.

"And Peaches?"

"That is a completely different issue and doesn't concern you now," he replied, his voice calm and authoritative, almost as if daring her to argue.

She didn't even know what else to say. It was obvious that whatever she had thought would happen went out the window when Peaches messed it up, or it was messed up for them.

Amber wouldn't argue if it meant staying here. This was her only chance now to stay and to weigh in one way or the other. She took a step back and said, "Fine, I'll go back to my place." She turned and, with the men still escorting her silently, she headed back to her place. She stepped inside and closed and locked the door. Almost immediately, a hard pounding came on the door. She looked out the window to find Brutus glaring through the window at her.

"What?" she asked, leaving the door closed and locked.

"What the hell are you doing here?" he asked.

"It seems like nobody gives a damn about Peaches around here. Actually it's good to know that's how it is," she snapped bitterly. "Pardon me for thinking the right thing to do was to try to help someone."

That seemed to stop him for a moment. "We have our own code here," he said, calming down. "I thought you knew that."

"A code is one thing," she argued, "but letting people die for lack of care is another."

"Peaches tried to commit suicide," he snapped. "Everybody knows that."

"Only because she was being pressured into marriage by one of the guys." She pointed her finger at Brutus. "How is that okay?"

He stared at her in surprise. "Seriously?"

She nodded. "Yes."

"Do you know who it was?"

"Russ." She told him about the argument they heard last night, and Brutus stepped back. "Interesting," he murmured. "That's not generally allowed either."

"Right! So who around here was looking after Peaches?" she asked bitterly. The next time she spoke, she was in tears again. "It doesn't seem like anybody around here gives a crap about her."

With that, she stepped away, refusing to talk to Brutus anymore. She wasn't sure what the hell would happen, but she knew that something was about to go down—or to come crashing in on her head. Screw the three-day ultimatum to get out of here. This was all about to blow up in her face, and, whether she wanted more answers about Annette or not, Amber needed to get the hell out before the decision was made for her.

She needed to get out before she wasn't able to.

Chapter 6

"THANK GOD." AMBER raced to Tomas, throwing herself into his arms, when he finally showed up.

He held her close and stroked her head. "Thank God you're okay. I really hated leaving you behind."

"There wasn't a whole lot of choice," she murmured. "I was called in to see Baxter, and he's making the decision about my behavior. But he also said that you wouldn't be allowed back on the property."

"Yeah, I got that message loud and clear," he noted. "So I left again, and the truck is parked down the way. Don't give him the choice to tangle you up here. Do you want to leave now?"

"Yeah, I don't think I have a choice at this point," she said hoarsely.

"I think you should. We know that Peaches is out and safe," he noted.

"Is she though?" she asked, looking at him.

"She's in the hospital under guard. Levi arranged that."

"Thank God for that," she murmured.

"I've also talked to the county sheriff, and it's the Baxter Levi thought it may be," he said cheerfully. "So, if you were expecting leniency, you can forget it. As far as Baxter's history goes, his rap sheet is huge. I am concerned that he has no morals, and, as such, no qualms about ordering somebody killed in a heartbeat."

She shuddered. "I was afraid of that. I'm not even sure what to say. I haven't got all the answers I wanted."

"You may never get all those answers," he stated firmly. "I'm not the kind of guy who would order you to go, but I'm certainly of the opinion—"

"You should go find Dezi," she murmured. "I haven't seen him at all."

"No, I haven't either," he murmured, "and I may check that out tonight."

"In which case we can't leave yet," she stated. "I won't leave someone here who came in to help me get out of trouble."

He smiled at her. "Believe me. If he's in trouble, you can't help."

"I might be able to …"

He shook his head. "No, our best move now is to get you the hell out of here."

She thought about it for a second, then remembered the look in Baxter's eyes and his words. She nodded. "I guess you're probably right, even as much as I hate to give in."

"I don't think it's giving in," he argued. "I think it's about making a good decision before all the options are bad."

She winced at that. "I can't believe that guy, … like he can get away with keeping people prisoner like this. And I feel bad for the women who are pregnant."

"Yeah, I'm sure they're wondering about their own options right now too," he noted, "but you have to understand that, in some cases, the women can be way worse than the men."

"That would be Mary," she confirmed.

Just then the door burst open, and Brutus was there, with a grin on his face.

"Now that's what I wanted to see," he said, with a jeer. "The fiancé is here."

Thankfully it was just Brutus. "What are you doing here?" she cried out. "How dare you just storm into my place."

"It's hardly your place anymore now, is it?" Brutus said. "It's not like little Peaches will be back. She was such a loser anyway."

Amber stared at him in shock. "That is hardly the way to speak about a woman who's obviously troubled."

"*Troubled?* She was nothing but a loser, and her husband let all of us know. Too bad he failed to get the information he needed before he screwed things up for himself," he said. "But you know how that goes. Or maybe you don't, but you will by tomorrow."

"Really?" she asked, as she dropped her arms from around Tomas. "What does that mean?"

"Oh, you'll find out," he snapped. "Soon enough, you'll find out. And you won't like it one damn bit."

She took a deep breath. "That sounds like a threat."

"Not a threat," he sneered, "a promise. As for your boyfriend here, You might as well say goodbye. I'll take him in now. That was supposed to happen tomorrow night, if and when this asshole ever got back. Otherwise, we would go hunt him down in town, but now I want that chance with him first."

"So … what? You take him, and you kill me? Is that how this goes?" she asked bitterly.

"Not if I buy you out," he said, "then you are all mine." There was such satisfaction in his words that she stared at him in horror.

"Did you say, *buy me out?*"

"Yep. Somebody has to pay for your sins," he explained, "but that's all right. I'm happy to do it."

"Jesus." She stared at him.

"But this guy has got to go first. I thought about making you do it, you know, as a way to make sure you realize that you'll never get free. To make you understand your place and what happens to people who can't follow the rules."

"What rule did he break?" she cried out.

"He interfered," Brutus said, "and he knows better."

She looked over at Tomas, who was just looking at Brutus, with a lazy smile on his face.

"That's all right," Tomas said, "just step aside, Amber. We'll settle this. He wants a fight, so he'll get a fight."

"No fight," Brutus argued, with a sneer. "That's a waste of my time and energy."

"Let's go for it then. Show me what you got."

OUTSIDE, AND SUDDENLY surrounded by two other men, Tomas walked past the houses, assuming they were heading in the direction of Baxter's house. However, they took several redirects and ended up in a clearing on the other side of trees. He looked around and asked, "Baxter doesn't want to see me?"

"No, he really doesn't," Russ said in a hoarse voice. "Traitors are like that."

Tomas stared at him in surprise. "Traitor? What did I do?"

"You took one of our women away."

"A sick woman," he said, feigning surprise. "Quite a sick

woman."

"Nothing wrong with her that a good man couldn't cure," Russ snapped. "She's just lonely."

"She lost her partner," Tomas acknowledged, "but obviously that's not all that was going on."

"It would have been, if you had left it alone," Russ said. "We were trying to solve that problem right away."

"What problem?" he asked carefully. "I mean, whether she was suicidal or not, I don't know, but she obviously needed care."

"But you don't get to make those kinds of decisions," said Russ. "That's not for you to decide."

"Ah." Tomas nodded. "So what you're saying is I overstepped my authority."

"Yeah, you think?" Brutus growled. "And we don't take kindly to that."

Tomas nodded slowly. "So, what now?" he asked. "Because, if you don't make the rules clear, how the hell am I supposed to know how to follow them?"

"You should have known. You already belong to a different faction of the same group," Brutus snapped.

"Yeah, but a faction where they look after their women," Tomas noted, with a deadly calm. "They don't leave them to suffer the way you left Peaches to suffer."

"She didn't suffer, not at all," Russ argued. "Like I said, she would be married before the week was out."

"That's not what you just said," Tomas murmured, wondering how bad this was likely to get. Not that he was worried because he had a lot of skills, but skills against one or two was one thing, Skills against four or five was another. He didn't know how this would go down with just these three idiots or how many more would be coming his way.

Meanwhile a wild bird called in the distance. Tomas cocked his ear and said, "Interesting birdlife you've got around here."

"Fuck the birdlife," Brutus said. "The only thing I want to hear is your screams of pain."

Tomas studied him. "Seriously that's what this is all about? You want to beat the shit out of me?"

"You'll be lucky if you survive," Brutus stated, snarling. "We don't take kindly to anybody interfering."

"I still don't understand why you're so upset," Tomas repeated. "She would have died. And you're worried that I saved a woman, so that you still have her in your group?"

Russ laughed. "Because it was my woman who you stole, asshole. So I get the rights to your first beating."

Tomas stared at him. "Yeah, I remember now. You're the one who she was *so happy* to see last night when she was screaming and woke me up. So you're the one who would force her to marry you? You can't get a woman on your own, *huh*?"

One of the other guys chuckled. Russ shot him a hard look and threatened Tomas. "You'll pay for that. Don't you worry. You'll pay."

"You'll only get part of this, Russ," Brutus stated. "You know perfectly well that he's mine to take down."

"What? So now you're fighting over me? Is that normal here?" While pushing their buttons, Tomas assessed his team—Saul was close, but where was Dezi?

"What Russ'll do to you is nothing," Brutus growled, looking over at Tomas. "That's my woman you're trying to claim as your own." Brutus glared. "Like you'll get a fine piece of ass like that for yourself. That's not happening. You're nothing but a busted-down piece of shit."

Tomas stared at the two men in wonder. "Is this really how you guys live? Threatening women to the point that they have no choice but to become your partners? You can't get somebody to *want* to be with you, so you take them by force? You do know the world has a word for that."

"Don't you fucking say anything to us," Brutus screamed. "We treat our women just fine, and they know perfectly well how to get along."

"How *you* live may seem perfectly fine to you, but I wonder if the women have any idea about what really goes on around this place," he stated calmly.

"What do you mean by that?" Pearson asked suspiciously.

Tomas turned toward him. "Do you think all the women will take kindly to knowing that they're forced into these arranged marriages, whether they like it or not?"

"What makes you think they don't know already?" Russ asked, looking at Tomas imperiously. "It's not like we've had to force any of them."

"Really? I guess the word *force* has different meanings for you guys," Tomas noted. "If women aren't free to leave, free to get medical care when they need it, free to get support when they need it, free to choose who they want for a partner, that sure sounds like *forced* to me."

Russ shrugged. "We run as a society here, and everybody does their part."

"And the women's part is to marry people they don't want to be married to? Is that it?" Tomas stared at him.

"We haven't heard any complaints yet."

"Of course not. And, even if you did, I'm sure you would have beaten that out of them. Don't you think?" Tomas said, with a sneer. "I wonder, if you got these women away from here, how many would willingly return?" he asked.

"All of them," Brutus piped up.

"Like I said, we haven't had any complaints," snapped Russ.

"Because they don't dare." Tomas shook his head. "God, this is a feudal society."

"And that's just fine with us," Russ said. "It works."

"No, it doesn't work," Tomas snapped. "Anybody who has to force a woman to stay with men who they don't want to be with, denying them proper medical attention when they need it, is not taking care of their own. This is using power and abuse to keep people prisoners, who don't want to be kept," he said, shaking his head. "Honest to God, you guys should be ashamed of yourselves. This is no way to build loyalty."

"What the hell are you talking about? It has been like this from the start," Brutus argued.

"The hell it has. Women in biker gangs, other groups, and women in general should have choices and should go with men they want to go with. Or be alone if they so choose."

"No, they are possessions. They can get passed around, just like everything else," Russ added. "And this system works for us."

"But it doesn't work for the women," Tomas stated. "Only you guys don't give a shit about it working for the women, do you? I mean, as long as you get a piece of ass at the end of the night and somebody to cook and to clean, you really don't care."

"What's to care about?" Brutus asked, with a harsh glare. "As long as they do what they're supposed to do, nothing else matters."

Tomas couldn't believe that any woman would even want to be here. But obviously these guys all seemed to think that the women were here willingly. "It would be interesting to bring it up in the next meeting," Tomas noted, "and to find out just how many women want to be here."

"You won't be at that meeting," Pearson stated, "so I wouldn't worry about it."

"Ah, so I'm not allowed to stay, is that it?"

"Hell no," Brutus yelled, staring at him. "You've caused enough trouble already."

Tomas nodded. "Of course. I mean anything that would cause the women to rise up against you guys and to claim their most basic of rights as human beings would be horrible, in your view anyway. Not to mention the women freely sharing their own beliefs and looking after themselves and their offspring, which you won't even let come into the world with any medical assistance," he said, shaking his head.

"Oh hell no. They don't need medical assistance. Women have been giving birth—"

Tomas snorted and interrupted. "And dying in childbirth for hundreds of years. Yeah, I get it. It's perfectly natural, and most births go well," he stated, "but there's a reason why we have modern medicine. It's to help make our lives easier and to relieve suffering and loss."

"We choose to not have anything to do with the outside world," Pearson said, his voice calm.

But Tomas knew he was the most dangerous of them all. There was just something about him and that killing acceptance in his gaze.

"I'm surprised that your clan does," he said to Tomas.

"They do because they also see the value of looking after

their people. And keeping them happy in the knowledge that they are well loved and cared for," he murmured. "Not like this bullshit here." He shook his head. "Women need physical assistance sometimes. Everyone does. You can't just wear them down to the bone, looking after you guys."

"I don't think that's really an issue here," Brutus snapped. "All the women here are in good shape. We wouldn't allow it any other way."

Tomas stopped and stared, chuckling. "Wouldn't *allow it* any other way?" he repeated, still staring at him. "Are you for real? You do realize it is the twenty-first century, not the thirteenth, right?"

And at that, Brutus took a swing at him.

"Hey, not here," snapped Pearson, who Tomas had found out earlier was the third man in line after Baxter and then Brutus. "Brutus, get yourself under control or get out of here. We have to get farther away from the houses."

"I don't give a fuck anymore," Brutus yelled. "I've had enough of this guy and his smart-ass insults."

"And I don't care if you give a fuck or not," Pearson said. "Now move it."

And, with great difficulty, Brutus managed to get himself under control and to go forward. "He's a dead man. He's mine, and he's dead."

"He's not," Pearson argued.

"You already told me that I could take him out."

"I told you that you could give him a good beating," Pearson stated. "Taking him out is a different story. You heard Baxter say so."

"Fuck that," Brutus yelled. "This traitor will just go back and make life difficult for Amber, and she's mine."

"Amber doesn't even want you," Russ snickered.

"She just doesn't know what she wants," Brutus snapped, glaring at his buddy. "Not with this fucker in the wings, filling her head with nonsense. Besides, who the fuck are you to talk? It's not like Peaches wanted you. Hell, she tried to commit suicide to get away from you. That says a lot for you, doesn't it?"

"Whoa, whoa, whoa," Pearson yelled. "Enough of that bullshit, you two. That stops right now."

The two men shrugged, but both were angry and still glaring at each other.

"Nice interplay you've got here," Tomas murmured. "Sounds like an awful lot more discord is here than anybody is letting on."

"There's always discord everywhere," Pearson snapped.

As they kept on walking, Tomas looked around, knowing that Saul would be somewhere close by. "So, is this what you'll do to Dezi now too?"

"Wish I could," Pearson snapped. "It's only because of Dezi that you won't get deep-sixed tonight," he murmured. "A beating he would understand, but, beyond that, it's not good."

"I'm glad you won't blame Dezi for this at least," Tomas noted.

"Anybody can have a bad seed in their group," Pearson noted. "It's what you do about it at the end of the day that counts. And tonight Dezi will prove to us that he's got the balls to do what needs to be done."

"Ah." Tomas nodded. "So you'll get Dezi to beat me up."

"Only after we're done," Pearson added, "then he gets to decide whether you live or die."

"Cute," Tomas murmured. "Nice society you've got

here."

"You keep saying that," Russ said in a gruff tone. "Just shut the fuck up."

"Why?" Tomas asked. "I mean, obviously nobody here gives a shit what I say, and nobody'll listen. That's the whole point of this, isn't it? To silence me because you don't want to hear anything I say, because you just don't like it. It's not what you want to hear because it doesn't give you permission to confine and serially rape a woman who doesn't want anything to do with you. I mean, that's all you'd be doing, … the whole lot of you, it seems. Neither woman wants to be married to Russ or to Brutus. Neither woman wants to share a bed with you. I mean," Tomas repeated, "Peaches even went so far as to attempt suicide. What does that say about your great society?" he asked, with a sneer.

At that, Pearson shoved him forward. "You're not helping your case."

"I don't give a fuck about my case," Tomas snapped, as he took two more steps. Then, in a move that completely caught them all off guard, he spun on his right foot and took out Pearson. He heard a satisfying crunch, as he hit his jaw, before he went down.

Pearson was out cold and didn't move.

Then Tomas turned to face the other two. "Now that the numbers are a little more even," he said, "bring it on, bitches."

Chapter 7

AMBER COULDN'T STAY. Baxter's orders be damned. No way she could stay here, knowing that Tomas was out there getting his ass kicked. When she went to open the door, Mary stood in the way.

"Where are you going?" she asked in a hard voice.

She stared at her in shock. "Mary."

"Yeah, me," she snapped. "I want to know what the hell you're up to."

"What are you talking about?" she asked, but the fear bubbled up inside. "We were helping Peaches, that's all."

"Like she fucking needed help," Mary snapped. "That woman is just a wuss."

"A wuss?" Amber cried out. "She's still grieving the loss of her husband, and you call her a wuss?"

"She wasn't grieving," she sneered. "She hated him with a passion. I figured, when he had the affair with Annette, she'd be happy about it. But, no, she just kept on whining that she wanted to leave. As if that would be allowed," she said, with an eye roll. "And, when both of them died, she found out just how hard her life here would be."

"It didn't have to be hard," Amber murmured, staring at the other woman. "She didn't have to suffer."

"Maybe not"—Mary shrugged—"but she did, didn't she? She could have made the best of it. That's what women have been doing since time began, making the best of it."

"What? And that's all we have to look forward to?" Amber asked. "Just *making the best of it?*"

"You'll be lucky if you even get a chance to do that after the shit you've just pulled," Mary snapped.

"You mean, helping poor Peaches?"

"Yeah, that's exactly what I mean, as if you didn't know," Mary spat.

"I'm not sure what I knew and what I didn't know," Amber stated, "but I hadn't realized how futile, outdated, and backward you all were," she murmured.

"Watch your fucking mouth," Mary said, her fists clenching.

Amber stared at her. "And why are you here right now?"

"Because somebody needs to teach you a fucking lesson. I don't know if Baxter will let you stay or not. He shouldn't, but I don't get to make that decision. So I just wanted to make sure that you know that, if you get the chance to stay, what your life will be like," she added, with a sneer. "Nobody'll trust you. Nobody'll want anything to do with you," she murmured, "and the minute Brutus is done with you, believe me. You'll be done with all of us. Good luck staying alive at that point." And with those cold, harsh words, she turned and walked away.

Amber now knew that it wasn't safe to stay in the house. She had planned to leave, but, as she looked around, curtains twitched in the houses around her.

She didn't know how much support she would have for any of her actions now. Likely none because it would all come back on the women. What kind of a society was it where women were punished for just needing help? Amber was glad she wasn't stuck in this place. Not like Peaches, not forever, but it certainly had been an eye-opener for whatever Amber was up against now.

She still didn't know why Annette had come here and if she really had hooked up with Peaches's husband. It was possible that was just gossip. And gossip was the death knell of everything. On the other hand, people would gossip until they figured out what was going on, whether you liked it or not.

It was deadly when it happened to somebody you knew. For Amber, that was hard because she didn't want to think poorly of Annette. Whatever she had done, whatever she had been caught up in, Amber wanted to believe in the decency of the person she had known. So far, there was no reason not to at this point. Amber didn't think that Annette had had an affair with a married man—an abusive man at that.

Yet it was easy to judge others and much harder to let go of that instant judgment. For Annette's sake, all Amber hoped for was that Annette had fallen in love and had had a choice. Maybe she'd been raped and was trying to get out herself. Amber had no idea, but she also knew that the longer she stayed here, the worse it would get. They didn't have three days to wait.

As she looked around, she wished she had a way to sneak out without being seen. It was obvious that whatever she did, and wherever she went on the property, people would track her movements. She stepped back inside and closed the door. And considering that, she walked to the bedroom, which was at the back. There was a window with no screen. Inside the room, she tried to look out into the night, studying what was directly around her. She realized that the bedroom was quite secure from prying eyes.

With that thought in mind, no way she would be here

when Brutus came back. Of that, she was certain.

She needed to get the hell away before that. She just didn't know how far she could go or even where. She studied the size of the window, looked around at the relatively small amount of possessions she planned to take with her. She wasn't sure if she'd get off the property tonight, but at least if she stashed everything someplace to collect later, then she would run as soon as an opportunity presented itself.

That couldn't happen fast enough because now, with Brutus taking Tomas somewhere, she knew it would get even uglier. She didn't even know for sure if Tomas was capable of looking after himself. He had seemed almost affronted by her concern, but, once the bullets start flying, it didn't matter what kind of ego anybody had. It would just be bad news all around.

She didn't want him to get hurt. She didn't want anybody to get hurt.

Well, no, that wasn't quite true.

She was totally okay if the assholes who took Tomas were beaten down or better yet beaten to death. She sent Levi a text, telling him what was going on. When the response came back immediately, asking if she could get out, she quickly texted back, saying that she could possibly crawl out the rear window, but she was under watch all the time.

His acknowledgment came right away. Followed by a warning. **Don't do anything that will get you in further trouble. Help is on the way.**

With that, she wasn't even sure what to do, but she finished packing up the few belongings she'd arrived with, which were about five different outfits and not a whole lot more, besides her secret cell phone and some books and hiking gear.

She did have a laptop, courtesy of Dezi, and she quickly packed that up to make sure it came with her. On it, she had all her notes on Annette's disappearance and Peaches's finances. Probably not something she should have on there. Frowning at that, she quickly sent everything in an email to her own personal account, then quickly deleted everything off the laptop, just in case they found it.

Then she emptied the computer trash can and set the system up to do maintenance, hoping that, by the time everything was done, no trace would be left.

Of course serious hackers would probably recover anything that she had had on there, but she did erase everything in a way that would deter a commoner. As long as it wasn't something that was set for her to open up when she turned on her laptop, then she would have a better chance of keeping the information private.

With that done, she packed it into her bag, and she headed toward the window. Levi had said don't do anything because help was on the way, but, the longer she remained here, the worse the feeling inside her stomach got. Then, almost as if she were given a go-ahead, she felt certain that she understood her time to leave was now.

If she didn't, there wouldn't be any other time to go.

She quickly opened the bedroom window and scrambled up with difficulty because it was a basement window and just above the normal height. Closing the window behind her, hoping it would delay her pursuers a little bit, she headed out into the darkness and away from everyone.

She would take animal predators over human predators any day.

AS FIGHTS WENT, it was pretty damn fast and efficient, but then Tomas wasn't exactly wasting time. He knew perfectly well that Amber was in trouble back at her basement suite. He just didn't know how bad it was and who was involved.

As soon as all three men were knocked out, he quickly did a search of their pockets, took their cell phones and anything else that he could use to screw up their lives. When Saul approached, Tomas studied him and said, "Nice timing, dude. All the work is done here."

"Yeah," Saul noted, smiling, looking at the three downed men. "I see that."

Tomas snorted. "What did you do, wait until I was done?"

"Pretty much," he agreed cheerfully.

"Come on. Let's go collect Amber."

"Why?" Saul asked, still not looking at him. "I was hoping she'd be okay, since Brutus was here."

"After what that asshole Brutus said to her, before I was escorted out of there," Tomas said, "We're all de facto here now."

"Yeah, you sure are," Saul confirmed. "And we still don't have enough evidence. What we need is to get a place in town, where we might be safe," he said, with an eye roll, "because, from what I'm hearing, they were planning to come into town and take us out anyway."

"Which defies logic, when you think about it. I mean, there are idiots, and there are bigger idiots. These guys don't think with their brains. They only think with their dicks," Tomas snapped, with a harsh tone in his voice. "The women are forced into marriages, whether they like it or not. Once they're married, everything they own is under the control of the husband."

"And yet the law isn't like that."

"State laws vary on the subject," he said. "It could very well be that way here. Some of these states are still incredibly backward, and they use religion as a shield in order to do whatever they want, all in the name of the Lord."

"Yeah," Saul agreed, "I never really understood anybody falling for that."

"I don't think we'll ever understand it," Tomas noted. "But you can see how badly they're functioning on that level."

"What about the boss man, Baxter?" Saul asked. He was on an information-seeking spree and wasn't about to be distracted.

"There's something off about him, and he told Amber to stay in."

"That doesn't mean that she will," he noted, "and it could have the opposite effect. Particularly if she's getting more and more panicked. Apparently somebody named Mary came to her door too."

"Oh, shit," Tomas replied. "She doesn't like Mary to begin with."

"And she happens to be Baxter's partner."

"To set the record straight, according to Amber, Mary is more of his spy," Tomas stated.

"That's how he keeps everybody in line then, isn't it?" Saul murmured.

"It is, but, at the same time, I'm not so sure what's happening with Baxter himself. He didn't look …" Tomas hesitated, searching for the right word. "Not so eloquently phrased, but he just didn't look right."

"No, and sometimes power like that can go to a man's head, and he can look really wrong."

"Yeah, but it wasn't even that," Tomas clarified. "I don't know for sure, but it's possible he's sick, like really sick."

"That would be an interesting twist for these guys, since they won't allow anybody to get help."

"Right, and maybe he's happy enough not to. Maybe he has a bad relationship with doctors or hates the medical profession as a whole," Tomas theorized. "Or maybe he just wants to die a martyr."

"I wouldn't be surprised at that, but it'll really shake things up once he's gone."

"I don't think there is anything imminent," Tomas noted, "but I could be wrong. But given the way that everything is operating, you must wonder what'll become of Mary when he's gone. She's not exactly making friends at a place like this."

"No, I don't imagine she is." Saul paused for a moment. "And that just means that there could be all kinds of issues that will come up that she may or may not solve. And she'll also have to consider her own future."

"Which is probably something that's going on behind the scenes already," Tomas stated. "She could very well be choosing who'll be boss number two."

"Or maybe Baxter's already done that, and she's trying to change it—in order to keep herself in power. In this place I wouldn't be at all surprised."

"But," Tomas explained, "from what I've heard, Baxter is number one. Brutus is number two. Pearson is number three in line of succession. But Mary's with Baxter. Brutus wants Amber. Russ wants Peaches. I don't know who Pearson wants or maybe he already has his concubine. Regardless, if Brutus is number two, no way he would hook up with Mary instead of Amber. So Mary must be working some angle to get Brutus deposed. But then who the hell is the new number two?"

"That's what we've got to figure out," Saul replied.

"And how the hell do we do that?"

"I don't know," he murmured. "It's not like anybody's talking."

"Except Amber and Peaches."

"Maybe so," Saul said, turning to look at Tomas. "You know what? That's a damn good idea. I think we need to go have a talk with Peaches."

"Once we collect Amber."

"Well, in that case," Saul replied, "let's go. We need to find her, before somebody else does."

At that, they headed to the basement suite, where she'd been staying. As they moved silently through the trees, a bird call came from the left. Saul pulled them off into the shadows and whispered, "That's Dezi, with a warning."

Just then they heard a set of footsteps up ahead. Someone was moving toward them, silent but creeping, as if trying to hunt or to track down prey. As Tomas watched, one of the other men came into view nearby, slowly moving through the area, searching for something, studying the grass.

As he walked past, just barely missing them, he muttered, "She's got to be here somewhere."

Tomas waited for the man to be out of earshot and looked over at Saul, mouthing, "It could be her. You know that."

He nodded. "It could be, but where the hell has she gone?"

"Anywhere she felt less trapped."

"Maybe she headed for the hills."

At that, they stopped and reoriented themselves. Then Saul said, "If she knows where the road is, she might have headed down there."

"Does she know where the road is though?" Tomas asked Saul.

"I don't know," Saul noted, "but she's not foolish. She's got a good head on her shoulders, so I'll say yes."

"In that case," Tomas replied, "we need to go in this direction to find her."

They watched in silence as the guy drifted farther away, his flashlight going from left to right and back again.

Tomas looked over at Saul, who shook his head ever-so-slightly, meaning that they wouldn't follow him. But his point was that, if he had already been down as far as the basement suite, and Amber wasn't there, where the hell had she gone?

And how the hell would Tomas find her before somebody else did?

Chapter 8

AMBER CREPT THROUGH the darkness, careful of where she placed each foot. The ground was dry, and it seemed like every time she took a step, the sound was loud enough to wake the dead. The fact that there was dead silence around here terrified her even more.

She hadn't gotten information from anybody about Annette except what Mary had admitted tonight. And Amber knew that, if there would be a police investigation, they would want the bodies exhumed—once found—which she was pretty sure wouldn't happen anytime soon. More so, it wouldn't make anybody very happy.

But to bring this to a successful conclusion without getting herself killed was the mission now. Getting out was the most important thing. Amber had to get the hell away from here, and hopefully then she could come back with reinforcements to get her guys free and clear as well. She couldn't stop thinking about the three guys who had walked Tomas out here somewhere. She could only hope that Dezi had been around to give him a hand, or at least Saul, but she didn't know that for sure.

No way to know or to find out. Absolutely no way to know anything. This place was built on secrecy, and the members weren't open to anybody jumping into their problems. It wasn't a matter of problems as much as a case of leadership issues, and she wasn't even sure if that was quite fair because something seemed to be going on with Baxter.

While he had certainly been intimidating, he hadn't let her get near enough to have a good look at him. It was quite possible that he was ill, and a power struggle was happening here. That thought kept her occupied, as she continued walking through the darkness. Was that even possible? Is that what Mary was trying to hide? Who was the logical successor? The number two in command typically. Was Mary playing both sides, trying to secure her own future position?

Amber thought about it and then realized that the number two would likely have been Peaches's husband originally. And, when that happened, he probably would have gotten rid of Peaches, one way or the other. He would have found a traditional divorce out of the question, especially since he rejected government involvement of any kind, and any financial settlement suitable to the courts would have been out of the question too. He probably would have been fine seeing Peaches get nothing at all, even if she did live.

There was really no way to know what her lousy husband had been up to, but, now that he was dead—and her friend Annette potentially along with him—Amber had to wonder who would have replaced him as number two. And who was after that? Why take out Tristan in the first place though? Had he not been loyal enough? Was a relationship with Annette against the code?

There were so many possibilities that Amber didn't have any way to know about. It was mind-boggling, yet strangely fascinating because somebody knew something. It's just that nobody ever wanted to talk, and talking is exactly what they needed in order to get the information to answer all these questions. If nothing else, each of these people had learned the importance of keeping their mouth shut. Clearly for their own safety, yet how could she blame them?

This all appeared to be one huge cloak-and-dagger scenario. Was it always like this? If it was, what brought the women in on it, and what made them accept this horrid criminal behavior? Or was it different at first and had slowly become more futile over time, as the men gradually made more rules and kept the woman out of the decision-making process, eventually turning them into servants and victims, who saw to their needs and desires, whether they wanted to or not.

What a disgusting thought that was.

There was a reason why humanity had moved in the opposite direction over the decades. But obviously still enough self-serving assholes were drawn to that life, who moved here so they could freely keep the women downtrodden and under their thumbs. But to go so far as to deny them medical care? That … that had really surprised Amber. It didn't make any sense because, without the women, these men had little else, though maybe they didn't want anything else. Maybe it was just a way to keep the women trapped here.

It was all too confusing, and, by the time she cleared a crest and stared out over the moonlit fields around her, she wondered where she'd ended up. She thought she had been moving parallel to the road, but she definitely saw no sign of a road here, and that, in itself, was terrifying. She looked around once more, and, after a moment, she realized—to her horror—that she was good and truly lost.

The good guys coming to look for her wouldn't find her, but the bad guys wouldn't find anything else either, and they wouldn't be happy about that. When they realized she had taken her things, they would know that she had booked it, never to return.

She shook her head, considering her plan. Finding a unique tree nearby as a landmark, she stashed her bag here, hoping she would find it later. But, should she get caught tonight, it would be bad enough without having her contraband laptop and cell phone on her person too.

Who was she kidding? The clan really wouldn't be happy at all regardless. She imagined what Brutus would look like, when he discovered she was gone. Though it made her happy, it also gave her chills. The last time she had seen him, he had stated his intent to resolve the issue of her punishment by buying her, thus taking ownership.

Maybe being lost wasn't so bad.

Swearing to herself, she put one foot in front of the other and kept on walking, wondering again what had happened to Tomas. Three against one were odds he couldn't have overcome on his own, so it didn't seem likely that he would be coming to her rescue anytime soon.

There had to be some way out of this nightmare, even on her own.

She should have stayed in town when she had the chance. That's about the only thing that would have made sense at this point. Even now, in hindsight, she could see how dangerous this was, and she wondered just what had brought Annette into this mess.

Surely Annette had had some thought processes that had warned her that it was just a crappy idea and to get the hell out of Dodge. Yet, if there had been some process like that, her friend hadn't listened because apparently Annette was dead, along with several others, according to the information Amber had been able to glean from this place. She just didn't know why they were dead, who killed them, or how they died. If someone was responsible for their deaths, then what was the rest of the clan planning on doing to keep it secret?

Murder more people?

Maybe that's what it was all about, trying to keep it a secret. Maybe they knew that if it all blew up and came to light, they would all be incriminated for their parts. Of all her various theories, this one would be worth remembering because, if one person was guilty, but they'd all kept the secret, chances are everybody would be culpable to some degree.

That would mean they all had something to hide, and that threat might be enough to keep the women here and quiet, even though they were miserable and not where they wanted to be.

"I really need to talk to Peaches," she whispered.

Maybe now that Peaches was safe and out of that place, she would talk. But Amber had no way to know without getting to the hospital and seeing what Peaches's state of mind was. And to make that happen, Amber had to find her way out of this damn maze.

She slipped up to a tree and leaned against it for a moment, trying to think about what was the smartest way to handle this scenario. When she heard footsteps close by, swearing softly, she melted tight against the tree, as she much as she could.

She closed her eyes, so that she wouldn't stare at whoever was coming around the corner. She did know that, when the prey were noticed, any immediate automatic response—a gasp, a sigh, a reflexive movement—gave away their position, an early warning so that the predator was alerted. And that was the last thing she wanted to do. She also didn't want to let anybody know that she was here and to give them a chance to hunt her down.

Because she wasn't ready to defend herself. She was just trying to get the hell out of here. When a man walked past and didn't even notice her, she frowned because what the hell was he doing out here? When he murmured something about *where the fuck has she gone*, her blood ran cold. If the clan members were already out looking for her, she had lost this contest. And, if they found her, she already knew she would be dead.

Soon.

HEARING ANOTHER OWL call up ahead, Saul pulled Tomas from the direction they were going and quickly disappeared into the trees. Tomas followed as closely and as swiftly and as quietly through the bush as he could, while studying the area and looking for her. When they came to a small lookout point, the two of them stood and waited, until Dezi suddenly appeared to their left.

"What the hell's going on?" Saul asked.

"She's out there," Dezi said. "I caught sight of her moving through the trees. You guys are heading in the wrong direction."

Tomas turned and stared, shook his head and asked, "Why is she going up there?"

"She lost her way, I think," Dezi said. "She started parallel to the road, but then came up against that dense brush. Instead of going left, she went right. While it veers off the road, getting easier and easier, it leads her in the wrong direction completely."

"Well, crap," Tomas whispered. "We have to get her and

get her back to where she's safe."

"If that's even possible at this point in time," Dezi stated. "They have guys out here looking for her now."

"I saw one," Tomas confirmed in a low voice. "I'm not sure he had anybody with him though."

"I'm not sure either," Dezi agreed, with a nod of his head. "But we should split up, and we need to get going, and we need to do it fast." He looked over at Tomas. "Nice job on those men by the way."

Tomas just looked at him and shrugged. "They're all idiots. They're just assholes trying to keep these women tied here. Some of the women probably can't escape, no matter what they want to do."

"Meaning?" Saul asked.

"I think something's been going on here that nobody can really get out of," Tomas stated. "And that's causing them more trouble. Whether it was somebody dying or getting killed somehow, I don't know. But there's a fear level here that most people won't deal with, and fear makes some people trigger-happy and makes others cower."

"Yeah, you're not kidding," Dezi muttered. "And that is bad news."

"It's very bad news," Tomas stated. "There are all kinds of trouble to be dealt with here, but first of all, let's get Amber back."

"Obviously if she's running like that, she'll run right into trouble," Dezi noted.

"Mary was down at her place," Saul added, "and it was a conversation that didn't last very long."

"No, and, after the promise of punishment from Baxter," Dezi added, "and then what Brutus said, she knows that she'll be bought and sold as his personal property, assuming he can pay enough money for her."

"Jesus, it's ridiculous they even think that way," Saul said, staring at Tomas.

"I know. The words sound inane," Tomas noted. "But don't worry. I gave Brutus an extra boot in the groin."

"Good choice," Dezi muttered. "Now let's split up and find her," he said, "and be aware that at least one guy looking is close to her."

Tomas looked over at Saul. "Let's do this."

Saul nodded. "I'll take the left. You got the low side to the right, Tomas, and remember somebody was after her."

"And somebody is after you too, Tomas," Dezi added.

"And yet, not after you. I wonder why?" Tomas added.

"Yeah, I wouldn't count on it," Dezi said. "Goodwill only goes so far."

And, with that, Tomas disappeared, knowing Dezi was quite correct in that assessment. At this point in time, all of them were in danger, particularly if they were caught out here, with no decent explanation. He quickly raced down through the brush to the right. All he could hope for was finding her quickly and getting her farther down the road, where he had his truck parked. He just didn't know what that would take. He admired the fact that she had run, but he wished she had stayed long enough to at least let somebody know.

She had apparently contacted Levi, and that was probably one of the best things she could have done. Tomas himself wasn't used to having somebody like Saul around. And the fact that Amber trusted him said a lot about her state of mind too. It also said a lot about the friendship she had with Levi's team, since that's who she'd gone to early on, when she realized she was in over her head. The fact that all

Saul had to do was ask, and Dezi and Levi had immediately stepped up to lend a hand, all spoke well of that organization.

Now it would be anybody's guess who got out of this first. Dezi and Saul were quite talented, each in their own right. But Tomas smiled into the darkness and whispered, "Come on. I haven't lost this fight yet."

With that, he picked up the pace and started to run.

Chapter 9

AMBER KEPT ON walking, hoping she was heading toward the road but feeling doubtful. She was afraid she was lost. She could have easily gotten turned around, which would put her directly in the path of the guy who was out here looking for her.

Now she didn't know what to do. Was it even safe for her to move? She was pretty sure that, when lost, you were supposed to stop and to wait until you were found. However, in this case, being found was the last thing she wanted. And that put her in a quandary. How the hell did she get out of this scenario without dealing with whichever assholes found her first? Then, just as she stepped out from behind a tree, she felt rough arms grabbing her.

"Nice job," he noted. "Thought you would escape, huh? Not happening."

She turned to study the man—Mojo, she believed was his name—who had grabbed her so roughly, almost throwing her to the ground in his rush to make sure he caught her. She stumbled to her feet, and he quickly knocked them out from under her.

"Don't bother," he said, looking at her keenly. "A lot of people want to have a talk with you."

"And why is that?" she asked, struggling to remain calm, when all she wanted to do was scream.

"Because … you look like money to me right now." His evil grin shone in the dark. "So I can't let you go."

"*Money?*" she asked, staring at him, confused.

"Yep, Brutus knew you well enough to know you'd try to take off. He said to keep an eye out and to follow you if you left, and, if I brought you back, he would make it worth my trouble." Laughing, he added, "I could use the money. So here we are."

"What will you do with the money?" she asked. "You don't get to spend it here. You don't get to do anything."

"Sure I do," Mojo replied. "You women may not have a need for cash, but men do. We spend it on more guns, more toys, and favors with each other," he explained. "So I get that you don't understand, … that it's probably too complicated, but, for men in a feudal society, we do have financial needs."

She shook her head. "It doesn't make any sense what you're doing. What did I ever do to you that you would turn me over to a jerk like Brutus?"

"Nothing," he said cheerfully. "And I really don't care what he wants to do with you. At this point in time, you should be damn happy he wants to buy you. In the end, you'll be willing to go with him regardless."

"And how do you figure that?" she asked stubbornly.

"Brutus wants to buy you out of your punishment, but a price has not yet been decided. You'll still be turned over to Baxter. Unless Brutus has enough money to talk him out of it, Baxter will have everybody teach you a lesson." Her captor grinned. "*Whoop!* I'll get a piece of the pie too. I can't lose."

She felt sick to her stomach, when she realized what that punishment would be like. "Good God." She stared at him. "Is that how you guys really want to live?"

"It *is* how we live, and it's great," Mojo replied. "I'll get brownie points all the way around for bringing you in." He grinned, as he eagerly rubbed his hands together. "So you've done me a huge favor. I can't lose on this deal."

"God." She tried not to throw up at the thought.

"Yeah, well, it's a little late for second thoughts," he noted. "I mean, you pulled a pretty shitty stunt by leaving him in the first place, but, … if he didn't want nothing to do with you, I could understand it." His shook his head. "But old Brutus, he may not even want to spend his money trying to get you out of trouble now."

"Maybe not," she repeated, staring at him. "So all that effort to get away was for nothing? Is that what you're saying?"

"Yep," he agreed. "You've got to pay the piper some days."

"I don't have to if you don't turn me in," she stated, changing the tone of her voice.

"Ah, no, not happening," he replied shortly. "Nice try."

She stared, studying Mojo, while trying to figure out what made him tick, and, out of the corner of her eye, she caught a movement. Sitting still, she said, "I do have money though."

"Yeah, sure you do." He sneered. "Not like what he'll pay me."

"What's he paying you?"

"Don't know yet. As long as I have you as a bargaining chip, I can drive up the price." He started to laugh now. "This is perfect, like my lucky day." He held a gun in his hand, which she hadn't seen earlier.

"Have you ever used that thing?" she asked, pointing at it.

"Sure have," he said, "and not just on animals." With

that, he went off into raucous laughter again.

She felt sick to her stomach. "Oh my God, you're the one who killed Annette," she cried out in pain. "She was my friend."

"She was also a two-faced bitch, especially after she got herself into the sort of trouble that nobody could get her out. Even if we wanted to, that one wasn't somebody we could save. Once Baxter puts down the rule, that's it," he noted. "The rules are the law, and nobody gets to go back on it."

"Poor Annette," Amber muttered. "She didn't want to cause any trouble."

"She sure went about it the wrong way then," he snapped in a voice of disgust. "And, if you're anything like her, you better take heart and understand how things work around here because you won't get away with that bullshit."

"Like she didn't get away with what?" she asked sadly. "I don't understand. Why did Peaches's husband die at the same time?"

"Because he was a fucking idiot," Mojo explained. "He made a move to take over Baxter's power."

"Oh, ouch," she noted. "That's not cool."

"No, it's not. Number one stays number one"—he nodded—"and anybody who tries to screw up that system has to pay."

"No, that's a given," she agreed. "I'm surprised Tristan didn't understand that."

"I was too," he replied, looking at her. "You'd have thought that anybody who'd been here as long as he was would have understood that."

"I would have thought so," she said, frowning. "That's just doesn't make a whole lot of sense."

"Doesn't matter if it does or not," he snapped, "because

that's what happened."

She shrugged. "I don't know what Annette's part in all of that was, but I'm still sorry for her. She was so very young and had no idea what she was getting herself into."

"She was also ambitious and cheeky. She didn't have a chance against the others here."

"No," she murmured. "It's a tough place to be."

"Particularly if you're the kind to get your ass kicked all the time. Once you go against Mary, you might as well just commit suicide," he stated. "Peaches was smarter in that regard and saved herself a lot of pain because Mary won't tolerate anything from anybody."

"Yet I didn't do anything to Mary, and she's still been mean as a dog the whole time."

"She *is* mean," Mojo agreed, with a nod. "So the best thing you can do is just live and learn from it."

"Maybe," she noted, "but nobody can live and learn when you don't get that chance." She didn't even know why she was talking to him, except to buy time for someone to find her. "Anyway, what are we doing now?"

He looked around. "I'll take you back in, but I also must make sure only Brutus gets you because, if one of the other guys sees us, he could take you from me."

"What happens then?" she asked curiously.

"Then Brutus has to deal with him, and I don't get my money or my brownie points."

"But you're the one bringing me in," she protested. "How is that fair to you?"

"It's not," he noted, "but it's our way."

She shook her head. "God, I just can't imagine."

He nodded. "You know that you can't just be stupid all the time. Sometimes life gives you a little bit of a wake-up call, and you realize it is what it is, and you must deal with it, if you want to survive."

She nodded. "At least somebody decent picked me up," she murmured.

Mojo looked over at her, then smiled, but it wasn't pleasant, "You're right about that. I am decent, but, even if Brutus doesn't want you anymore, I won't take you for myself."

"Oh, that's interesting," she noted. "What's wrong with me?"

"That guy, … your fiancé. He's trouble. I don't know if they took him down a peg yet, but that guy'll come back after anybody who touches you, guaranteed. If they don't kill him, they'll pay the penalty down the road. I took one look at that guy's eyes, and I knew he was a bad deal for everyone."

She snorted. "At least you were smart enough to see it. I don't think anybody else thought anything of him."

"Yeah, they probably saw the limp and forgot about the rest of it, but not me. Oh, no. … I like keeping myself safe, and the look in his eyes said loud and clear that anybody who touched you was dead."

She really liked that idea. To think somebody out there was a champion for lost causes, not just somebody who wanted to rape, pillage, and burn, like this group. "And you're really taking me back, so Brutus can *buy me*, is that it?"

"Yeah, but he'll do more now. Once you tried to escape, that changed things because Baxter won't put up with that. Brutus will know that my silence will cost him, and it will cost you too." He laughed. "I just might milk you dry too."

"For the same reason?" she asked.

"Hey, money is money. If anybody knows you tried to escape, you are history here."

"No free will, no choice, a prisoner? … I got it," she stated.

"They don't put up with much," he replied.

"I still don't understand letting people suffer. I don't understand how I did something wrong by trying to get medical attention for Peaches," she stated sadly. "The woman needed help."

"Yeah, she probably did. Clearly somebody else didn't want you to step in and to help her. That's the price to be paid now, unless Brutus can get you out of it."

At that, she slowly looked at Mojo. "Are you saying that somebody might have given Peaches something?"

"I didn't say nothing," he snapped, but then he grinned. "And remember. That's the only way you survive in a place like this. You keep information to yourself, until you need to use it."

She nodded. "I did smell chloroform when I was looking after her."

"I wouldn't be at all surprised." He laughed. "Just think about it. If Peaches was in the way and if somebody didn't like her, who knows what the hell went on?" He just shrugged and grinned.

"Mary," she said instantly.

"I told you that one is one mean dog. You would do well to keep away from her."

"I tried that, but she kept coming at me."

"And, if she did that because something in you triggered her, that's bad news. It also means that you're on Baxter's radar now." He pondered that for a moment. "You know something? Maybe I better take you straight to Baxter. I wouldn't want him to get wind of the fact that I was asked to take you directly to somebody else."

"I suppose that would get you in trouble, wouldn't it?"

"Hell yeah," he said, "and that's trouble I'm not sure I could get out of. They would take that as being the wrong motivation for doing the right thing."

She followed his words, realizing how this was probably the worst turn of events for her. Dealing with Brutus was one thing; dealing with Baxter was something else entirely. She sucked in her breath. "On the other hand, you need money, and Brutus sure seems to have a ton of it."

"Not according to him." Mojo stared at her suspiciously. "That's not what he said anyway."

"He told me that he had lots of it."

"He's always been a big liar. I guess I'm not sure on this one." He pondered that statement, as he looked at her. "Now I have to decide what my best deal is. I'm not exactly sure."

"If not Brutus, then who?"

"I'm not sure," he admitted. "Baxter would reward my loyalty with favors, but he sure as hell isn't giving me any money, and I need money."

"Money for what?" she asked, trying to figure out what drove this guy.

"I'm not telling you," he snapped. "It's none of your business."

That just made her all the more curious. "Maybe," she noted, "but it is fascinating to watch how you work."

"Of course it is. You just think that you'll find out what I want, so you can get out of here," he said, sneering. "That ain't happening. There is no getting out of here for you."

"So what difference does it even make?" she asked, wincing. "I'll probably be dead anyway."

"I wouldn't be too sure about that," he noted calmly. "Brutus wants you bad."

"Yeah, as a punching bag," she stated bitterly.

Mojo looked at her, then nodded slowly. "That would be Brutus. But it ain't no skin off my nose. I mean, if you do right by him, he won't be that tough."

"Some guys just like to be tough, whether you *do right by them* or not." She stared at him, frowning. "You know that's true."

He shrugged. "You don't see me trying to find a partner in here," he murmured. "Besides, my wife died."

"Yeah? Did you help her along?" she asked bitterly.

He shook his head. "No, I sure didn't. I loved her. We came here looking for a life without government, without authority, but it didn't work out that way."

"How quickly after you got here did she die?" she asked.

"It wasn't long. Unfortunately I didn't even know she was sick."

"How long have you been here?"

"Oh, a long time," he replied. "No other life for me now."

She nodded. "Got it."

"This is the life that she wanted."

"I don't know about that," she argued. "She certainly didn't want to be sick."

"I couldn't help her," he said.

"You really didn't do anything to help her?" she asked, staring at him, "I thought you loved her."

"I did," he said. "I loved her so much. And yet ..." He grimaced. "I couldn't help her. When it came time for her to see a doctor, it was just not allowed."

"Jesus," she said, "if that's love, it's an ugly deal."

"Sometimes love is rough, and, well, it's also love of a cause, love of the leader, plus the understanding that, once you're in, there is no getting out."

"Yet you regret it, don't you?" She read the nuances in his voice. "When you lie in bed at night, all alone, you realize what happened to you. You lost the one person who understood you the most, who cared about you, and worried if you were getting enough to eat and were looking after yourself. And I'm sure you do wonder if it is right for you to be here, especially when you remember all that you lost. Simply because you couldn't even take her to a doctor." She shook her head. "That must still eat at you."

"Enough talk," Mojo snapped, turning his back on her. "I'm not responsible for her death. That was God's will."

"And yet God gave us hospitals," she said. "God gave us medical facilities, where people could get help. He gave us medicine to help those with problems. You don't even know what was wrong with her, do you?"

"No," he replied, "and no way to know now."

"Right, because she's buried somewhere out there in the middle of nowhere. Nothing is left of her, not even a grave, where you can go honor the dead."

He looked at her in surprise. "There's a grave."

"Sure there is." She gave him an eye roll. "I haven't seen any graveyard anywhere on the property."

"See? That means you don't know as much as you think you do. It's not even far from here." He turned around. "Let's go." He forced her to her feet and said, "You want to see the graves? Let's do it. You might as well see where you'll rest," he added, "because I don't think Baxter is likely to let Brutus keep you. Honestly, I'm seriously thinking about just taking you to Baxter and forgetting about the whole money thing."

"It depends on what you need the money for," she stated.

He shook his head. "I'll think about this."

"You do that," she agreed, as they stumbled along. "I'd like to see where everybody is buried." As they arrived at the oddly shaped cemetery, she looked around. "Headstones?"

"Yeah, but they're flat, just stones marking the sites. No names, just initials if anything. No dates." He shrugged. "Apparently that's not something we need."

"But gravestones are for the living," she murmured. "So you can come and see where your wife is buried."

"I know where she's buried," he snapped roughly, as he pointed to a grassy knoll.

She walked over, with him standing close by, and asked, "Is this her?" Her voice was soft.

"Yes," Mojo replied, his voice the opposite of soft.

She recognized the harshness in his tone. "And you miss her, don't you?"

"Every damn day," he snapped angrily. "And I still don't know why she died."

"No," she murmured, "yet how are you going along with all this? You're still here, at the place that killed her soul, her mind, her body."

"She's here too," he muttered, shaking his head.

"I'm sorry."

"Fuck, I am too, but it doesn't change anything."

"If you hadn't come here, I guess she'd still be alive, *huh*?"

"I won't think about it that way," he stated. "That way leads to madness."

And she realized that he really did care. He had loved his wife and probably couldn't get her any medical care, and that was destroying him. "Of course the guilt will probably kill you."

"Why would it?" he asked, glaring at her.

"Because you didn't do anything to help her," she murmured, studying him. "Doesn't that matter to you? But I'd bet you did what you could to make her last days comfortable."

"She went quickly," he murmured. "There weren't any days to spend making her comfortable."

"Interesting. … She wasn't poisoned by any chance, was she?"

Mojo stared at her in shock. "No, of course not."

"Okay, sorry. I just wondered because of … Mary."

"What about Mary?" he asked.

"I think Mary is changing the numbers in this community by design," she explained. "You know? Helping to establish the power base that she wants to see."

"She wouldn't do anything without the leader," he argued, shaking his head.

"No, she probably wouldn't, and maybe Baxter's behind all this," she suggested. "I don't know. It just seems so sad that everybody is so focused on how they can personally profit or advance, instead of how they can help each other, like with Peaches."

"Peaches was a different case entirely," he noted. "She was spoken for."

"Sure, she was spoken for, but not by choice. She didn't want anything to do with Russ."

"That's not what he said, and you can't listen to women anyway," he stated, with a wave of his hand.

"Really? Is that how you felt about your wife? That she was brainless? That she wasn't *allowed* to have an opinion? Couldn't be trusted? Couldn't even speak up?"

"Every woman but my wife," he said harshly. "She was special."

She nodded. "I'm glad to hear that. I'm glad that you made her last few years special," she told him. "And that you loved her. Because everybody deserves to be loved." At that, she turned and looked around. "This is a nice resting space."

He nodded. "It's the best place on the property for that."

"It's well hidden too."

"Why hide it?" Mojo asked, with a shrug. "They're dead already. What else can happen?"

TOMAS STOOD IN the trees, watching Amber with one man. Tomas wasn't even sure what they were talking about. The guy stood there, pointing at something on the ground. Then, after hearing a word here and there, Tomas put it together and realized that they were at a graveyard.

That was huge.

At least now they had a place to get the bodies. He quickly marked the spot on his phone's GPS. No matter what happened, at least he could get some assistance to clean up this mess. As he stared, he watched the other guy angrily motion at Amber a time or two, but she seemed to appease him and talked to him a little bit more. Then soon he was angry again.

But then everybody here seemed angry. Everybody seemed to have a chip on their shoulder or a belly full of hate. Tomas wasn't even sure what was going on, but it was obvious some level of disregard for life existed here for each situation these people found themselves in. They were disassociated from society, and it was a very strange thing to witness.

In many ways, they were normal, and yet, in their minds, everybody else out there was looking for trouble. They had this feudal thing going on here, but he wondered, how many really worked to give this place a soul? Tomas wondered how many were just sucked into a life that got worse and worse the longer they stayed, and they couldn't get free.

When the man grabbed her roughly and motioned her toward the main houses, Tomas heard more of their conversation, and most of it he could make sense of.

"Maybe she didn't have to die," Amber said. "Did you ever think of that?"

"No point in thinking about it," he snapped. "Now shut the fuck up about my wife. It's got nothing to do with you."

"I don't know about that," she muttered. "It seems like somebody around here is doing some indiscriminate killing for their own purposes."

As he heard her words, Tomas twisted around and stared at her in shock. *Is that what was going on here?*

Were more bodies there than he expected? It made sense in a way. Apparently this place had been running for a good ten or fifteen years, so no telling how many people had been killed in the process of establishing their version of law and order in this hellhole. It was a sad state of affairs when that's the way "order" was established, but it happened all over the world. Those with power took control, but losing was the end of control. And quite possibly something along that line had happened in Baxter's world.

It would sure as hell be nice to get to the bottom of it,

but first Tomas needed to get the good guys out of this. As Amber kept walking and talking to the man, something was earnest about her voice. When they approached, Tomas heard her saying. "I don't know who's killing, but I have my ideas. I don't know why she's killing people, but you may want to consider that Mary might have had something to do with your wife's death."

"There's was no reason for her to do that," he argued, with a scoffing tone.

"No?" she asked. "How about because it made you stick with the group? Or maybe … Mary saw Laura as competition in some way. Or maybe Mary thought that, you know, if you didn't have that distraction, you would take a larger role in the group. Maybe Laura pissed off Mary because Laura was looking to leave."

"But she wasn't looking to leave," he replied. "She was looking to get pregnant."

"That also means she couldn't seek medical attention related to getting pregnant, could she?"

He stared at her for a long moment, his jaw working. "No, it wasn't allowed," he replied reluctantly.

"Maybe that's why," Amber added.

"That doesn't make any sense," he stated, arguing with her.

"If you think about it, you'll see that it does."

"It doesn't. Mary was already in control. It's not like my wife had any power here."

"No, of course not. No one has power here, except Mary. Simply because that's how she likes it," Amber murmured. "And you can see that it's something Mary isn't willing to give up either."

"Why would she?" he asked, staring at her. "I mean, if

you had that kind of power, you wouldn't let it go, would you?"

"But what happens when Baxter goes?" she asked calmly. "What happens to Mary then?"

"She'll step down," he replied, "because number two will step up."

"Who is number two?"

"It was Tristan, Peaches's husband," he said, "but, with him dead, I'm not even sure right now."

"And who killed Tristan?" she asked. "Because his death seems very convenient."

He stared at her, his lower jaw working. "That's not true."

"What? It wasn't convenient?" she asked, with a dry tone. "Of course it was because now whoever was number three moves up to number two."

He nodded. "That's true. But number three is somebody who's been here forever."

"Yeah, what's his name?"

"You met him earlier. *Pearson.* He took your fiancé out for … a walk," he said, with a mocking tone.

"The guy I barely recognized?" she asked.

"Yep, some people don't like to come out of the shadows much," he noted.

"Who's his partner?"

"He doesn't have one."

"Right," she noted. "Any chance Mary is working that angle?"

He stared at her in shock. "You really don't like Mary, do you?"

"I really don't like what's going on here," she stated. "And as far as I can see, Mary seems to be working the angles to make sure she stays in power."

"And yet," he argued, "Baxter is doing just fine."

"I don't think he's fine at all," she replied. "I think something is wrong with him. Like an end stage of a disease."

He stared at her. "What the fuck?"

"Think about it," she said, "and, if that's the case, who will run this place?"

He shrugged. "It won't be me. I'm in the bad books."

"Why is that?" she asked.

"Because I wanted to get medical attention for my wife," he muttered, with a shrug, "and having asked for that put me in the bad books."

"For all time? And you aren't angry at them for that?"

"Doesn't matter if I am or I'm not," he told her. "She's dead and gone. I can't do anything to help her."

"No, but that guilt is steadily eating away at you. Aren't you curious at least?"

Tomas was amazed at how Amber was cleverly getting the conversation to nag away in the back of this guy's head. Tomas almost wanted to let her continue to investigate, but, while the conversation could certainly continue, so could the disaster. This was the one chance Tomas had to get her out of here and to take down one of the enemy.

Without another thought, he stepped out from behind the trees in a movement so sudden that her guard wasn't even aware as Tomas came at him, and down Mojo went. He didn't argue or even put up a fight. "Interesting conversation," Tomas said, looking over at her. "Any truth in any of that?"

"I think there's a whole lot of truth to much of what Mojo just said." She seemed in shock, staring at Tomas.

"Where did you come from?"

"I've been here for a while, waiting for you to get closer," he explained.

"And listening to the conversation." She nodded. "His wife died here, not all that long after they arrived. He wasn't allowed to get medical attention for her. It's something that's been eating away at him, even though it was a long time ago."

"Of course it has, particularly if he loved her."

"In this case, I think he did. I'm not sure love is something many of these other guys even know about, but, in Mojo's case, yes," she murmured. "And now it's something that still nags away at him, maybe more than ever."

Tomas nodded. "Guilt is a powerful thing. It has a way of separating right from wrong, and sometimes the result is something that nobody is particularly happy with."

"When you think about it, there'll always be some of that going around. I think more is happening here. Something is sick and evil here."

"No doubt." He smiled. "But now that we've got him, what do you want to do with him?"

"I would just let him go, but they'll probably kill him," she noted and sighed.

"Seriously?" he asked, clearly stunned.

"I wouldn't be at all surprised. Something is definitely rotten in this *lovely* little society of theirs."

"Oh, I'd agree with that," he replied. "It's definitely rotten. It's just a matter of how to get to the bottom of it, so we know where the rot is."

"I think we start with Mary," she murmured. "Mary and Baxter."

"Do you really think Baxter's dying?"

"You saw him. What do you think?"

"Something was definitely off about him," he agreed. "I'm not sure what it was though."

"That's the problem," she murmured. "Nobody can get close enough to him. He's always in the shadows, and nobody is allowed to argue with him. Nobody gets a say about anything."

"And always Mary is in the middle of things, isn't she?"

"Yep," she confirmed. "Mary's always there. Like his little guardian, watching over him and the clan. And the question is whether she's really watching over him or actively helping to kill him?" She took in a deep breath or two, unsure if she was in a better position now, or worse, but very happy for the reinforcements.

"I think she's more of an advocate for all these rules than most of the men here," she suggested. "I'm not quite sure how any of it fits together, but I can tell you that this guy here, Mojo, was undecided on what to do with me. He was supposed to take me back to Brutus for payment, but, if it becomes known that he did that for money, then Baxter is likely to punish Mojo, and it won't be a light one."

"Will he kill Mojo?"

"It's also possible that Baxter is starting to lose it, or it's really got nothing to do with Baxter at all," she guessed. "It's also possible that's Mary's behind it all and that Baxter really doesn't give a crap anymore."

"Oh, I think he gives a crap," Tomas stated. "When I met him, it seemed like he wasn't quite normal—as if all the killing and the evil life that he's lived has had a very negative effect on who he is."

"I wouldn't be at all surprised," she agreed. "He may no longer be a sane person, not after living with this much death, hate, betrayal. So anything that anyone has to say, be it for or against him, is likely to cause this poison to deepen."

"Maybe so," Tomas noted, "but the bottom line is that we still need answers."

"I know," she said, "but what do we do with Mojo? I really didn't want him to get hurt." She stared at the guy on the ground.

Tomas looked over at her and smiled. "I get that, but we can't always get what we want." He cheerfully picked up Mojo, threw him over his shoulder in a fireman's carry, and moved toward the road.

She raced behind them, overwhelmed that she was no longer a prisoner. Seeing a familiar tree, she told Tomas, "Wait. My bag is here." She took a quick detour, while staying in Tomas's sights, and returned to him. She had to admit to being worried about Mojo. "What will you do with Mojo?"

"I think we should take him into town and have a talk with him."

"Well, town sounds good, but I don't know. He'll still end up in trouble with these guys."

"Yes," Tomas agreed. "I wouldn't be at all surprised. Enough is going on to make me suspect that they probably have fingers in town too. They'll probably come after Mojo, but Levi is sending some men to help. So we'll see what we can get out of Mojo in the meantime."

"Good," she said. "I admit that I'm damn glad to be leaving this place. Mojo could provide evidence against people here, but I don't think he will. I think he's still far too indoctrinated."

"Unless we can prove that his wife was murdered," Tomas suggested, looking at her.

She winced and nodded. "Now that might do it. I think he really did care for her."

"Yet they came here and signed up for this."

"And I think that was more out of desperation for something different in their lives, something that had more meaning than everything they had experienced beforehand. She really wanted a child, and they hadn't been able to have one, and I think that was the crux of the matter. But, when they got here, she wasn't allowed to continue with any medical treatments. That may have been the end for her."

"Of course," Tomas agreed, with a nod. "It's very hard for anybody who wants to have a child and can't. It would be interesting to see what Mary has to say about all this."

"Good luck with that," Amber said, with a snort. "I mean, I get it. These guys are dangerous as hell, but you haven't seen the spite and the absolute joy in seeing somebody suffer that you see in her face. That woman is malicious and evil. She's just bad."

Tomas nodded, and just then came another owl cry. He froze, then picked up the pace. "Come on. We need to hurry." He was almost running, as he called out softly to her, "Move it."

Still carrying his captive and, with Amber racing behind and not even able to ask questions, they moved fast, as he took her to a spot deep in the woods. Once there, she asked, "What was that for?"

"We're being followed," he said quietly, "and they're still after us. So, not a word and let's pick up the pace and keep going." He looked over at her and added, "Otherwise you'll wind up being somebody else's prisoner."

Chapter 10

ONLY FORTY MINUTES had passed but it seemed like hours when Amber stepped into the small hotel room, still feeling shocked and shaky on the inside. The trip out had been hard and fast and had seemed incredibly wrong. Her captor was now their captive, not that she wanted to accept ownership of Mojo. At any rate, he was still unconscious, which just made her worry that something could be seriously wrong with him now.

As they stepped inside the hotel room, Tomas nodded toward one of the two beds. "I'll lay this guy down over there."

She stepped out of the way and wrapped her arms around her chest. "This is not how I thought the evening would end up."

"No," he said, shooting her a glance. "When shit goes wrong, it tends to go wrong in a big way."

She nodded slowly. Her phone vibrated just then, and, with relief, she read her Caller ID. "Hey, Levi. I sure hope you've got help on the way."

"They should just about be at your door in, three, … two, … one," he murmured.

At that, a knock came at the door. She stared down at her phone and then spun to look over at Tomas, but he was already opening the door.

"Yeah," she told Levi, "I don't know how you guys do that. It's frigging scary. But somebody is here."

"Good," he said. "How badly injured is your captive?"

"I don't know. I don't even want to think about that or to look at him," she shared. "Let's just say that he's not awake at the moment."

"I've sent a couple people, and one is a doctor," he replied, "so we'll see how bad it is." And, with that, he hung up.

She didn't know what to say, but the two men stepped inside, nodded to her, and then their gaze went to the man on the bed. As they headed straight for Mojo, she stepped out of the way, hoping that whatever was wrong wasn't too severe. One was definitely the doctor, and the other guy was his assistant, she assumed. She frowned and joined Tomas, standing at the far side of the room. "Do you think he's badly injured?"

Tomas shook his head. "No, I don't, unless we don't know something about him—and couldn't really expect it—like if he has shrapnel in his body or maybe a heart condition."

"Right. The hidden stuff. Yet I don't think his jaw is broken. I haven't heard any bones grind," she said, wincing. What a horrible thought that was.

He smiled, stepped closer to her, and put his arm around her shoulders. "It'll be fine."

She nodded but didn't have any confidence in this assessment or in the entire nightmare actually. Nothing she felt agreed with Tomas at this point. "It's not how I thought it would go down."

"Did you put any thought into how this would go down?" he asked, looking at her in surprise. "There wouldn't be too many options."

She stared at him, feeling like a fool. "Of course not," she noted belatedly. "I just … I guess I blanked it out."

He nodded. "That's pretty standard, when we come up against something like this. It's easier to just ignore that side of things."

She looked up at him, frowning. "Have you done a lot of this kind of work?"

"I certainly have experienced it. I did a few tours in the navy. But you know what? Those ops were organized, so that experience was pretty fast in, fast out, and really no time for talking."

She winced. "I can't even imagine that. There's just so much wrong on so many levels with this."

He smiled at her. "But you know that a lot of people are doing a lot of really ugly shit at that place, and we need to make sure that it comes to an end."

She nodded. "And preferably before anybody else gets hurt."

"Maybe, but I can't guarantee it."

"Do you really think that they killed his wife?"

"I wouldn't be at all surprised, but it would depend on what the reasoning was. Maybe just through the lack of not helping her get medical care," he offered, "but then he would have also allowed that to happen."

"And I think he did, and it's been eating away at him," she murmured. "He believed their storyline and then didn't know how to unbelieve it. And, once everything blew up in his face, there was really no getting out."

Tomas nodded. "Getting out is one thing, getting out intact is another. You sign up for a better life within the organization because it's almost impossible to do anything else."

"The whole thing just blows me away. I mean, for somebody who supposedly loved his wife—and I saw the grief in his eyes—how is it that he would be okay with her not getting help for something when she needed expert help?"

"He might not have believed that she needed it."

"Maybe," she murmured, staring down at the man who was even now still unconscious, but the two men were still at his side. "It's scary to think that anybody could consider something like that."

"I know," Tomas agreed, "but that doesn't make it any less real."

She nodded. "I just haven't had any exposure to that kind of willful blindness."

He smiled at her, then gave her a gentle hug. "I need food."

She looked at him in surprise. "Right, you probably expended a lot of energy."

He nodded. "I have, and I need food now. I'll ask Levi if anybody's around we can get to help."

"What about Saul and Dezi?"

"They're making their way around the clan property, setting up a surveillance, so we can see what happens now that this guy is missing."

"*If* anything will happen. He was asked by Brutus to keep an eye on me, away from anybody else."

"That's good to know," Tomas noted. Pulling out his phone, he made some phone calls. She only heard his half of the conversation, with almost all her attention focused on the men checking over the unconscious man.

When they straightened up, then looked over at her and

smiled, she felt some of the relief in her system sagging. "Thank God for that," She walked closer. "Will he be okay?"

"I think so," the doc replied. "He's got a hard head."

"Maybe," she noted, "but he's been out for a long time, and that's a concern."

"It is," he agreed, "but I suspect he should come to very soon." He looked over at Tomas, who was still talking on the phone.

"Do you need him?" she asked.

He shrugged. "We can wait a minute."

She looked over toward Tomas, who now studied the group of them, and she motioned with her head. "You're needed."

"Right," he said, as he put away his phone. "What's the verdict?"

"I think he'll be fine," the doc said. "Obviously we want to see him wake up, so we know for sure, but I don't think it'll be an issue."

"Good," Tomas replied. "I didn't think I'd popped him too hard."

"Nah, he's got a hard head. Plus, there's always the chance that he'll play a little possum at some point."

The other man shrugged. "We've seen them pull all kinds of stunts."

"Yeah, me too," Tomas agreed, his gaze hard, as he studied the man still unconscious on the bed. "It just means I can't leave him alone with her."

"No, definitely not," the second man agreed, then hesitated before offering, "If you need an extra hand, I could hang around."

Tomas looked at him, his gaze searching.

The guy pulled out his phone and called Levi. "I can stay

if you need the extra help," he told Levi, "but your man here isn't so sure that I'm vetted." With that, he handed his phone to Tomas.

She watched in fascination as Tomas did a full visual check of this second guy, before nodding and accepting the phone, just listening to whatever Levi said on the other end.

"Fine," Tomas said, "you can stay. And, besides, now I know where you live." Then he gave him a wolfish smile.

The other guy studied Tomas. "Yeah, so you know where I live," he replied. "Yet I've got to tell you that people like Levi and his crew are not ones to screw over."

"No, they sure as hell aren't," Tomas agreed calmly.

Amber glared at him, Tomas turning to her. She bent closer and whispered, "What the hell are you thinking about here?"

"I need to go get food," he stated, for all to hear.

"Send them," Amber suggested. "They at least will look normal around town."

He frowned at her and then turned to look back at the men. Both of them nodded. "That's not an issue," they replied, almost in unison.

The doc nodded. "We can get supplies. This guy could use a bandage and something for the headache he'll feel, once he's awake."

"Maybe," Tomas said reluctantly.

The second guy added, "I go out for late-night munchies all the time," he murmured. "As long as you're not fussy about what you eat."

At that, Tomas shook his head. "No, just bring lots." Then he watched as the second man left. Tomas turned to the doc, who was bandaging up the head wound on Mojo, still unconscious. "And what's your story?" he asked suspiciously.

The guy turned toward Tomas. "I'm a doctor, who has had the benefit of Levi's assistance a couple times in my life," he replied. "Don't worry. I've got absolutely no reason to hurt him at all. You never know when you'll need somebody like Levi in your corner. Screwing around with that is not a good idea."

Tomas nodded. "That's the truth," he noted quietly.

Wow. He wasn't giving anybody an inch, which Amber found fascinating. Obviously something inside him still didn't trust anybody. And considering where they were and what they were up against, she had to appreciate it.

As soon as the head wound was bandaged, the doc stepped back. "Now I'm not sure what your plans are for him," he began, "but he should be available to question pretty soon."

"I hope so, but the real question is what we'll do with him afterward. I could have left him behind, but he looked like a source of information we needed to explore."

The doctor nodded. "I assume you don't knock them around, if you do find *resistance*," he noted, with a hard emphasis on the last word. "If you need more medical help, I can leave you my number." Pulling out his phone, he gave him his number. "It's just, let's say, not what I would prefer."

"Of course not," Tomas agreed. "I can't say that I'm into it either." And, with that, the doctor was gone. Tomas turned and looked at Amber. "How are you holding up?"

"Okay," she said. "Maybe we shouldn't have brought him with us."

"Maybe not," he agreed, "but there wasn't much time to figure it out. If the clan had found Mojo and had any idea that I'd knocked him out, they would have just started the manhunt sooner."

"Maybe," she murmured. "Now we have an extra person to look after, and somebody always has to be here then."

"Maybe, but we'll also get more help."

"If you say so." She looked around the small room and shrugged. "I'm cold, and I'm tired. And I'm really rethinking this whole thing right now."

"Of course you are," he noted. "It's obvious that you can't return to that property."

"That doesn't mean that I can get away either though," she murmured. "They made it very clear that they have people in town."

"Exactly, and Levi is trying to find out if anybody within law enforcement is trustworthy."

She winced at that. "What a thought, to consider that he has to vet people within local law enforcement."

"When you get a case like this, where more people are out to cause damage, and you know they've clearly worked their way forward to keep everything running smoothly without law enforcement's interference," he explained, "not really a whole lot of options for us. There are good and bad people everywhere, and law enforcement can play both sides too. Every once in a while, you get a situation where it's just plain all bad."

It was a horrible thought that sent a chill up her spine. She walked over to the other twin bed, sat down on it, and asked, "Will you stay awake? Can I crash and close my eyes for a bit?"

He looked at her in surprise. "Yeah, if you can sleep, go ahead. I don't know when you'll get another chance. I'll put restraints on this guy regardless."

Again, not something she wanted to hear, and she didn't even know if she could sleep, but hell, … it would sure be nice if she got a few hours in. "I do need to talk to Peaches."

"Yeah, and she's under guard right now," he noted. "I'm hoping we can get there soon."

"Or," she said, looking at him, "if she's not badly hurt, could we bring her here? It seems like the more people who see us around town, the worse off we are."

"That's another consideration as well," he muttered. He pulled out his phone and quickly sent off some texts.

At least they had a support system and somebody who seemed to know what they were doing. It was a little unnerving to realize just how much of this stuff she had no exposure to. Looking back, she had no idea what she'd been thinking, jumping in this hellhole. This wasn't her world, and she knew nothing of the things going on in the underbelly of the world around her. "How do people even get involved in crap like this?" she muttered from her bed.

"First, they decide they want to live off the grid," he said, "and then end up meeting all kinds of people like this. I can't say that they're all bad by any means. All I can tell you is that they end up with a whole load of characters who they didn't really understand existed out there. Sometimes they all hit it off, and they're absolutely their kind of people. And other times it doesn't matter what they do or say because they're so far out of their element. Yet they don't find out about it until it's too late, and they're stuck. Then they can't do anything about it."

"Which is also a very disconcerting thought," Amber murmured, "because I know Peaches didn't want to live with the clan. Yet Mojo's wife *did* want to come. However, I don't think she wanted to stay very long."

"Probably not," Tomas murmured quietly. "If she was looking to get pregnant and to have a family, then found out nobody out there would let her seek out medical help, then that was probably not a lifestyle she wanted to continue with. Finding out that her husband wasn't willing to help her either left her with nothing to do but keep up the charade of a life they had committed themselves to. That would have changed things for her as well."

Just then came an odd sound from the bed beside her. She turned her head to see herself staring into Mojo's eyes.

He glared at her. "What the hell did you do to me?"

She motioned to where Tomas stood.

Mojo rolled over ever-so-slowly, then took one look at Tomas and groaned. "Jesus Christ. Brutus couldn't even take you down properly, could he?"

"Nope, not even close," Tomas replied.

"You can sure as hell bet that I'm not going back to become somebody else's property," Amber told Mojo.

He closed his eyes, sighed. "Yeah, of course not. And the way you said that suggests we're not on the compound, are we?"

"Nope, we sure as hell aren't," Tomas replied, walking toward him. "I just had a doctor check your head."

"Oh, it depends which one," he murmured. "Because, you know, if you picked the wrong one, you'll have all kinds of people coming down here to rescue me." He winced and closed his eyes.

"But will they rescue you?" she asked gently. "Are you paranoid much? Or are you just one of the disposable ones in that place?"

His eyes flew open again, and he stared at her, and she noted the understanding in his gaze. "I honestly don't know," he replied. "Things are changing there. They have been for quite a few years. I just didn't really see it happening until … my wife," he muttered.

"And now things are happening that you weren't expecting, right?" she asked him.

Mojo nodded. "I don't think anybody could expect what's been going on there."

"Maybe not," she murmured, "but it's definitely something that people in the compound need to understand, so they can make fully informed decisions on their own."

"You do that, and you'll break up that place," he said, looking at her. "I don't even know what your stake in all of this is."

"My friend Annette died there," she stated, "You admitted to it. Based on what I've seen, I can't believe it was an accident or even a case of being in the wrong place at the wrong time."

"Nobody in this mess is innocent, including her. I think she got involved with the wrong person, before she realized just how severe her punishment was, and then got taken out for the same reason."

"Maybe," Amber admitted, "and I'm not saying she was innocent in all things, but I can't see that she needed to be killed for her indiscretions either."

At that, Tomas stepped forward, looked at the man on the bed and stated, "So now you have a decision to make."

"Nope," the other guy said, spitting out his words. "If you were seen taking me out of there, they'll know I've been compromised, and they'll come for me. But, if you have implied in any way that I was helping you, I'm already as good as dead."

Tomas looked at him, with a narrowed gaze, then he

nodded. "Yeah, and will they ever trust you again?"

"I doubt it," Mojo replied, glaring at him. "I was pretty happy there, you know?"

"That's a lie," Amber stated calmly. "You weren't happy at all, but you figured you couldn't get out, and there was no forgiveness for you, so you might as well stay and take your punishment, like a man."

He turned slowly and stared at her. "Who the hell are you to say that to me?"

"You think I don't know what you went through with your wife?" she asked. "Do you think I don't understand how much her loss has affected you?"

He shrugged. "Everybody has loss in life. We can't all just live our lives as if it's some big party. Shit happens."

"It does, indeed," she murmured. "But it doesn't always happen, does it?" At that, his gaze fell. She nodded. "Your wife didn't have to die, and you know it, but you let them dictate your actions, and both of you paid the price." She could almost see him try to fight back mentally, only to finally give it up.

"So," he admitted, "that is my penance to pay."

"You don't have to pay it forever," she noted calmly. "And you might want to make sure that something else is in your life, outside of all that pain."

"That pain is part of my punishment." He glared at her. "It's not like I'll walk away from it."

"No, maybe not," she murmured, "but maybe there is something you can still make of the rest of your life."

"No, there's no life after this," he noted. "And now you've made sure that there's no life at all. What the hell did you have to interfere for?"

"*Me* interfere?" She gave a snort. "Don't you remember

the part where you were trying to force me to be with Brutus, who was trying to buy me, to pay for my punishment, so he could own me? I fucking told you that I will not be somebody else's possession," she snapped, with a sneer. "Do you think it's okay that I don't have a choice in my own life?"

"Yeah, I do. The women there are okay with it," he muttered.

"No, they aren't. They're just biding their time, and they're petrified," she murmured. "Mary makes most of them so scared. They aren't capable of speaking out because they know they'll get whacked back into line."

He nodded slowly. "I know that really bothered Laura. It did bother me too, but, I mean, from the guys' point of view, it was a tune-up, that's all. Women needed a tune-up to keep them in line."

"A *tune-up* is what you call *physical and sexual abuse*?" She stared at him, her stomach revolting. "So that's how it is, *huh*? You too? Did you *tune-up* your wife?" she asked bitterly.

He glared at her. "I never hit her in my life."

"And yet," she murmured, glaring at him, "you're okay with other men hitting women, raping women?"

"You certainly can't argue in a place like that." He raised his hands and then shuddered as the pain ran through his body. "It's ruled by men, and not the kind of men you can call out or challenge. What could I say? 'Hey, I don't like what you're doing. Stop beating up on your wife.' That would get me killed in no time flat."

"I get that," Amber agreed, "but your wife didn't like it, did she?"

He shook his head. "No, she didn't."

"She wanted to leave, didn't she?"

His shoulders sagged, and he nodded. "She did, toward the end anyway. Yes, she really wanted to leave."

"Of course she did, and she wanted to get medical care. She wanted help, and she wanted to have a life again," Amber glared at him. "And you refused her."

He stared at her, but there was no argument in his eyes. "In my own defense," he added, "we were too far in already. I don't think we would have been able to leave."

"But you didn't try, and now she's dead, and she doesn't have a second chance."

"Do you not understand? There are no second chances with this group," he said bitterly. "Believe me. Once you're in, you're in for good. There's no getting out of there."

"Maybe that's true. Maybe you're right," she noted, "but a guy like you, a guy who's got that kind of firepower behind him, you still didn't give a shit about her and what was important to her."

"I did care," he roared, "but it was too damn late. I don't know whether she was too sick and couldn't fight anymore or what, and then she fell into a coma. There wasn't anything I could do. And there was nothing else they would allow me to do."

"Did you ever consider that it was very similar to the coma that Peaches suddenly fell into, when Tomas took her to the hospital, which is why I got in so much trouble?"

He stared at her. "If you're implying that my wife tried to kill herself," he said in outrage, "that's not fair."

"I'm not implying that at all," Amber replied. "What I think happened, though I can't prove it yet, is that Mary killed her. I think she poisoned her, hoping that Laura would die slowly, or even quickly, depending on what Mary ended up giving her for a dose, and it worked. And she did the same to Peaches. Only we got Peaches out of there, or she would be dead too. I think it was meant to be a warning to me that, if I didn't toe the line, I would get the same treatment."

Mojo stared at Amber in shock. "Mary wouldn't do that." And then he blew it by asking in a hesitant voice, "Would she?"

"Oh, yeah," Amber said, "she would, indeed. I don't know if you have any idea, but she is one of the scariest women I've ever seen."

He nodded. "Honestly, Laura didn't like her either."

"And that's because Laura had seen the threat in her eyes and understood just how dangerous Mary was."

Mojo stared at Amber for a long time and then turned to look at Tomas. "Now what?"

"As I started to say before, that's largely up to you," he murmured. "If you want to go back, and you think they'll believe whatever story you tell them, you can go back—after you've given us the information we need from you of course. I don't give a shit if you throw away your life on that place. I'm pretty sure that's not where your wife would want to see you, but I don't think you cared enough about her to get her even a little justice back then or now either."

Mojo glared at Tomas for a long minute. "What do you want to know?"

"How many men are there? How many guns? And that's just a start."

At that, he shrugged. "There's an armory." He turned and looked at her. "You know about that."

"I do," she confirmed, "but I never got to see it. And I also want to know more about all the graves."

"I don't know anything about them," he replied. "I know a couple people got sick."

"Yeah, *sick* my ass," she snapped. "Didn't it make you wonder when it was mostly the wives who were disappearing? Wives who had money?"

He stared at her, his eyes widening. "What?"

"You heard me," she said bitterly. "Are you telling me that you didn't help your wife because you inherited from her?"

"I didn't inherit anything from her." Frowning, he added, "That's not the way we work."

"Not the way *you* work maybe," Amber replied, "but did you ever wonder why you have no money and why everybody else does?"

The breath slowly escaped from his chest, as he contemplated her words. "What the hell?" he said. "Is that what's going on?"

"You tell me. We do know of a few of the women who died and understand where their money is now—with their still-alive men," she stated. "I figured that's why Peaches was being forced to marry Russ."

"Why?" he asked. "Because she inherited money from her husband? I inherited from my wife. What's the big deal."

"You just denied it."

"It's not much," he said.

"Okay. But you're a guy, and you're allowed to have money in that clan."

He winced at that. "Maybe," he muttered, staring off into the distance, lost in thought. "Good God." He shook his head. "A couple women were only there for a short while, and then next thing I knew they weren't. One guy said his wife decided to leave, and he couldn't stop her."

"And you believed him?"

He frowned, thinking about it. "We hadn't been there very long, and I think maybe that's when Laura decided to bug me about leaving too. Once she realized that somebody had left, then maybe she could leave too."

"I'm pretty sure that the discussion of leaving led her to that nameless, headstoneless grave," she said calmly. "If you've got any names, we can check it out."

He immediately supplied a couple.

At that, Tomas stepped back and started making phone calls to get the names checked out.

"And if you find out that these women have just disappeared and gone off the deep end somewhere, would you believe it then?" he asked her.

"No, because, even if they're no longer at the clan property, you can't prove that they aren't somewhere else. I mean, if they wanted to leave, I imagine they had to *really* leave, like get the hell away, like witness protection, before these guys changed their mind."

He winced.

"Right," she said, with a knowing smile, "at least you've got that part figured out."

"It never would have occurred to me that they were killing the women."

"Maybe they didn't, and I'm completely wrong," she stated, "but I just don't believe that Annette died on her own."

He looked at her, then shook his head. "I'm pretty sure she was involved with Peaches's husband."

"And why would that get them killed?"

"That alone wouldn't," he said, with a shrug. "But Tristan tried to oust Baxter. And that would never go down."

"Honestly, I tend to agree with that," she stated. "In a place like that, power is everything. But did Annette have to die too?"

He frowned. "She would have known about it. She was smart enough to know that it would never be allowed."

"And what about Peaches?"

"Honestly, I don't think they were after Peaches," he said. "At least, not as a risk to anyone. They didn't seem to think she had enough brains to be a danger."

"Or it could be," Amber suggested, "that they just thought they'd marry her off to the next person."

"Definitely some guys wanted her," he admitted. "I heard a lot of talk about it."

"About them moving in on her?"

"More or less. I mean, it really did make sense that she shouldn't be alone."

"And of course she's got a substantial amount of money in her name now. So, if she marries, it goes to her next husband. So how long before somebody would knock off Peaches to get control of that money?"

He stared at her, then frowned, shaking his head. "I think you're barking up the wrong tree on that. I don't think that's what Baxter had in mind at all."

"That may well be true, but what if it's happening without Baxter's knowledge? Or what if he knows but isn't well enough to really give a shit?"

Mojo stared off, shaking his head. "No, you've got it all wrong."

"And yet you said you're totally okay with Peaches's husband getting killed."

"That would have been self-defense, if you think about it," he said, shrugging. "I mean, once you start trying to overthrow the leadership and to go against the boss like that, … that really is just a fact of life."

"I get that," she admitted, "so maybe Tristan's death was a little more understandable, but what about Annette's?"

"Like I said, she would have known about Tristan's plan to take down Baxter, and being involved in a deal like that is taking a terrible risk. Such a person could never be trusted, even if they did survive."

Amber shrugged. "So, no law of the land there. As long as you don't know anything, you might get away with it for a while, is that it?"

"I don't think anybody involved in that scenario got away with anything," he murmured. "And I'm not sure that I'm totally against it either."

"No, of course not, but what about your wife?"

"I really think you're wrong there," he stated, some of his equilibrium returning. "They had no reason to kill her."

"Except that, at the end, she was talking about leaving for good, wasn't she? Maybe it was causing unrest with the others. Maybe some people were more affected by her wanting to leave, and others were asking about it too."

He stared at her. "How did you know that?"

"Because it's a reasonable and predictable scenario. Once one woman wants to leave, and others are there against their will—or once they finally see some light in their very nasty tunnel—it makes them sit up and pay attention. Not wanting to miss out on an opportunity, they would waste no time in requesting a chance to leave themselves."

He stared into space for a long moment. "I'm not sure where you're getting all these insights from, but there was a bit of a kerfuffle because Laura wanted to leave, and they didn't want her to."

"Of course they didn't. That would start a chain reaction, right? And, after all, what did Laura know?"

"She didn't know anything," Mojo said in surprise.

"So, nobody disappeared around that same time?"

He shook his head. "No, of course not. It's not like they were sitting around murdering people right and left."

She smiled softly at him. "Maybe you should think back a bit. Think back to something Laura might have seen or might have known about that might have been a problem."

"There wasn't anything," he stated immediately.

"It doesn't have to be something huge. How about something strange or out of place?"

Then he stopped, frowned, and considered her words. "She did see Mary at one point in time."

"What was Mary doing?"

"I didn't really believe Laura at the time."

"Great, so your own wife tells you about something that she saw, and you don't believe her either?"

He glared at her. "That's enough out of you," he snapped. "I loved my wife, and I don't have any illusions about who she was, but, at the end, she was getting more … *desperate*, I guess is the best way to describe it. At the time, it seemed like she might be making all this shit up."

"At least to you, it seemed like she was making it up, but, to her, she was seeing things more clearly, and it was making her more panicked and even more worried about everything."

He nodded at that. "True," he admitted, as he frowned and thought about it. "There was one couple," he began, frowning. "They were around a lot. And then they moved off."

"Ah, and how long were they around there? Did Laura

get to know them?"

"Yeah, to a certain extent."

"Any chance they would help her leave?" Amber asked.

"I don't know," he replied, "but anyway they disappeared one day, and she was devastated." He frowned, then shook his head. "I don't even want to think about that. It would mean that she betrayed me at the end."

"You mean, just as you betrayed her?" Tomas interrupted-ed.

Mojo turned and glared at him. "I didn't betray her. I loved her."

"And yet … you wouldn't help her when she needed it. She was sick or not doing well. She wanted to leave, and you wouldn't let her. She had worries and fears, and you didn't believe her."

"We had put everything into that place. To leave with nothing would have been suicide. We would have to start all over again."

"Right," Amber murmured. "And this other couple? You know who they were?"

He frowned, as he thought about it. "Murphy, I think it was. Yeah, Jim and Gina Murphy," he said. "They weren't around very long."

"Maybe not," Tomas agreed. "Have you ever looked at those graves?"

A shadow crossed his face now. "No, why would I?"

"Ah, maybe you should because one grave marker has *JM* and *GM* on it."

Mojo stared at Tomas and then made the connection. "Oh no, no, no," he said. "No, no."

Amber just stared and waited for him to work his way through it all.

"No way," Mojo cried out. "You must be making that up."

"I'm not." Tomas pulled up his phone and quickly flicked through the photos he'd received, after he'd provided the cemetery location to Levi, who had shared it with Saul and Dezi. Holding his phone out to the man, it clearly showed a rock with a small *JM* and *GM* on it.

"Good God," he said, "surely it's got to be somebody else."

"I don't think so," she replied. "You don't really know the people you've been sucking up to for years, do you?"

He stared at her, looked at the gravestone photo again, and started to shake. "No." He shook his head. "It can't be."

"Did you know them?"

"They were just a nice young couple, looking to find a life away from all the authority and rules. They were young, you know? Vibrant. They would have been among the hippies of the '60s, had they been born at that time."

Both Amber and Tomas kept silent for a few moments, letting Mojo process the information. Finally it looked like he might be ready now to understand what they were up against.

"Assuming that is them in the cemetery," Tomas asked, "what are the chances that they would help your wife leave and got killed for it?"

Mojo shook his head, wordless, but in obvious pain. "Oh my God, you have to be wrong."

"And *you* have to be right? Look at what you were willing to do to me," Amber said quietly. "You would take me back to Brutus, against my will, in order for him to buy my supposed sins away, so I wouldn't be killed on Baxter's orders. I would continue to be a prisoner, and Brutus would own me. *Own me*, and, therefore, do whatever he wished with me. And you were okay with that. Is that what your wife would have wanted? A husband who was participating in the buying and selling and raping of women?"

He stared at her, as some of the color faded from his face again. "Jesus."

"Yeah, you didn't think about it that way, did you?"

He slowly shook his head. "No, no, no." He looked around, almost frantic. "What the hell happened?"

"How do you think I feel?" she snapped in a snarly tone. "Everybody seemed to be quite happy to take care of me as long as I was willing to sign up for some of this bullshit you guys were part of."

That reality was starting to set in on some level with Mojo.

"So I wonder just how much you have changed over the years. Now that you realize how your life is being led by these guys, how do you feel?"

Mojo shook his head, almost in denial of everything she said. "It just can't be," he said, but he rubbed his face and whispered, "Dear God! What have I done?"

"You mean, what have you become?" she asked in a hard note.

He slowly lifted his head, as he stared at her.

She noted the realization on his face. "Right," she murmured. "So I guess that takes us back to what your wife would think about all this and you?"

"She'd hate it," he said instantly. "She'd hate me."

And, at that, he fell silent.

TOMAS WAS IMPRESSED with Amber's way with words and

with Amber getting into this man's psyche. And had maybe changed his mind. That would be good because they needed somebody to inform them on further details regarding the rest of the group.

Even if it wasn't very much and if he was somewhat in the dark or in denial on some points, Mojo was the best they had in terms of somebody to clarify how the place was functioning. They needed to determine who was really at the helm of this nightmare. Tomas could see how, over time, the grief, loss, and guilt had allowed Mojo to slowly sink into this state of depression that would have a major effect on his future.

Tomas wasn't even sure what kind of future that would be at this point. Considering his involvement in this mess to date, what future could he even have?

He'd been taken in, pulled into the terrible web so slowly and with such a light touch that he didn't even realize what was happening.

Tomas for one had just no forgiveness when it came to this kind of BS. Life happened, and then so did shit. But it didn't mean that life had to stay that way. Sometimes, there was no better answer than trying to figure out who could be helped and who could not.

It all came down to the choices they made. Right now, it looked like this Mojo guy might be on their side now. And maybe he would help them save a few others.

Tomas, even in his few days there, had seen more than a few women who were friendly enough on the surface but hadn't been terribly keen about their life in the clan. The fact that also several pregnant women were there who needed ongoing medical care, which they had no way to get, meant that Tomas and Amber needed to use anything they could get from Mojo.

Tomas was quite concerned for those other women as well, and he'd like to give the police every advantage to help the innocent that he could.

Just as they pondered these questions, a knock came on the door.

Chapter 11

AMBER SAT UP, startled at the knock on the door. Wide awake, she looked from the door to Tomas.

He shrugged. "Should be the food."

She relaxed, just as the door was suddenly thrust open, and Dezi was thrown onto the floor, facedown. She bolted to her feet, as two gunmen stepped into the room and ordered in calm, but hard voices, "Hands up."

At that, she immediately tossed her hands in the air and looked down at Dezi. And, sure enough, one of the men was Brutus.

He just smiled at them. "What the hell do you think you're doing?" he asked, smiling at her with a horrific grin on his face. "You know better than that."

She was too shocked to answer. She opened her mouth and then closed it again, not sure what to say.

He snorted. "Yeah, it's about time you kept your fucking mouth shut for once, and, if you haven't learned that lesson by now"—he pointed his gun at her—"I'll take a great deal of delight in teaching you."

She stared at him, a sick feeling in her stomach. She knew exactly what he meant. Brutus's vile actions and words didn't mean all men were assholes, but the fact that the clansmen had signed up for something like this made her doubt humanity as a whole. She dared not look at Tomas.

Even now, with his arms crossed over his chest, Tomas leaned stiff as a board against the wall. "How'd you find us here?" Tomas asked.

"Do you really think we don't have this town sewed up?" Brutus snapped. "God, nobody can make a move here without us knowing."

"That still doesn't tell me how you knew," Tomas stated, with a shrug.

Brutus looked over at him and sneered. "Did you think you would get food tonight?"

"I guess not," he said, "but did you kill the delivery guy?"

"Nope, I didn't need to. He knows what side his bread is buttered on."

She stared at him in horror. "Wow, talk about a traitor."

"Yeah, he has to pick where he'll live and who he'll work with, and, in this case, he knows what's good for him. Don't worry. We pay him well."

She nodded slowly. "I know somebody who'll be very sad to hear that."

"Whatever." Brutus shrugged. "Everybody betrays everybody. You just have to be smart about which side you're on."

She didn't even have a retort for that. She risked a glance at Tomas, but he hadn't moved. He still leaned against the wall, but now a muscle twitched in his jaw. Obviously he was less than impressed over the whole scenario. Tomas had let in the two guys earlier—one a doctor—based on Levi's say so, and now they were in trouble.

"As for that doctor," Brutus added, "he'll get a warning, and, if he ever crosses us again, he'll wish he hadn't."

"You don't even believe in doctors anyway," Amber replied, with a snort, "so what difference does it make?"

"Maybe none." Brutus shrugged again. "But I know the townsfolk might get a little upset if they lose their doctor," he noted. "We don't give a shit, but they probably will, and they wouldn't like it if we took him out. So we try to keep him alive, just for the sake of not ruffling any feathers, but even that has a limit."

She nodded. "I guess that makes sense. I mean, you must have somebody to let you keep operating in this scummy little world of yours."

"You don't know anything about it, and you never tried to figure it out."

"I did try," she replied in protest. "I just couldn't understand why everybody was staying and letting you guys call the shots, even when it was so obviously wrong."

"See? That's the thing that you didn't try hard enough at," he explained. "And, if you think we're to blame for this, you're wrong."

"Right. Of course not," she murmured. "You're never wrong."

"Exactly," he stated, "at least we try not to be. It's a very different world here, and all of us think it's the best way to go. The world out there"—he waved his hand around—"is a mess. If you have law and order and if you must have rules, it's better that we make our own."

"But you get to make the rules, and everybody else has to follow, right?"

He just stared at her, his gaze flat. "Everybody makes rules. You must be smart about which ones you'll agree to. Ours are nice and simple, so it keeps everything organized. Only when you screw up majorly—like you've just done— then things go wrong. You were already on a tight leash," he sneered, "and your time was up. They were giving you to me for a chance to coax you into line and be part of us. Now nobody gives a shit, and I won't keep you either." He shrugged. "So that's just the way it is."

"*You won't keep me?*" she repeated, but inside her a horrible sickness was taking over. "That sounds like something you'd say about a pet."

"More or less, but I would have tried. Although I would have married you first, but then this idiot showed up." Brutus lifted his chin toward Tomas. "And I realized that you thought you would get away from here."

"I didn't realize I was a prisoner," she stated. "And the other women?"

"They do what they're told," he snapped, "otherwise they face the consequences. And, if they do something against the entire compound, the men hand out their punishment." Brutus looked over at the injured man. "Just like good old Mojo here," he went on, pointing to the man on the bed. "When his wife screwed up, we knew her days were numbered, but we didn't have anything to do with it. Seems the good Lord had a hand in that."

"Or Mary," Amber added, her voice harsh.

Brutus stared at her for a long moment. "Oh, so you know just enough to be dangerous, don't you?"

"Mary is a law unto herself. She's got that entire complex going in directions none of you guys even have a clue about," Amber snapped.

"She's the boss's partner, and, if she's doing his bidding, it's got nothing to do with us," he said immediately.

She stared at him. "You really believe that, *huh?*"

"Of course," he replied, his gaze wide open. "Why wouldn't I?"

"Maybe because she's killing people who don't deserve it."

"If she says so," he admitted, "we're not arguing."

"So she has a free hand at killing off whoever she wants? No one cares?"

"I don't believe she's killing anybody," he clarified, with a shrug. "The fact of the matter is, some of those women probably need killing. Particularly Mojo's wife. She was trouble right down the line."

"And what about the couple who died around that same time?"

He gave her a fat grin. "What about them?" he asked. "Remember the rules? If you don't follow them, then you pay the price."

"So … what? They deserved to die? Why?"

"Because they were trying to help Laura escape," he snapped, his voice harsh. "Whether Mojo likes it or not, his wife became a hindrance. She became somebody we couldn't allow to stay around. Or the nosy couple who decided to help her. It was too damn bad, as we could have used some young blood, but they didn't really understand the old ways."

"No, of course not," she quipped, "and you couldn't take a chance of them bringing new ways in either."

He shrugged. "Not my choice."

"But you had a hand in it," she snapped, with a sneer, and he looked at her in surprise.

"Of course I did," he stated. "We all had a hand in everything. Nobody is innocent, but we're all doing our own life, our own way, within our own laws."

"But it's not a lawless land," she argued, "and the rules are for everybody, including you."

"No," he stated. "The rules aren't for us. We have law enforcement here wrapped around our little finger. Absolutely ly nobody will go against us."

She snorted. "*Great*, so I'm stuck with you?"

"Oh, I wouldn't worry about it," he replied, "by the time I'm done with you, you'll be grateful for the bullet." She sucked in her breath at that, and he nodded with a smile. "Now you're starting to understand."

"And did you rape Mojo's wife too before she died?"

"No," he stated. "I don't touch what belongs to another man. But this idiot doesn't count." He pointed to Tomas.

"Yeah, you think so?" she asked. "So it doesn't matter to you that I'm not willing, does it?"

"Nope, you had your chance," he explained. "Willing or not, you'll be leaving with me tonight, and, by the time I'm done with you, you won't care who I hand you over to."

"And just who would you hand me over to?"

"Baxter," he replied. "The boss wants to see you. But, if you get killed trying to escape, I won't be too bothered." He looked over at his silent buddy. "Will you?"

The other man laughed. "Nope, but I want a turn."

"When I'm done and not before," Brutus stated briskly.

And that, more clearly than anything else, showed Amber what her future would have been. She looked at Mojo, wondering how much of this he had heard too. "Did you know that's what happened to your wife?"

He shook his head slowly. "Jesus, no."

"What? Come on. You knew she was stupid and getting into shit she shouldn't be," Brutus replied. "We warned you."

"Yeah, you did," he murmured, "and I warned her."

"Well, like we said, the women are stupid around here,

and they just don't accept what'll happen, even when they're told. We told you to shut her up, Mojo. When you didn't, she got other people killed too."

"She hardly got them killed," Amber protested. "They were trying to help her."

"Maybe," Brutus said, "or maybe they were just looking to be do-gooders, while they were trying to get out of here themselves. They were already causing trouble, and we were wondering what to do to shut them up. We tried to convince Jim that this wasn't the place for him and his wife, but that wasn't going down too well. They seemed to take that almost as a rejection."

"It was a rejection," she stated. "And it would have immediately turned their attention to something else, once they started looking a little closer."

Brutus nodded. "That's what the Murphy couple did, but we couldn't let them look too close."

"Particularly with all those graves," she noted.

He glared at her. "What do you know about the graves?"

"I stumbled on the graveyard, when I was out for a walk," she said, instead of implicating Mojo. "That's where I found the rock inscribed *JM* and *GM*, presumably the couple you guys wiped off the planet. Even though they didn't do anything to you and were just a young couple starting off in the world."

"Yeah, they started off wrong," Brutus snapped. "They wanted lawlessness, and they got it. You think we don't understand or haven't seen more than a few of these young kids out there? They think life is easy. They don't want to do the work. They don't want to pitch in, and we sure as hell don't want a lowlife in the group. These young kids just want what they want, and they want it easy."

"I think that's everybody, including you guys," she snapped. "You hooked up with Baxter early on, so you guys formed the society you *guys* wanted, and everybody who came afterward had to toe the line that you guys set."

He nodded. "Nothing wrong with that," he said, as he turned, looked at Tomas, and the smile fell off his face. "Until you brought in this piece of shit. What would you want with him? He's not even a whole man."

"He's more man than you," she stated calmly.

At that, his backhand came out of nowhere, and her head snapped against the wall, almost knocking her out for a second. There was dead silence in the room, and then Brutus laughed. "See what I mean? You'll learn fast enough," he said. "Too bad you didn't learn earlier, so you would survive this, but not now, not with Baxter's law coming down on you."

"Are you sure that it's Baxter's law and not Mary's? Are you sure you're not all being manipulated by a woman? It's ironic that you hate women so much," she snapped, with a sneer in her voice, "but you're being played by one."

He shook his head. "You don't know shit."

"I'm damn sure."

"No, you don't know shit, and that's the way we'll keep it."

"Says you," she muttered. "You blindly follow the rules because you like them, because they make you happy, and because they give you that sense of power and manhood that you need," she murmured. "But, at the same time, it's not giving you anything but more blind obedience in your world."

She didn't know if Tomas had a plan, but she sure as hell hoped so.

She looked back at Brutus. "So, now what?"

He smiled, then stared to rub his hands together. He looked over at the unconscious Dezi and then at Tomas, who even now was just leaning against the wall, near the door.

"We'll tie up your guy, drop him on the floor beside your buddy here, and then we'll have a little fun," Brutus said, with a raucous grin.

She looked over at Mojo. "This is your friend," she told him, with disgust. "This is the kind of people you are."

He shook his head. "Not me."

"If you didn't do anything to stop it, then it is you," she stated bitterly. She stepped over to where Tomas was even now just staring at Brutus, as if he were some bug.

She threw her arms around Tomas and gave him a big hug. "Thanks for trying," she murmured.

Holding her a moment longer, he whispered, "Count down from three and then duck."

She stepped back, confused, but her mind was already going—*three, two, one*—and then she dropped to the floor. She barely had a chance to even see what was happening, but Tomas immediately exploded in some martial art format that she had never seen. Before she even saw it all, both men were on the ground, and Tomas stood, his fist clamped around Mojo's throat. "You get one chance to decide," he stated, his voice hard. "You can either join these assholes on the floor, or you can give up that entire lifestyle and help put them away."

Mojo nodded. "I'm not a rapist," he said, glaring at the men on the ground. "And that's nothing for anyone to be getting involved in. That's not what this—our—life was supposed to be."

"Yeah, and how do you know they didn't have their way with your wife first," she asked bitterly, as she picked herself up off the floor.

He shook his head. "If they did, I'm killing them myself."

"That won't help anything now," she murmured. "These guys have been a law to themselves and have been causing all kinds of shit for everybody who crossed them. And it hasn't helped them, has it?"

"I was cut out," Mojo explained, now rubbing his neck since Tomas had let go. "Once they realized that my wife wanted to leave, I was put on a distant pathway, where they could keep an eye on me, but I couldn't do anything about it, and I couldn't do anything to regain their trust." He got up, then kicked the nearest man in the face. "I don't know what the hell they think they're doing," Mojo said, "but that's enough of this bullshit."

TOMAS TURNED AND checked on Dezi, still out, then looked at the two clansmen and quickly secured their hands and feet behind them. Then he pulled out his phone and called Levi. "I have two thugs, who busted their way into the hotel room and delivered a very unconscious Dezi. He's got a walnut-size knot on the side of his head, getting bigger by the minute," he said. "No other wounds I can see."

"Damn it," Levi snapped. "What the hell happened?"

"Your supposedly good-to-go guy turned us in."

"Really? The doc?"

"Not the doc, the other one. At least according to these goons from the clan."

"Cronus?"

"Yeah. We have Brutus and some asshole I don't know. Also, after hearing some of the discussion with Brutus, the captive we brought has decided that he's done with them. I'm really not sure how much we can trust him, but Mojo is a source of information and is willing to share what he knows."

"Got it," Levi replied. "Sending men over now."

"I also don't know where Saul is."

"I've just had word from him, An army is gathering at the compound."

"*Great*," Tomas noted. "So we're likely to have a civilian militia uprising."

"It's quite possible."

"Brutus also said that everybody in the town is in their pocket and that the doctor has been warned. They've let him stay in practice to appease the locals."

"*Great*," Levi murmured. "I'll handle this. Don't you worry. Just hold on a minute." He returned a moment later. "You may want to change rooms."

"Okay, I'll find another room right now," Tomas confirmed, as he put away his phone. Then he turned and looked at Amber. "When I go out, you lock this door behind me."

He looked over at Mojo, shook his head, and, without warning, slammed his right hook straight into Mojo's jaw, knocking him out once more. Tomas quickly secured Mojo too, as she gasped.

"Why did you do that?"

"Because I can't leave the two of you alone. He might overpower you, and then what?" he asked. "I'll go find another room and be right back. Lock the door, until I return. You'll know it's me if I give three quick knocks, a pause, and then another one. Nobody else gets in, no matter what they say."

She nodded, and he was gone. Moving quickly, he checked out several other rooms and found one at the far end. Even only six doors away, it was enough to keep them alive hopefully. Leaving the door ever-so-slightly open, he went back, gave the proper knock, and she opened the door.

"Go down six doors to the right," he said. "The door is cracked open a bit. I'll bring these guys."

And, one at a time, swearing under his breath at the weight of the men, he quickly transferred them to the other room. As he propped Dezi up on his feet to throw him over his shoulder, Tomas heard a groan. "Hey, bud. You awake?" he asked. "You're one big-ass motherfucker, and I don't want to pack you, if I don't have to."

At that, Dezi's eyes popped open, and he glared, until he understood who it was holding him upright. "What the hell happened?" he croaked.

"Too much," Tomas murmured. "Let's get down to our new room, and I'll tell you."

And with that, shutting the door quietly behind them, he helped Dezi walk to their new room. When he got inside, satisfied to see the three clansmen were still unconscious on the floor, he helped Dezi settle on a chair. "Now," Tomas asked, "how are you feeling?"

"Like shit." Dezi reached up to check out the big knot on his head. "Some asshole knocked me out."

"He sure did. I'd bet on Brutus."

At that, Dezi looked at the three men and nodded. "Yeah, that'd be about right. Mojo's here?" he asked, now trying to stand.

"Yeah," Tomas noted. "Brutus had him watching Amber, so, when she bailed, Mojo was on her tail and grabbed her. When I came across them, I brought him along, so the clan wouldn't find Mojo right away and be on to us."

Dezi shook his head, then winced. "So Mojo is bad news, *huh*?" Dezi was upright, still holding his head with one hand.

"We're not sure about that," Amber stated defensively. "I don't think he had any idea how bad it was and what all was happening there."

Dezi looked over at Mojo sideways, then he shrugged.

"I was trying to get as much information as I could from him," she muttered, "but trying to get anything useful from these guys is pretty futile."

"That's because they're all assholes," Dezi muttered, as he rotated his head slowly. "Crap, that hurts." Dezi sighed. "I didn't know if they were on to me or not. If they weren't on to me, then maybe they were neutralizing me from potentially helping you."

"That could be," Tomas agreed. "Let's just hope Saul is still in play."

"According to Levi, Saul is, but I don't know for how much longer. He provided intel that the clan was amassing an army."

"They'll be here in town anytime now, if that's the case," Dezi muttered. "Bad news for all of us."

"More or less, yes," Tomas agreed, "but, at the same time, we do what we can to save the day. We're now in a different room than they know about. With any luck, we can bar the door from having anybody enter, but, at the same time, we can't just stay here holed up either."

"No," Dezi noted. "I can't believe that Cronus ratted on us."

"He might have had some undue influence. According to these two guys, the clan has been running this town for a long time."

"Of course they have. The clan had to have outside help. They must have connections to rely on in order to maintain the free and unfettered lifestyle they claim they have. But they still need the town and what it can do for them, and they still need minions to do their bidding."

"The same old bullshit," Tomas said in disgust. "They reject authority, yet have become what they are rebelling against, only one thousand times worse. Levi says he's sending reinforcements, but I have no idea who or what that will be."

"Right now?" Dezi asked. "I know a team was on the way already, but, if they can't trust the local law enforcement, Levi will have to bring in somebody from outside."

"Like who?" Tomas asked.

"In this case it could even be the opposing local militia, the anticlansmen," Dezi noted. "Levi's got strings and threads that we could never ever hope to pull."

"That's a damn good thing," Tomas agreed, "because, with the trouble we've brought upon us, that whole mess up there is probably preparing for war."

"That *is* bad news for us all," Amber said, from the bed, "including Peaches."

"I know." Tomas nodded.

"We do have somebody over at the hospital, watching her," Dezi shared.

"But that doesn't mean they're prepared for what could be coming," Tomas noted.

"I don't think anybody is prepared for that," Dezi replied.

"The National Guard maybe, but that would require a declaration from the governor or something," Tomas suggested.

"Don't you worry," Dezi told Amber, "when it comes to this kind of shit, Levi's got some pull."

"I hope so, and I hope it's resolved fast," she replied, "because our time is running out."

Chapter 12

AMBER WASN'T EXACTLY sure what would happen, but she knew that everything Dezi and Tomas discussed was fanning the flames of the mounting fear rising in her.

"God, I didn't think this through," she admitted, shaking her head. "I mean, I thought it would be simple. Like I'd get some information and find a way to bring them down. I had no clue that bringing the law down on them was enlisting help on their side, not ours."

"That's another reason why this thing must get blown up once and for all," Tomas told her. "I'm not even contacting the sheriff because, if he's involved, nothing'll happen. It's quite possible that he wants something to happen but doesn't have enough power to make it happen," Tomas added. "All these people have families at risk as well, so, even if someone isn't on their side, opposing them is a terrible risk, and they know it."

"I get that," she murmured, "so it's great that Levi's in charge."

"He's not really in charge though," Dezi explained. "Remember that. He is limited in everything that he does in this area, and his movements must be watched very carefully. It's quite a tightrope that he walks, especially right here in his backyard."

"I get it," she said, "but hopefully he's got somebody to

bring in."

Just then Tomas got a call. "Hey, Levi. What have you got?" He turned and glanced at the others. "By the way, Dezi is awake, talking, and seems to have no lasting damage beyond a killer headache. Wait a second. I'll put you on Speaker."

"That's great news," Levi said, "but our intel is bad news. The clan is amassing their weapons for something really big."

"Yeah, they may be coming to get Mojo," Tomas suggested.

"*Huh?*"

"I'm not sure if they want to rescue him or to teach him a lesson. He's had a lot of second thoughts about what's going on up there. It sounds like he was shut out of quite a bit, when things went down with his wife, and he probably avoided really seeing what was happening. He was kind of stuck there after her death and didn't know how to get out, and I suspect we'll find a lot of people in the same boat when you talk to the people there, especially the women, the pregnant ones."

"Honestly, the best thing would be to get the armed guys to come into town and nab them all here," Dezi noted. "That would let us know how many people are left behind and what they're likely to be doing there at the compound itself."

Seeing a wave of a hand, Tomas glanced up at Amber. "Hang on a sec. Amber is saying something."

"Don't forget Mary," she told him. "I'm pretty sure that Mary is the one who poisoned Peaches and who knows who else was killed or what else Mary did. That woman is deadly. I'm sure of it."

"Right," Tomas stated. "Did you get that, Levi? We need to raid the compound, and Amber is a firm believer that Mary, the partner of the current leader, Baxter, may have killed several other people in their group and likely poisoned Peaches."

"She may be right about that," Levi agreed. "We did receive the tox screen on Peaches, and she was definitely poisoned, so we'll keep that in mind. I need you guys to stand firm where you are. I've got a group to raid the town and another one at the compound simultaneously."

At that, Dezi frowned. "Hey, I want in on that," he said. "Saul is up there, and I don't like leaving him alone."

"He's not alone," Levi stated. "He'll be fine."

"You don't know that," Dezi argued. We don't leave anybody in a situation like that without backup, and this is bound to be a bit of a free-for-all. He could easily be mistaken for one of them."

At that, Levi hesitated. "You're injured," he noted. "So you can't go anywhere, and you could *definitely* be mistaken for one of them, since you have been."

"I can do it," Tomas offered. "I can leave Dezi here to cover this." Turning, Tomas said, "I'm on the way."

"If they see you, they'll shoot you," Levi warned.

"Yeah, well, they've got to see me first." He disconnected the call and faced Dezi. "You can look after her?"

"I can," he confirmed, "but I don't love the idea of you getting all the action."

Tomas grinned. "That's what happens when you get caught unaware like that," he teased, chuckling.

"Is this a game to you?" Amber asked in horror.

Tomas's smile faded from his face. Walking over, he pulled her up off the bed, wrapped his arms around her, and held her close. In the last few days it seemed like, every time they were together, he was hanging on to her in one way or another. But, when her arms wrapped around him, and she tucked in even closer, he whispered against her ear, "No, it's not a game to us. It just helps us deal with the severity of what we're facing."

She tilted her head back and looked up at him, worry in her gaze. "I don't think you should go either."

"I can't just sit here though," he argued. "Saul is out there alone."

"I know," she said, with a frown, "but I don't want you to get hurt either."

"No buts," he replied. "Hold that thought." He leaned over and kissed her, a kiss intended to blow her socks off. And, from the look in her eyes when he stepped back, he knew he'd succeeded.

"Where the hell did that come from?" she murmured.

"Don't you worry," he added, "more of that when I get back."

She gave her head a quick shake, as if to clear the fog. "Jesus, I had no idea you were packing that kind of a punch."

"Hey, it's a two-way street," he said, with a bright smile. "Now, you look after Dezi. He's injured."

With that, and Dezi still protesting loudly, Tomas bolted outside. But rather than going for the same vehicle he came in, he hotwired a different vehicle, recognizing it as the one Brutus typically drove.

And, with that, Tomas headed back to the compound and whatever was waiting for him.

AMBER CLOSED THE hotel room door and then turned to face a grinning Dezi. She shook her head. "I didn't really see that coming."

"I don't know why not," he said. "Everybody else did."

She stared at him in surprise. "Oh no," she murmured. "I mean, sure he came in as my fiancé, but that was all."

"And you took to it like a duck to water," he noted. "The sparks were flying, and that's probably what set off old Brutus here." He motioned at the three men, who were still out cold. "What did Tomas hit these guys with anyway?"

"Honestly, some weird martial arts moves. Now, in Mojo's case, it was his right fist."

"He used to be a hell of a boxer," he murmured. "The guy's got a right hook that you wouldn't believe."

"Oh, I believe it," she admitted. "I saw it firsthand. It was deadly."

"I'm sure it was," Dezi said, "but it's also effective, and that's what we need."

"He'll be in a lot of danger, won't he?" she asked, worry gnawing at her.

Dezi thought carefully and then shrugged. "Yeah, this whole thing has been dangerous from the beginning," he noted, "but it took you a while to really get that message."

"I know. I thought it would be a lot easier than it's proven to be," she murmured. "And I also didn't really see the larger picture of what I was up against."

"Hey, you did it for all the right reasons. The challenge for us was trying to keep you alive at the same time."

"Not only alive apparently," she muttered. "I didn't want to be gang-raped by this cult," she snapped bitterly. "And that's what they were planning on. Even Mojo here was supposed to be taking me back to Brutus and getting paid for delivering me. Until I started talking to him about what might have happened to his wife and about how we could find out a little bit more. Brutus here wasn't forthcoming about everything to Mojo, and a lot has gone on there that he didn't know."

"I'm not entirely sure that Brutus knows everything either," Dezi added. "When you think about it, there really is a limited amount of information that anybody knows, downwind of the top boss."

"I know," she said. "And it's just all bullshit."

"But it's a classic cult-style organization." With that, he smiled, then stood and walked around, stretching, while she watched.

"How's the head?" she murmured.

"Feels like crap," he replied cheerfully. "But don't worry, I'll hold."

"Are you guys all made of steel or something?" she asked, staring at him in surprise.

"Nope. But we've got a lot of experience. And, at times, you can let down your guard, and, at other times, you can't." Dezi stared off into the distance. "This is one of the *can'ts.*" Then he leaned down and checked the ties on all the men and nodded. "They'll hold too."

"I feel bad about Mojo."

"I don't. I didn't hear him confess, and I didn't hear what was on his mind all day today as he was tracking you to capture you," he reminded her. "So I don't trust him at all. Particularly now that I know that Cronus turned."

"Not sure he had any choice either. He was supposed to be getting food because, for some reason, Tomas needed to eat in a bad way. Which he never got."

"Tomas will hold too," Dezi stated.

"I know, but he expended an awful lot of energy today, and he hasn't eaten in quite a while."

"That's okay. I'm wondering if he deliberately sent Cronus out."

"You know what? It did strike me as strange at the time. Eating was the last thing on my mind, and suddenly Tomas was desperate for food, like it was the most important thing ever."

At that, Dezi laughed. "Yeah, that would have been a ruse. Something must have tipped him off."

"I don't know what it would have been," she admitted, turning up her palms. "It's like you guys have these supernatural senses that nobody else has a chance to figure out."

He grinned at her. "We call it *experience*."

"Maybe," she murmured, "but it's not the type of experience most people have access to."

"Maybe not," he agreed, as they heard shouts from outside in the hallway. He looked over at her. "Get down or maybe jump in the tub."

Amber winced, as she lay on the floor. "The clan must have found the empty room."

He nodded. "I wouldn't be at all surprised."

At that, more gunfire sounded all up and down the hallway.

"I hope nobody leaves their rooms," Dezi murmured.

Amber cocked her head. "Is that opposing gunfire added in?" She frowned, staring at Dezi now.

Dezi nodded, as he pulled his own handgun from his pocket.

"They left you a handgun?" she asked, glad to have something to distract her from the war in the hallway.

He showed her the hidden holster he wore under his

shirt.

"Jesus, the clansmen really weren't thinking that you were a cop or anything, were they?"

"Well, I'm not," he said, with a smile. "And that is just as important."

"I guess." She nodded. "Yet, at the same time, we're damn lucky it's you."

He nodded. "That we are, but we also must ensure that nobody comes through that door who isn't allowed."

"That would only be Saul and Tomas," she stated. "As far as I'm concerned, everybody else is guilty of something."

"Even the women?" he asked her curiously.

She frowned, then shook her head. "No," she said forcefully. "Except Mary of course. But I can't say that about the others. I think they've had a pretty rough deal."

"Maybe," Dezi agreed, "or maybe it's not as rough as you're thinking, and it'll all come out in the wash."

"Not if they were afraid for their own lives," she argued. "And hearing what Brutus here was planning to do to me, it's pretty easy to see that nobody would go against him."

Then the noise in the hallway abruptly stopped. She blew out the breath she had been holding.

At that, Mojo opened his eyes and glared at her. "Why the hell am I tied up?" he bit off.

Amber almost laughed. He had slept through all that and only woke up when the silence came. "Because this is Dezi, and he doesn't trust you," she said, with a shrug. "And honestly, at the time, we had to move rooms, and Tomas couldn't leave me alone with you, just in case."

At that, Mojo sank back onto the carpet. "I've been such a fool."

"Yeah, and you paid the hard way," she noted. "Unfortunately it's not just you who's paying."

He glared at her. "I'm still not sure they did anything to my wife."

"Maybe not, but you didn't do anything *for* her either."

He had the grace to look ashamed. "That's true," he admitted, "and that's not something I ever want to think about again."

"Well," she added, "you may not have an option because, as sure as hell, this will be a really long night."

"What do you know?" he asked, his gaze sharpening, as he shifted away from the two men beside him. He shook his head. "Jesus. They've got more balls than brains," he said. "Anybody could see that Tomas wasn't somebody to cross lightly."

"Not your guys," she argued. "Your guys were all swayed by the limp."

He nodded. "He's got one hell of a kick though. I saw him take down Brutus with just one leg, so I don't know how much of a limp that really is."

"I also know he's worked damn hard to make sure he's not deemed as handicapped," she stated calmly, as she looked over at Mojo. "And limp or not, Tomas can damn sure handle himself." Even though she totally believed that, she was still terribly worried. She sank back on the bed. "I wish somebody had brought food."

Dezi looked over and smiled. "You guys can go get a big steak when this is over."

"I will hold you to that," she said, with a smile.

He grinned. "One thing I know for sure is that Tomas is hell on wheels," Dezi stated, "so don't you worry about him."

TOMAS MADE IT to the compound without seeing anybody, so he wasn't sure if they had all taken another route into town or if anybody knew about this backwater route he had taken several times before.

If somebody was watching him, Tomas had no clue, and he didn't care right now. His priority was looking for Saul. As Tomas exited the vehicle—now hidden under a bunch of trees as well as he could for the moment—he slipped farther into the woods and sent out a birdcall. He walked close to the compound, hearing noises as he approached.

He let out one more owl call and then held to the silence around him. When he heard a response off to his right, he headed in that direction. It didn't take long before Saul showed up. Tomas crept up beside him and squatted out of sight. "What's going on?" Tomas asked Saul.

"The militia is getting ready to move."

"Good, we want them off the property," Tomas admitted. "Levi sent reinforcements."

"What about Dezi?"

"He's fine," Tomas said, with a snort. "He's got a knot on that hard head of his and is bound to have a headache for a while, but, at the moment, he's pretty pissed off."

Saul grinned, his teeth flashing white in the darkness. "Yeah, none of us like getting caught."

"No, we definitely don't," Tomas admitted. "And these guys are assholes, each and every one of them." With that, he filled Saul in on what he had heard so far.

"Jesus. Any idea who Levi is sending?"

"No."

"Who would they even send for something like this?"

"No clue. But if he's got anybody, it must be someone with more clout than the locals, who look like they are heavily involved with the clan in one way or another." Then he mentioned what had happened with Cronus.

"Yep, that's the problem. We can't keep these guys loyal all the time. They tend to screw you in the back. I'm surprised Levi found that out so fast."

"It's one of the reasons I sent Cronus off to get food," Tomas said. "The way he was shifting his gaze and searching the room, not to mention staring at Amber, all worried me. I just didn't get the feeling he was as reliable as Levi thought. And, sure enough, he took the bait, and, before we knew it, Brutus and one of his thugs showed up."

"I get it. So where are Amber and Dezi now?"

"Moved to a new room, with the clansmen trio, all under guard by Dezi."

"He'll keep her safe," Saul noted.

"I hope so," Tomas said. "I also hope he keeps Mojo safe because if anybody'll turn it all around for us, it could be him."

"Seriously?" Saul looked over at Tomas in surprise.

"Yeah, there was talk suggesting that the clan may have killed Mojo's wife."

"Shit."

"Seriously. She wanted to leave, and he wouldn't go. She needed medical attention, and the clan wouldn't let her get it. She ended up dying, and he's not sure how, but that is suspicious in itself. A young couple in the group who had befriended her also turned up missing at the same time and are likely in the clan graveyard. Amber thinks Mary is pretty handy with the poison and may have killed Mojo's wife that way. Peaches's tox screen came up positive for poison too."

"*Mary.*" Saul shook his head at that. "From what I've seen of that woman, she's bad news."

"Amber sure has bad feelings toward her. And we've seen women be the worst of the lot sometimes. I don't know who will be the worst of the lot in this mess," Tomas noted, "but definitely some shits are in this group."

"Too many of them. I know they've been trying to chase down who the various members of this group really are, but I didn't get an update from Levi."

"That could be the power he's using to get help over here, like if anybody is wanted within multiple jurisdictions and across state lines and such. He may pull in all kinds of officials from various jurisdictions."

"True enough." Saul nodded.

"Sounds like Baxter is somebody they've wanted for a long time."

"He is, so that's what we can expect—maybe FBI."

"Is that who we want to visit the clan?"

"If I were in trouble, no, they wouldn't necessarily be my first choice. I'd prefer my fellow SEALs," Saul explained. "But, given the fact that we operate within the parameters of the law right now, the FBI will do just fine."

At that, Tomas laughed. "I hear that."

Just then, several vehicles fired up, and they heard sounds of yelling, as everybody raced to the vehicles. Tomas peered through the bushes and nodded. "All the better to get these armed idiots the hell off the property. The lot of them."

"You think?"

"Yeah, because I'm not sure what else is going on here, but I'd sure like to search Brutus's place and Baxter's."

"Do you really think he'll stay?" Saul asked.

"I do. I'm not sure he's that physically capable of leaving, at least not without revealing his weakness. I suspect he's in a wheelchair, hiding in the shadows."

"That would be something that would severely cut back his power and authority and standing with the clan."

"There have already been a couple power plays to oust him," Tomas noted. "So I wouldn't be at all surprised. And then there's Mary, who even now wants to get rid of everybody, so that she stays on top."

"They are all messed up," Saul stated. "And it won't be the same, once the leader is gone."

"No, it won't be. Not unless they can make the transition of power smooth and easy, but I don't think it'll happen for this clan, and this leader's a rattlesnake," Tomas added. "Don't ever think that, just because he's in a wheelchair, he's weaker."

"And yet that's what you would assume," Saul noted.

"I think he isn't letting anybody know just how bad it is. He trusts Mary and has given her a free hand in killing whoever the hell she wants to kill to make it work in her favor, just to keep them in power. But I think he'll have trouble hanging on to his position here soon."

"The only way they'll take him out is if they kill him."

"Exactly, but I don't think that's today's issue. I think it's very much a case of them wanting to take out Mojo, Dezi, and me," he acknowledged. "They have no idea about you."

"Let's keep it that way, if we can," Saul teased.

As the vehicles raced past, with everybody hooting and hollering through the windows, Tomas shook his head. "What a bunch of idiots."

"Hey, they think they are powerful men with an admirable cause," Saul explained. "Wars have been started for less."

"Isn't that the truth," Tomas muttered. "Let's go." With that, they headed up to the leader's house. As they approached on the backside, Tomas whispered, "Don't forget Mary. If she's still here, count her as one of the worst of the lot."

At that, Saul nodded.

"I wouldn't even give her a chance to talk, given a choice," Tomas noted. "No doubt she's got her own guns and is just as feisty as the rest of them."

"I'll remember that," Saul replied and disappeared on the other side, leaving Tomas to enter on his side. As he slipped up to the front, he listened inside. Several women were talking.

"I don't know whether this place is safe or not anymore," one of the women whimpered.

"Doesn't matter whether it's safe or not," Mary snapped, her voice hard. "We support our men."

"I know that," she replied, "but I'm scared."

"Oh, for God's sake," Mary yelled. "What are you scared for?"

"I'll give birth soon," she said, crying out.

"It's normal to be nervous."

"I am beyond scared. I mean, this is a huge day," the woman explained.

"Sure it is, and you'll get through it just fine," Mary stated, in an awkward attempt at a soothing voice.

The other woman started to sob quietly.

"Oh, for fuck's sake," Mary yelled again, "just shut up. I don't have any patience for this. We need to keep an eye on what's happening here."

"But the men are gone," the woman cried out.

"What difference does that make? They'll be back,"

Mary snapped, "and, when they are, we let them know that we've done our jobs in keeping this place safe."

"Fine," the woman muttered. "I'll go lie down, so I have some strength for later."

"Yeah, you do that," Mary sneered, with a barely veiled disgust in her voice. "The rest of you go too but keep your eyes open."

As soon as the other women exited and sadly trotted back down the path, Tomas slipped inside.

Mary turned and yelled, "What the hell do you want now?" She stopped when she saw Tomas. A smile like none other crossed her face. "Well, look who we have here." She smirked. "Trouble found its way home."

"I don't know about *home*," Thomas corrected, "but you are one rattlesnake, bitch."

"Whatever," she said, waving her hand about. "The rest are just simpering weaklings."

"Maybe, but you're not supposed to be killing off your loyal members," he replied, with a hard smile.

"I need to sometimes," she stated, "especially if they won't take a hint and won't at the least take care of it themselves."

"Is that how you get people to commit suicide? Or do you just drug them and give them the suggestion?"

"No, if I drug them, I take care of the business myself. Why would I want to leave it open to interpretation on their part?" she admitted, with a headshake. "That won't do anybody any good."

"And what if they don't want to die?" he asked.

"Doesn't matter. When their usefulness has expired, it doesn't fucking matter."

"Does your partner know? Does he know all of what

you've been doing?"

"You think I don't?" Baxter asked, cocking a gun from the side.

Tomas turned toward Baxter. He nodded. "Nice to see you, Baxter. I wondered about the wheelchair."

Slowly Baxter moved into the room in his wheelchair. "How did you even see it?"

"I saw it last time I was here," he stated. "And I heard it too. I understand the sound, having come back from a ton of rehab myself. So you might be trying to hide it, but anybody who's heard the sound of wheelchairs for long won't be fooled. And, by the way, you should expect another challenge for your position," he shared, leaning against the door. "And soon."

He had his handgun hidden inside his folded arms, knowing it would all come down to noting the tiny details. But with Mary also being a decent shot, the chances of getting out of this unscathed weren't looking good for Tomas.

Baxter glared at him. "I don't think so," he snapped.

"Oh, I do, especially seeing how your wife killed your previous number two after she tried to persuade Tristan to take you out."

"What the hell are you talking about?" Mary asked, staring at Tomas, but he caught the glimmer of fear in her gaze.

"But Tristan didn't take the bait," Tomas stated, as he turned his focus on Baxter. "It's one thing to be all-powerful, but it's another thing when the power is gone, and your wife doesn't like giving up her position," Tomas noted calmly. "And, if you do know exactly what she's been doing, then you're perfectly aware of the fact that she's been erasing all competition, so she can keep her position and can jump right into bed with your current number two, by the time you're dead and gone."

Baxter stared at Tomas and then Mary, his eyes jet-black, like a snake, as his gaze went from one to the other.

"Don't even listen to him," she said in disgust. "God, that doesn't make any sense."

"Sure it does, Mary," Tomas argued. "You took care of Peaches's husband—and Annette for that matter. And of course you got Peaches to poison herself."

"She didn't poison herself. I poisoned her," Mary admitted. "Do you think Baxter doesn't know about that?"

"Sure he does," Tomas agreed, "but he also understands that keeping a viper close to his chest is one thing, but what happens when he gets weaker and he can't handle life? Have you already told him how you'll kill him, like you killed Annette?"

"You don't know jack shit," she snapped, staring at Tomas, as she turned toward Baxter. "You're not listening to him, right?"

"He has a couple good points," Baxter noted, fingering the gun in his hand.

"Absolutely I do," Tomas agreed. "And you know that yourself. You've seen the change in Mary. You've seen how she's a little more affectionate, how she's looking after you better, and how busy she is dealing with everybody in the complex."

Baxter nodded slowly. "Yes, yes, and yes."

"I wonder how many other people noticed."

"Only people who are looking for betrayal, so that doesn't make for very many," Baxter noted. "What the hell are you even doing here?" he asked Tomas.

"The fact of the matter is, Amber is my fiancée," he stated. "And I don't take kindly to men who decide they should gang rape her because they feel like it."

At that, Baxter's eyes widened. "What the hell are you talking about?"

"Oh, you didn't know what Brutus had planned? Since Amber's been slated to die, unless Brutus pays the price, and seeing how now the price will be too high, he'll just take what he wants, then throw Amber to the others and forget about her, before she is killed."

At that, Baxter shook his head. "Rape is not condoned here."

"You've got to be kidding me," Tomas snapped, laughing. "Maybe not by you, but it sure as hell is by her." He nodded his head toward Mary.

At that, Baxter turned and looked at her.

She shrugged. "A couple of the women needed to be punished," she noted. "You left that punishment up to me."

"But never rape," he snapped. "We need the women willing."

"None of the women at this place are *willing*," Tomas yelled. "They're all here by force, all here under extreme duress and held by fear. So much for your nice little compound. You haven't seen it rotting from the inside?"

At that, Baxter's gaze narrowed, but it was obvious he was contemplating the information he'd just been given.

"You're so full of shit," Mary snapped. "All you're doing is trying to cause trouble between the two of us. We've been together a very long time."

"Sure you have," Tomas agreed, "and you don't like giving up the top dog position."

She shrugged. "He's good for many more years yet, and I'm making sure that everybody toes the line to him."

"Don't you mean, *toes the line to you?* Are you sure you're even still considering Baxter in this equation? I mean, if you had a way to make it so that you were the one in power, I'm sure you would handle that quite nicely too, wouldn't you?"

She glared at him. "I don't know what the hell you think you're doing," she spat, "but this is bullshit."

"Maybe, but I don't think so, and believe me. The longer Baxter thinks about it and the implications of what I'm saying, he'll figure it out too."

She shook her head. "No, because that would imply that he didn't trust me. And trust and loyalty is everything." She turned, looked at Baxter, and said, "You trust me, right?"

Even as she spoke, she was convicted by the note of fear and uncertainty in her voice.

Baxter turned and looked at her. "What the hell?" he finally said. "Just what the fuck have you been doing when I haven't been watching?"

She shrugged. "Keeping the place as you wanted," she cried out. "You know that."

"I know that *now*"—he shook his head—"and I know that I've let you run wild a little too long," he murmured, his gaze narrowing.

She stiffened in outrage. "What? You'll listen to him and not me?"

"Apparently I need to listen to somebody because I didn't see this happening. It goes along with me being sick," he added.

"Presumably it's terminal?" Tomas asked.

"I have no idea," he replied, "and I won't find out either. That's the last thing I need to deal with."

"You mean, you can't, being a wanted man and all."

At those words, Baxter's gaze narrowed.

"The best thing for you would be to go out in a gunfight. So maybe she's just trying to make your last wish come true."

She gasped at that. "I would never do that," she cried out.

But obviously Baxter had had a little bit more time to think about it, and, as he turned to face her, she pulled up her own gun and pointed it at him. "You can't believe him," she snapped. "It's an outrage."

"Why is that?" Baxter asked, his voice like a deadly viper, whipping through the silence.

"We've been together for a very long time," she stated painfully. "You should trust me."

"Again, why is that?" he asked, his gaze never wavering from her. "Especially in light of what I'm hearing."

"This asshole?" She pointed, shaking her head. "He's nobody."

"Maybe not," Baxter agreed, "but some of what he's saying is true."

She shrugged. "Okay, so I had the men use rape to keep the women in line," she admitted. "At least the threat of it, and a couple of them are in line, and the others? They deserved it."

"Like Annette?"

"What she was doing was causing trouble," Mary snapped. "Creating an uprising!"

"Hardly," Tomas argued. "Annette wanted to leave. But Tristan wanted to leave Peaches behind, and you guys couldn't get him to sign over the paperwork, so you could get his fortune. That's why you've been trying to marry Peaches off to the next guy, so Russ could get the paperwork signed to secure the money. But she wasn't willing to be a punching bag again."

Mary glared at him. "You don't know anything about how this place is run."

"It's run by fear and intimidation," he stated flatly. "Just like everything else around this place. There isn't anybody here on loyalty anymore, except for your gun-toting men who want to abuse women and to pretend they have everything they want whenever they want it, running over anyone in their path, except that's a lie too. They have no real freedom either." Tomas shook his head. "You're leading quite an army here, Mary. I just wondered if Baxter knew about it all."

"He can't know about what doesn't exist," she snapped.

At that, they heard the cocking of a gun from Baxter's direction.

"Yes, shoot him," she said. But when it didn't happen, she's spun to look at Baxter, only his gun faced her.

She shook her head. "No, no, no, no," she said. "You don't understand, Baxter. Everything I did, I did for us."

"You mean, for *you*," Tomas spat in a hard voice.

When it happened, he didn't even see it. There was a harsh *boom*, and she remained upright for a moment, then leaning against the counter, she slowly sagged to the floor.

Tomas already had his gun out, pointing at Baxter. "You really had no clue?" he asked him harshly.

"No, I had no clue," Baxter replied. "I didn't look any closer because I didn't really want to know, I suppose," he admitted. "I've been sick for a long time. No saving grace here. But I trusted in her to hold my position until the end."

"And all she was doing was furthering her own influence to make sure that the end included her moving up the scale.

And that's what Tristan was supposed to be, but then he found Annette instead, and, all of a sudden, it didn't look quite so good to Mary. Then he decided to take over as number one and to keep Annette here and to keep his money from Peaches," Tomas explained.

"He wanted to take over all right, but that didn't happen," Baxter snapped. "I'm still strong enough to look after that. Any uprising from my men won't go over well."

"That depends on who it is who you leave in power," Tomas muttered.

"And the fact of the matter is, Mary turned out to be a poor choice. Did she really try to kill Peaches?"

"Yes, by poisoning her," he replied. "She's still in the hospital."

Shaking his head, he said, "I can't believe it all went off the rails so badly. I appreciate you taking her in to get medical attention. That makes more sense now. Thank you for that."

"Now, what the hell will you do?"

"Me?" Baxter shook his head. "I'm not sure." He looked around. "Where is everybody?"

"They've all armed up to go to town to get Mojo, Brutus, and possibly Amber back."

"What the hell happened to them?"

"Brutus and another guy attacked me, Dezi, and Amber."

"Jesus Christ," Baxter muttered, "there was a simpler way to solve this, and you sure as hell don't go into town with it."

"Oh, but you know everybody in town is either beholden to you guys or terrified, so you can do whatever the hell you want. You run the town and this compound ragged, and you can do it because everybody's terrified due to Mary's violent reign," Tomas snapped, with that hard glance. "At this point, almost anybody could betray you because even the code of honor you once had has been broken, and now everybody wants the power position, and no reliable leader is left to run point for you. Looks like you have a decision to make."

Baxter nodded slowly. "The beginning of the end."

"Oh, I'd say so," Tomas agreed. "But it depends on what you'll do from here." The two men locked gazes, taking each other's measure.

"You going to shoot me?" Baxter asked.

"If I have to, yeah," Tomas confirmed. "After the thugs you sent to take out my friends, you can bet I won't let you live."

"No, of course not," he acknowledged. "And there's enough still happening that I can't be sure who is on which side."

"No, I don't imagine you can. Don't suppose there are any records of anything around this place, are there?"

"You'll find them at some point, I'm sure," he replied. "Why should I make your job easier for you?"

"You don't have to. I know that Mary was responsible for a lot of deaths, like the young couple who wanted to help Mojo's wife leave this place."

"That was a bad deal," he noted, "but that was an accident."

"That was no accident, Baxter. That was Mary killing them."

He stared at him, looked down at Mary, shaking his head. "Fucking bitch. Killing indiscriminately like that? We're not angels, but that shit? That's not what we were about here."

"You gave her the freedom to do it, and she took advantage. She molded everybody here as she wanted to," Tomas explained calmly. "And you are just as responsible."

"It always comes back to the boss, doesn't it?" With that, Baxter fired a shot. But Tomas was on the move and it just burned his shoulder.

Baxter grabbed his bloody hand, yet stared at his gun, as it hit the floor. "I can't even bend," he mentioned in a conversational tone. "Why don't you just put a second bullet right in my heart."

"I don't think so," Tomas noted calmly. "I think that's too easy of an end. You've been involved in way too much shit here, all which started well before Mary took over," he noted. "Where do you think she learned all that? I'd say from you."

"She probably did," he agreed, with half an affectionate eye on the dead woman on the floor. "She was always a fast learner."

"And no way she would go down to a lesser status than what she's had up until now," Tomas noted, as he walked closer and kicked away Baxter's gun.

"What now?"

Pulling out his phone, Tomas said, "Now maybe we can get some closure to this mess."

"I don't think so," Baxter argued.

"That gunfire should have brought somebody, right? So why isn't this place littered with your minions? I'm pretty sure most of them are in town, with just a few women here. Women who have been denied medical care and who have been kept in line with beatings and threatened with rape—or worse. So, what do you think?"

Baxter was glaring daggers at this point.

"Do you really expect them to support you at this moment? They are terrified and have been for some time."

"Shit," Baxter snapped. "So what will we do then, just sit here?"

But Tomas had already sent a message to Saul, who stepped forward through the kitchen.

"No," Saul stated, "we won't just sit here." He smiled and added, "The rest of the house is empty, and I've sent word that the compound is secured."

"It's not safe to leave the compound," Baxter snarled. "My guys know better than that."

"They all headed to town," Tomas muttered. "Nobody wanted to miss out on the opportunity to shoot the town up with all their weaponry and ammo."

Baxter stared at him, dumbfounded, then shook his head. "Fucking idiots."

"Yep. Without you at the helm, they've gotten wilder, crazier, and don't give a shit," Tomas noted. "They've come to think that they're invincible and that the world will just keep tolerating everything they do."

"Christ, that's downright embarrassing," Baxter sneered. "I suppose that you've got a whole mess of law enforcement on the way. You at least would have thought those idiots would have seen that coming."

"They should have, but they were too interested in playing war games, and they didn't think of anything else fast enough," Tomas stated. While he reached to answer his vibrating phone, Tomas looked over at Saul, who nodded.

"Go ahead," Saul said. "I'll search this guy."

As soon as he'd searched Baxter, Saul asked him, "Can you walk at all?"

Baxter shook his head. "I haven't been able to walk for some years," he replied bitterly. "My world became encapsulated in this damn chair—the beginning of the end."

"Yeah, it sure was," Saul agreed. "They would have followed you, but they wouldn't have followed her for long, especially not after all the damage she'd done to the command structure and to the code. They would have fractured under the pressure of figuring out who was strong enough to take over and to hold control."

Baxter nodded. "Life's a bitch."

"Then you die," Saul finished for him, with a note of satisfaction. He wheeled him outside onto the porch.

Tomas was behind him, saying, "Law enforcement is here."

As he headed out, FBI agents stood there, looking at Baxter, wearing smiles of satisfaction. "There you are," the lead agent noted cheerfully. "We've been looking for you for a while."

"Of course you have," Baxter stated, disgust in his voice. "Here I am, and you can bet I'll demand my rights too."

"Yeah. We'll see how much rights you'll get when we figure out how many murders you are involved in."

"I didn't murder anybody. Hell, I've been in this chair for years."

"Maybe not, but your word is law here," the agent stated. "And your minion Mary wasn't your wife?" He caught Baxter's backwards glance and went inside to take a look. He returned and glared at Baxter. "What the hell?"

Baxter remained silent.

"The world is a much better place without that vindictive bitch," Tomas stated. "She was as dangerous as hell. But, as far as I'm concerned, Baxter, you are just as culpable for the murders. She followed your law." Baxter looked over at the agents, then nodded and asked, "Any word on town? On Peaches at the hospital?"

"It's all good," the lead agent replied. "And your Cronus guy has been picked up too."

"And what about Amber and Dezi?" he asked.

"They're waiting for you," he murmured.

At that, he nodded and asked Saul, "Are you ready to go in?"

"Hell yeah."

As more FBI agents arrived, exiting their vehicles, Tomas counted at least twenty men. Turning to the FBI lead agent, Tomas added, "Quite a few women are here, several who are pregnant, and all of them are likely terrified. Some might try to defend the compound on some level, but I doubt they'll put up much of a fuss, especially if you tell them that Mary is dead and that Baxter is in custody. Most of them have been threatened with rape and murder, and several people have been killed on the property."

Saul smiled. "There's a graveyard too." Then he stopped, looked over at Tomas, and said, "Why don't you go on to town, and I'll stay a bit and show these guys around." Not waiting on Tomas's reply, Saul set off with a large group of agents to show them where the graves were.

Tomas hopped into Brutus's vehicle and headed back to town, back to Amber.

Chapter 13

I T WAS ALMOST anticlimactic to return to the hotel room to see Dezi, sitting inside with an ambulance driver checking his head to make sure he was okay. Even though he was protesting loudly and long, nobody was listening.

When Tomas walked inside the room, Amber took one look, cried out, and threw herself into his arms. He pulled her up close and whispered, "Now that's the kind of welcome I like."

She chuckled. "Seems like, since we first met, this is the only place I've been."

"And that's a good thing," he said. "You know you belong here." She raised an eyebrow. He grinned. "Hey, and I mean that in the nicest of ways."

"Good thing," she stated, "because, if you ever think I'll be part of a group like this, well, holy crap, are you misguided."

"Nope, not at all," he murmured. He smiled, tucked her up close, and looked over at Dezi. "How's the head, Dezi?"

"Solid, like a rock, just the way it's supposed to be," he snapped. "I'm fine." Then he turned serious and asked Tomas, "Get your shoulder cleaned up."

Tomas glared at him, but with Amber not listening to his protests, he submitted to the treatment.

Smirking, Dezi asked, "And where do you go from

here?"

"I'm staying in town to help sort out everything, especially to see that Peaches is set up and that the other women in the clan have a second chance, especially those who are pregnant. Saul is showing the FBI agents around the compound, like that graveyard, right now."

Dezi looked over at Amber. "What about you?"

"I need to sort out my life, I guess. For one thing, now that I have answers, and this has finally been brought to a close, without anybody else dying," she added, with an eye roll, "I guess I need to figure out what I'm doing with my life."

"I'll go get food and book a different room," Tomas noted, as he looked around. "This isn't even ours."

"Of course not, and, by the time we get out of here, it'll be too late to drive anywhere," she admitted.

"So we could stay here for the night then," Tomas said. He looked over at Dezi. "What about you?"

"Saul and I will bunk somewhere, so you two kids go have fun," he said, but such a disgruntled tone filled his voice that they both laughed.

Tomas hugged Amber as they walked outside. "Are you okay to just grab something here in town?"

"You think it's safe?"

"I think so. Levi got word that the clansmen in town were all arrested, even some of their more loyal spies too. Plus, I hear no more gunfire," he noted. "Or, if you prefer, we can just drive through somewhere, then take it back to a hotel room."

She thought about that and said, "You know what? I don't really trust too many people in town. A drive-through might be okay, but I would just as soon continue driving and never look back."

"We need some rest soon, but after we get food. Plus, I do kinda need to stay in the area, so I can help out at the compound, as needed."

"So let's drive out of town a little ways, get some food there. And what's this about a hotel room?"

"We'll stop and book one on our way out," he said, and that's what he did.

By the time they picked up burgers, fries, and some drinks, including coffee, and made it to their newest hotel room, it occurred to her that she hadn't even asked questions about their sleeping arrangements. "I automatically assumed there would be double beds again," she stated, staring at the one large bed, turning to face him with an accusatory look.

"And I did too," he said, studying the layout with a frown. "If you want, we can get it changed."

She thought about it, then shook her head. "No, it's probably not an issue."

"*Probably* not an issue?" he asked, turning to look at her.

"*Definitely* not an issue," she replied, with a smile.

"I'm glad to hear that," he said, with a teasing eye roll.

"What?" she asked. "You just lay one of those kisses on a woman, and they melt at your feet?" That got her a bright laugh.

"Wow, not what I expected you to say."

"That kiss of yours is deadly."

He shrugged. "Glad to hear it."

As they set down the food on the small table, he said, "It smells good. Let's have at it."

"Yeah, you're finally getting food."

"I wasn't particularly hungry last time, but I just didn't trust that guy."

"Why though? How did you know?"

"It was the way he kept looking around the room, like he was searching for stuff, trying to get information or something," he noted.

"*Huh*," she murmured, "I didn't get that at all."

"That's fine," he said. "You don't need to."

"What if it ever happens again?"

"Hopefully you'll find a much easier way to occupy your time now."

She laughed. "Actually I have a job. Or I had a job anyway. It may not still be there when I get back."

"What kind of a job?"

She smiled. "I've been working in insurance."

"There you go," he murmured. "They always need people in that field."

"Isn't that the truth?" she agreed.

By the time they had everything cleaned up after eating, she stretched out on the bed and said, "God, I'm so full."

"Too full?"

"Too full as in what context?"

He grinned. "Well, we could try something else to take your mind off this mess," he suggested, climbing onto the bed beside her.

"We could," she agreed, "but that doesn't sound terribly romantic."

"Is it romance you want?" he asked, as he rolled onto his side and looked down at her.

"Actually," she said, sliding her arms around his neck, "what I really want is another one of those kisses."

His eyebrows shot up, as he smiled, then pulled her close. "I'm pretty sure I can handle that, no problem."

When he lifted his head a second time, she just stared at

him, wordless. But a distant, almost clouded look was in his eyes too. "So it's not just me," she asked.

"Nah," he replied in a bit of a daze. "Definitely not."

"I was afraid I was the only one affected."

He shook his head. "And I was thinking that you were deadly."

"Not alone, I don't think so," she argued, "but I will admit that maybe it's the combination of the two of us."

He smiled, leaned over, and kissed her gently. "And that could be," he murmured.

She whispered, "I think we should check again." With her arms around his neck, she pulled him until he was fully on top of her. She smiled. "We definitely need to explore this further."

"And I'm definitely open to exploration," he teased, grinning broadly.

She reached up, kissed him gently, and then not so gently, until finally she laid one on him that she'd been wanting to do ever since she'd met him.

"I wasn't expecting this," he murmured. "Honestly, I didn't book the room for, … for this."

"Oh, I get it," she said, wiggling beneath him. "But honestly, I'm not wasting such a grand opportunity."

He would have chuckled again, except she had plastered her lips against his, and, wrapping an arm around him, she held him close.

"God, you feel good," she whispered. "I don't know, but maybe it's just the whole thing about coming so close to dying, plus I came so close to being trapped into a lifestyle that I wanted no part of, but this? … This feels right."

"If you're sure," he murmured. "It is awfully fast."

"I don't know about you," she murmured, "but I don't

need to be told a second time about what's important in life."

"No." He leaned over and kissed her gently. "And I know that. I get it. I'm just so damn happy that you're okay."

She smiled. "See? Now that's the right answer. Because life's been pretty shitty for a while, and I know that other people didn't have the benefit of your rescue, so I really appreciate it."

He nodded, kissed her gently, and whispered, "At least maybe you can walk away from this now."

"Yes, I plan on it," she stated. "I'm sorry for whatever decisions Annette made, as they obviously got her killed, but it's no longer in our hands." Smiling, she added, "What I want in my hands now"—she laughed, as she wiggled underneath him—"is you."

And, as she flipped him onto his back, she kneeled and quickly pulled her shirt over her head. "See? This is good."

He shook his head, stunned. "I've got no doubt." He grinned. "I'm just grateful."

She stopped, then looked at him when a confused expression. "For what?"

"That we're here, both of us together," he stated. "A couple times tonight I doubted if it would happen."

She stared at him, noting a fresh wound on his shoulder. She frowned at him.

"Baxter's shot just missed me, but his shot at Mary hit her."

Amber nodded. "I'm not sorry to hear about Mary. That was one evil woman. But I'm so very glad that you lived through that encounter with Baxter and Mary." And she unbuckled her jeans, then slipped off her shoes and socks, kicked them aside, her jeans coming off soon afterward. She clambered back onto the bed, just wearing her panties, and climbed atop Tomas once more.

"You know what? One thing that I really noticed about you," she admitted, "was how you always looked like you were completely bored, not even paying attention."

He flashed her a grin. "It throws everybody off," he shared. "They can't quite figure out what move I'll make next."

She chuckled. "I wasn't even sure myself for the longest time. But, after I saw you take out the first guy, I figured you knew what you were about and that I was just along for the ride."

"That's a wise move," he murmured, and he reached up his hand, stroking her flat belly to her rib cage and her plump breasts. "Good God," he whispered. "You are so damn gorgeous."

She looked dispassionately at her body. "If you're happy, I'm happy."

He chuckled and flipped her over to her back, then hopped up. "My turn."

"No," she said, "I want to undress you."

"Too bad, not this time," he replied, as he quickly divested himself of his clothing.

Once he was naked, already erect, she kneeled on the bed and reached out both hands for him. He sucked in his breath, as she wrapped one hand gently around him, moving up and down his tender skin. He felt the heat growing under her ministrations, as she smiled and whispered, "This won't take very long at all."

"Not the first time," he promised. "But the second time, I'll make sure you get more and more." And, with that, he flipped her until she was tucked up on the bed and underneath him.

She stared around in amazement. "I don't know how you did that." She giggled.

"It's a skill," he replied, then he lowered his head. "But not to worry. I've got a few more tricks to show you, but not right now. Right now … there's something much more important."

He lowered his head gently, then kissed her with all his might, and whispered, "This time is for us—no more bad memories, no more bad thoughts, no worries about friends or worries about me or about what'll happen," he said. "This is all about us right now."

She smiled, then kissed him gently, and whispered, "Thank God for that."

He nodded. "Sometimes you just have to park stuff, then let it go and move on." And he lowered his head, his tongue gently waging war with hers, before outlining her lips and slipping inside and out, mimicking what was to come.

She opened her thighs and wrapped her legs around him and whispered, "I've got absolutely no problem worrying about tomorrow," she added, "particularly if you have any plans of being a part of it."

"I would love to be in your life," he murmured, his kisses deepening with every word. "But only if that's something you want."

"Oh, it's absolutely what I want," she agreed. "Nothing like finding out that your life is passing you by and that you haven't fully lived it or enjoyed very much of it because you've spent so much time working and looking after other people." She shook her head. "It's time for a change." She flicked her tongue against his neck and whispered, "One of the first changes is doing what I want. And what I want is to spend time with you."

"Done," he said instantly. "But I do have a position with Levi. Or I might have a position with Levi anyway," he added, as an afterthought.

"If you do, then I'll be here when you get back, from whatever jobs you've got to go do. And, if you don't have to do something for Levi for some reason, I highly suggest we take a few days and spend them together." With that, she tilted her pelvis and nudged him gently. "But first I think you belong somewhere."

"Where's that?" he asked, almost in a daze.

"Home," she whispered and pushed up against him. Taking her meaning, he'd lifted back ever-so-slightly, then repositioned himself, and, in one smooth motion, drove into the heart of her.

She groaned and arched underneath. "God." Ecstasy and pain racked her with such an incredible feeling.

"You okay?" he asked, as he tried to hold back, but that was the last thing she wanted.

"I'm more than okay," she whispered. "I'm better than I've ever been." She twisted beneath him. "But you've got to move."

He chuckled. "And if I don't want to?" he teased.

"I might manage it on my own," she noted, gently pulsing underneath him. "But that'll just drive both of us nuts."

"Okay, I'm game," he whispered.

Frustrated, she immediately started to lift, as he drove down faster and deeper and harder, until she was screaming beneath him.

Tomas threw her over the edge and followed her with a groan and a shout of his own. Afterward, he cuddled her close and whispered, "I really didn't think anything like this was possible."

"But you wanted it to be," she said against his lips.

"And how do you know that?" he asked, studying her.

She smiled. "Because I know when a man wants me. I was just afraid it would only be for a short time."

"Nope, I don't do short-term," he stated. "I'm all about here and now and the future as a package deal." He paused, then asked her, "And you?"

She murmured, "Absolutely." As she snuggled up against him, she whispered, "Thank God."

Epilogue

ONCE AGAIN IN the massive dining room at their compound, Levi looked over at Tomas and Amber, sitting close together at the huge dining room table. "Ah, the magic strikes again?"

"Maybe," Tomas said, with a nod. "Although I didn't know anything about your matchmaking plans, so a little more warning would have been nice."

"Nope," Ice stated, as she joined them, walking from the big kitchen area. "It happens with or without warning. You just can't escape it." She looked over at Carson and grinned. "You are next."

"Like hell," he replied. "I just started working for you guys. I'm not next at all."

"Yep, you are," Levi confirmed. "It always happens, so you might as well just accept it now."

"I haven't met anybody," Carson noted, shaking his head. "So it's hardly an issue at the moment."

"Well, you're likely to, on this next job," Ice added seriously.

He looked at her and smiled. "Oh, boy, what have you got planned for me?"

"Only the best for an old friend," she teased, smiling back at him.

He groaned. "That could mean anything though."

"True," she said, with a bright smile. "We've got an interesting case."

He shook his head. "I'm not convinced. Sounds more like a job you're just trying to give me to get me out of your hair."

"If that were the case," she said, "I would just put you to work out on the back forty. But, in this case, we have an old friend of mine. She's local, so she's in town here, but she thinks somebody is trying to kill her."

He stared at her in surprise. "Do we do that kind of job?"

"Not often, but, like I said, we're doing it as a favor for a friend. She's eighty-two."

He winced. "And?"

"I think she could be right."

He stared at her in shock and asked, "What about the police?"

"She already talked to them. She has no proof, no motive, no nothing. There are no suspects and nothing for them to go on. I've been talking to the police myself," she admitted. "They don't know how they can help because they don't have anything to go on with any of this. They can drive by her place every once in a while, but that's it."

"So, I'll provide security to an eighty-two-year-old woman, who thinks somebody is trying to kill her?" he asked in horror.

"And her granddaughter."

He narrowed his gaze at Ice. "What granddaughter?"

"Her name is Eva, and she's an art student."

"*Great*," he replied. "That'll get her a job and a steady income—not."

She laughed. "Oh, I wouldn't say anything about that

until you see her art," Ice said, with a bright smile. "But the bottom line is that they need somebody there to see if anything's going on or not."

"Somebody who's not connected. A fresh pair of eyes, I presume?" Carson asked.

Ice nodded. "Exactly. So I said I'd send you in for a week, but, beyond that, I can't do much more."

"Even at that," he noted, "that's generous of you."

"Like I said, she's a friend. And her influence helps us quite a bit too," she added. "I help my friends whenever I can."

"Good enough," Carson said. "How hard it can be?"

"I wouldn't say that because it could be serious. She has a lot of money, and I don't know if that has anything to do with the threats or not. I haven't delved into her financials or anything else because she is such a good friend," she explained, with a wry smile. "If you find anything or see anything that's suspicious or if you think something's going on that needs further investigation, you let me know, and I'll be on it in a heartbeat," she stated.

"And when am I going?" he asked.

"Now," she said, looking at her watch. "By the time you get there and get settled in, you should be just in time."

"For what?"

At that, Levi started to laugh. "I noticed Ice left this part to the last." He looked at his wife affectionately, as she grinned.

"For the haunting," she added.

"*Haunting*?" Carson asked.

"Yeah," she stated, staring at him intently. "Apparently things go bump in the night. So I want you to find out what it is, who is behind it, and whether any of those bumps are intended to kill her."

"If she's that old, anything like that could cause a heart attack," he noted cautiously.

She nodded. "And that's for you to figure out. Oh, and, by the way, say hi to Eva for me."

This concludes Book 27 of Heroes for Hire: Tomas's Trials.
Read about Carson's Choice: Heroes for Hire, Book 28

Heroes for Hire: Carson's Choice (Book #28)

Carson is pleasantly surprised by the job Levi assigns him, until Carson hears all the details. An elderly friend of Ice's believes someone is out to kill her. But she has no proof, no suspects, no motives. The police think she's imagining things and won't look into the case any further. However, after meeting this lady … and her granddaughter, Carson has his own suspicions.

Eva doesn't want Carson in the house. She doesn't want anyone in the house, if she were honest. As an artist, she loves her space, her freedom, and especially her privacy. This man is a distraction and soon could become so much more—her muse. And that is dangerous on various levels.

But, if his presence saves her grandmother, then Eva will do anything to keep her safe even put up with the man that makes her feel things she had never expected.

Find Book 28 here!

To find out more visit Dale Mayer's website.

https://geni.us/DMCarsonUniversal

Other Military Series by Dale Mayer

SEALs of Honor

Heroes for Hire

SEALs of Steel

The K9 Files

The Mavericks

Bullards Battle

Hathaway House

Terkel's Team

Ryland's Reach: Bullard's Battle
(Book #1)

Welcome to a new stand-alone but interconnected series from Dale Mayer. This is Bullard's story—and that of his team's. All raw, rough, incredibly capable men who have one goal: to find out who was behind the attack on their leader, before the attacker, or attackers, return to finish the job.

Stay tuned for more nonstop action as the men narrow down their suspects … and find a way to let love back into their own empty lives.

His rescue from the ocean after a horrible plane explosion was his top priority, in any way, shape, or form. A small sailboat and a nurse to do the job was more than Ryland hoped for.

When Tabi somehow drags him and his buddy Garret onboard and surprisingly gets them to a naval ship close by, Ryland figures he'd used up all his luck and his friend's too. Sure enough, those who attacked the plane they were in weren't content to let him slowly die in the ocean. No. Surviving had made him a target all over again.

Tabi isn't expecting her sailing holiday to include the rescue of two badly injured men and then to end with the loss of her beloved sailboat. Her instincts save them, but now she finds it tough to let them go—even as more of Bullard's team members come to them—until it becomes apparent that not only are Bullard and his men still targets … but she is too.

B ULLARD CHECKED THAT the helicopter was loaded with their bags and that his men were ready to leave.

He walked back one more time, his gaze on Ice. She'd never looked happier, never looked more perfect. His heart ached, but he knew she remained a caring friend and always would be. He opened his arms; she ran into them, and he held her close, whispering, "The offer still stands."

She leaned back and smiled up at him. "Maybe if and when Levi's been gone for a long enough time for me to forget," she said in all seriousness.

"That's not happening. You two, now three, will live long and happy lives together," he said, smiling down at the woman knew to be the most beautiful, inside and out. She would never be his, but he always kept a little corner of his heart open and available, in case she wanted to surprise him and to slide inside.

And then he realized she'd already been a part of his heart all this time. That was a good ten to fifteen years by now. But she kept herself in the friend category, and he understood because she and Levi, partners and now parents, were perfect together.

Bullard reached out and shook Levi's hand. "It was a hell of a blast," he said. "When you guys do a big splash, you really do a *big* splash."

Ice laughed. "A few days at home sounds perfect for me now."

"It looks great," he said, his hands on his hips as he surveyed the people in the massive pool surrounded by the palm trees, all designed and decked out by Ice. Right beside all the war machines that he heartily approved of. He grinned at her. "When are you coming over to visit?" His gaze went to Levi, raising his eyebrows back at her. "You guys should come over for a week or two or three."

"It's not a bad idea," Levi said. "We could use a long holiday, just not yet."

"That sounds familiar." Bullard grinned. "Anyway, I'm off. We'll hit the airport and then pick up the plane and head home." He added, "As always, call if you need me."

Everybody raised a hand as he returned to the helicopter and his buddy who was flying him to the airport. Ice had volunteered to shuttle him there, but he hadn't wanted to take her away from her family or to prolong the goodbye. He hopped inside, waving at everybody as the helicopter lifted. Two of his men, Ryland and Garret, were in the back seats. They always traveled with him.

Bullard would pick up the rest of his men in Australia. He stared down at the compound as he flew overhead. He preferred his compound at home, but damn they'd done a nice job here.

With everybody on the ground screaming goodbye, Bullard sailed over Houston, heading toward the airport. His two men never said a word. They all knew how he felt about Ice. But not one of them would cross that line and say anything. At least not if they expected to still have jobs.

It was one thing to fall in love with another man's woman, but another thing to fall in love with a woman who was so unique, so different, and so absolutely perfect that you knew, just knew, there was no hope of finding anybody else like her. But she and Levi had been together way before Bullard had ever met her, which made it that much more heartbreaking.

Still, he'd turned and looked forward. He had a full roster of jobs himself to focus on when he got home. Part of him was tired of the life; another part of him couldn't wait to head out on the next adventure. He managed to run everything from his command centers in one or two of his locations. He'd spent a lot of time and effort at the second one and kept a full team at both locations, yet preferred to spend most of his time at the old one. It felt more like home to him, and he'd like to be there now, but still had many more days before that could happen.

The helicopter lowered to the tarmac, he stepped out, said his goodbyes and walked across to where his private plane waited. It was one of the things that he loved, being a pilot of both helicopters and airplanes, and owning both birds himself.

That again was another way he and Ice were part of the same team, of the same mind-set. He'd been looking for another woman like Ice for himself, but no such luck. Sure, lots were around for short-term relationships, but most of them couldn't handle his lifestyle or the violence of the world that he lived in. He understood that.

The ones who did had a hard edge to them that he found difficult to live with. Bullard appreciated everybody's being alert and aware, but if there wasn't some softness in the women, they seemed to turn cold all the way through.

As he boarded his small plane, Ryland and Garret following behind, Bullard called out in his loud voice, "Let's go, slow pokes. We've got a long flight ahead of us."

The men grinned, confident Bullard was teasing, as was his usual routine during their off-hours.

"Well, we're ready, not sure about you though ..." Ryland said, smirking.

"We're waiting on you this time," Garret added with a chuckle. "Good thing you're the boss."

Bullard grinned at his two right-hand men. "Isn't that the truth?" He dropped his bags at one of the guys' feet and said, "Stow all this stuff, will you? I want to get our flight path cleared and get the hell out of here."

They'd all enjoyed the break. He tried to get over once a year to visit Ice and Levi and same in reverse. But it was time to get back to business. He started up the engines, got confirmation from the tower. They were heading to Australia for this next job. He really wanted to go straight back to Africa, but it would be a while yet. They'd refuel in Honolulu.

Ryland came in and sat down in the copilot's spot, buckled in, then asked, "You ready?"

Bullard laughed. "When have you ever known me *not* to be ready?" At that, he taxied down the runway. Before long he was up in the air, at cruising level, and heading to Hawaii. "Gotta love these views from up here," Bullard said. "This place is magical."

"It is once you get up above all the smog," he said. "Why Australia again?"

"Remember how we were supposed to check out that newest compound in Australia that I've had my eye on? Besides the alpha team is coming off that ugly job in Sydney. We'll give them a day or two of R&R then head home."

"Right. We could have some equally ugly payback on that job."

Bullard shrugged. "That goes for most of our jobs. It's the life."

"And don't you have enough compounds to look after?"

"Yes I do, but that kid in me still looks to take over the world. Just remember that."

"Better you go home to Africa and look after your first two compounds," Ryland said.

"Maybe," Bullard admitted. "But it seems hard to not continue expanding."

"You need a partner," Ryland said abruptly. "That might ease the savage beast inside. Keep you home more."

"Well, the only one I like," he said, "is married to my best friend."

"I'm sorry about that," Ryland said quietly. "What a shit deal."

"No," Bullard said. "I came on the scene last. They were always meant to be together. Especially now they are a family."

"If you say so," Ryland said.

Bullard nodded. "Damn right, I say so."

And that set the tone for the next many hours. They landed in Hawaii, and while they fueled up everybody got off to stretch their legs by walking around outside a bit as this was a small private airstrip, not exactly full of hangars and tourists. Then they hopped back on board again for takeoff.

"I can fly," Ryland offered as they took off.

"We'll switch in a bit," Bullard said. "Surprisingly, I'm doing okay yet, but I'll let you take her down."

"Yeah, it's still a long flight," Ryland said studying the islands below. It was a stunning view of the area.

"I love the islands here. Sometimes I just wonder about the benefit of, you know, crashing into the sea, coming up on a deserted island, and finding the simple life again," Bullard said with a laugh.

"I hear you," Ryland said. "Every once in a while, I wonder the same."

Several hours later Ryland looked up and said abruptly, "We've made good time considering we've already passed Fiji."

Bullard yawned.

"Let's switch."

Bullard smiled, nodded, and said, "Fine. I'll hand it over to you."

Just then a funny noise came from the engine on the right side.

They looked at each other, and Ryland said, "Uh-oh. That's not good news."

Boom!

And the plane exploded.

Find Bullard's Battle (Book #1) here!

To find out more visit Dale Mayer's website.

https://geni.us/DMRylandUniversal

Damon's Deal: Terkel's Team
(Book #1)

Welcome to a brand-new series from *USA Today* best-selling author Dale Mayer, where dark-ops SEALs have special senses and skills, needed to solve intrigue, betrayal, and … murder. A series with all the elements you've come to love, plus so much more, … including psychics!

ICE POURED HERSELF a coffee and sat down at the compound's massive dining room table with the others. When her phone rang, she smiled at the number displayed. "Hey, Terk. How're you doing?" She put the call on Speakerphone.

"I'm okay," Terkel said, his voice distracted and tight.

"Terk?" Merk called from across the table. He got up and walked closer and sat across from Levi. "You don't sound too good, brother. What's up?"

"I'm fine," Terk said. "Or I will be. Right now, things are blown to shit."

"As in literally?" Merk asked.

"The entire group," Terk said, "they're all gone. I had a solid team of eight, and they're all gone."

"Dead?"

Several others stood to join them, gathered around Ice's phone. Levi stepped forward, his hand on Ice's shoulder. "Terk? Are they all dead?"

"No." Terk took a deep breath. "I'm not making sense. I'm sorry."

"Take it easy," Ice said, her voice calm and reassuring. "What do you mean, *they're all gone*?"

"All their abilities are gone," he said. "Something's happened to them. Somebody has deliberately removed whatever super senses they could utilize—or what we have been utilizing for the last ten years for the government." His tone was bitter. "When the US gov recently closed us down, they promised that our black ops department would never rise again, but I didn't expect them to attack us personally."

"What are you talking about?" Merk said in alarm, standing up now to stare at Ice's phone. "Are you in danger?"

"Maybe? I don't know," Terk said. "I need to find out exactly what the hell's going on."

"What can we do to help?" Ice asked.

Terk gave a broken laugh. "That's not why I'm calling. Well, it is, but it isn't."

Ice looked at Merk, who frowned, as he shook his head. Ice knew he and the others had heard Terk's stressed out tone and the completely confusing bits and pieces coming from his mouth. Ice said, "Terk, you're not making sense again. Take a breath and explain. Please. You're scaring me."

Terk took a long slow deep breath. "Tell Stone to open the gate," he said. "She's out there."

"Who's out there?" Levi asked, hopped up, looked outside, and shrugged.

"She's coming up the road now. You have to let her in."

"Who? Why?"

"*Because*," he said, "she's also harnessed with C-4."

"Jesus," Levi said, bolting to display the camera feeds to the big screen in the room. "Is it live?"

"It is, and she's been sent to you."

"Well, that's an interesting move," Ice said, her voice sharp, activating her comm to connect to Stone in the control room. "Who's after us?"

"I think it's rebels within the Iranian government. But it could be our own government. I don't know anymore," Terk snapped. "I also don't know how they got her so close to you. Or how they pinned your connection to me," he said. "I've been very careful."

"We can look after ourselves," Ice said immediately. "But who is this woman to you?"

"She's pregnant," he said, "so that adds to the intensity here."

"Understood. So who is the father? Is he connected somehow?"

There was silence on the other end.

Merk said, "Terk, talk to us."

"She's carrying my baby," Terk replied, his voice heavy.

Merk, his expression grim, looked at Ice, her face mirroring his shock. He asked, "How do you know her, Terk?"

"Brother, you don't understand," Terk said. "I've never met this woman before in my life." And, with that, the phone went dead.

Find Terkel's Team (Book #1) here!

To find out more visit Dale Mayer's website.

https://geni.us/DMTTDamonUniversal

Author's Note

Thank you for reading Tomas's Trials: Heroes for Hire, Book 27! If you enjoyed the book, please take a moment and leave a short review.

Dear reader,

I love to hear from readers, and you can contact me at my website: www.dalemayer.com or at my Facebook author page. To be informed of new releases and special offers, sign up for my newsletter or follow me on BookBub. And if you are interested in joining Dale Mayer's Reader Group, here is the Facebook sign up page.
http://geni.us/DaleMayerFBGroup

Cheers,
Dale Mayer

About the Author

Dale Mayer is a *USA Today* best-selling author, best known for her SEALs military romances, her Psychic Visions series, and her Lovely Lethal Garden cozy series. Her contemporary romances are raw and full of passion and emotion (Broken But ... Mending, Hathaway House series). Her thrillers will keep you guessing (Kate Morgan, By Death series), and her romantic comedies will keep you giggling (*It's a Dog's Life*, a stand-alone novella; and the Broken Protocols series, starring Charming Marvin, the cat).

Dale honors the stories that come to her—and some of them are crazy, break all the rules and cross multiple genres!

To go with her fiction, she also writes nonfiction in many different fields, with books available on résumé writing, companion gardening, and the US mortgage system. All her books are available in print and ebook format.

Connect with Dale Mayer Online

Dale's Website – www.dalemayer.com
Twitter – @DaleMayer
Facebook Page – geni.us/DaleMayerFBFanPage
Facebook Group – geni.us/DaleMayerFBGroup
BookBub – geni.us/DaleMayerBookbub
Instagram – geni.us/DaleMayerInstagram
Goodreads – geni.us/DaleMayerGoodreads
Newsletter – geni.us/DaleNews

Also by Dale Mayer

Published Adult Books:

Bullard's Battle

Ryland's Reach, Book 1

Cain's Cross, Book 2

Eton's Escape, Book 3

Garret's Gambit, Book 4

Kano's Keep, Book 5

Fallon's Flaw, Book 6

Quinn's Quest, Book 7

Bullard's Beauty, Book 8

Bullard's Best, Book 9

Terkel's Team

Damon's Deal, Book 1

Wade's War, Book 2

Gage's Goal, Book 3

Calum's Contact, Book 4

Kate Morgan

Simon Says… Hide, Book 1

Simon Says… Jump, Book 2

Simon Says… Ride, Book 3

Simon Says… Scream, Book 4

Hathaway House

Aaron, Book 1

Brock, Book 2

Cole, Book 3

Denton, Book 4

Elliot, Book 5

Finn, Book 6

Gregory, Book 7

Heath, Book 8

Iain, Book 9

Jaden, Book 10

Keith, Book 11

Lance, Book 12

Melissa, Book 13

Nash, Book 14

Owen, Book 15

Percy, Book 16

Hathaway House, Books 1–3

Hathaway House, Books 4–6

Hathaway House, Books 7–9

The K9 Files

Ethan, Book 1

Pierce, Book 2

Zane, Book 3

Blaze, Book 4

Lucas, Book 5

Parker, Book 6

Carter, Book 7

Weston, Book 8

Greyson, Book 9

Rowan, Book 10

Caleb, Book 11

Kurt, Book 12

Tucker, Book 13

Harley, Book 14

Kyron, Book 15

Jenner, Book 16

The K9 Files, Books 1–2

The K9 Files, Books 3–4

The K9 Files, Books 5–6

The K9 Files, Books 7–8

The K9 Files, Books 9–10

The K9 Files, Books 11–12

Lovely Lethal Gardens

Arsenic in the Azaleas, Book 1

Bones in the Begonias, Book 2

Corpse in the Carnations, Book 3

Daggers in the Dahlias, Book 4

Evidence in the Echinacea, Book 5

Footprints in the Ferns, Book 6

Gun in the Gardenias, Book 7

Handcuffs in the Heather, Book 8

Ice Pick in the Ivy, Book 9

Jewels in the Juniper, Book 10

Killer in the Kiwis, Book 11

Lifeless in the Lilies, Book 12

Murder in the Marigolds, Book 13

Nabbed in the Nasturtiums, Book 14

Offed in the Orchids, Book 15

Poison in the Pansies, Book 16

Quarry in the Quince, Book 17

Lovely Lethal Gardens, Books 1–2

Lovely Lethal Gardens, Books 3–4

Lovely Lethal Gardens, Books 5–6

Lovely Lethal Gardens, Books 7–8

Lovely Lethal Gardens, Books 9–10

Psychic Vision Series

Tuesday's Child

Hide 'n Go Seek

Maddy's Floor

Garden of Sorrow

Knock Knock…

Rare Find

Eyes to the Soul

Now You See Her

Shattered

Into the Abyss

Seeds of Malice

Eye of the Falcon

Itsy-Bitsy Spider

Unmasked

Deep Beneath

From the Ashes

Stroke of Death

Ice Maiden

Snap, Crackle...

What If...

Talking Bones

Psychic Visions Books 1–3

Psychic Visions Books 4–6

Psychic Visions Books 7–9

By Death Series

Touched by Death

Haunted by Death

Chilled by Death

By Death Books 1–3

Broken Protocols – Romantic Comedy Series

Cat's Meow

Cat's Pajamas

Cat's Cradle

Cat's Claus

Broken Protocols 1-4

Broken and... Mending

Skin

Scars

Scales (of Justice)

Broken but... Mending 1-3

Glory

Genesis

Tori

Celeste

Glory Trilogy

Biker Blues

Morgan: Biker Blues, Volume 1

Cash: Biker Blues, Volume 2

SEALs of Honor

Mason: SEALs of Honor, Book 1

Hawk: SEALs of Honor, Book 2

Dane: SEALs of Honor, Book 3

Swede: SEALs of Honor, Book 4

Shadow: SEALs of Honor, Book 5

Cooper: SEALs of Honor, Book 6

Markus: SEALs of Honor, Book 7

Evan: SEALs of Honor, Book 8

Mason's Wish: SEALs of Honor, Book 9

Chase: SEALs of Honor, Book 10

Brett: SEALs of Honor, Book 11

Devlin: SEALs of Honor, Book 12

Easton: SEALs of Honor, Book 13

Ryder: SEALs of Honor, Book 14

Macklin: SEALs of Honor, Book 15

Corey: SEALs of Honor, Book 16

Warrick: SEALs of Honor, Book 17

Tanner: SEALs of Honor, Book 18

Jackson: SEALs of Honor, Book 19

Kanen: SEALs of Honor, Book 20

Nelson: SEALs of Honor, Book 21

Taylor: SEALs of Honor, Book 22

Colton: SEALs of Honor, Book 23

Troy: SEALs of Honor, Book 24

Axel: SEALs of Honor, Book 25

Baylor: SEALs of Honor, Book 26

Hudson: SEALs of Honor, Book 27

Lachlan: SEALs of Honor, Book 28

SEALs of Honor, Books 1–3

SEALs of Honor, Books 4–6

SEALs of Honor, Books 7–10

SEALs of Honor, Books 11–13

SEALs of Honor, Books 14–16

SEALs of Honor, Books 17–19

SEALs of Honor, Books 20–22

SEALs of Honor, Books 23–25

Heroes for Hire

Levi's Legend: Heroes for Hire, Book 1

Stone's Surrender: Heroes for Hire, Book 2

Merk's Mistake: Heroes for Hire, Book 3

Rhodes's Reward: Heroes for Hire, Book 4

Flynn's Firecracker: Heroes for Hire, Book 5

Logan's Light: Heroes for Hire, Book 6

Harrison's Heart: Heroes for Hire, Book 7

Saul's Sweetheart: Heroes for Hire, Book 8

Dakota's Delight: Heroes for Hire, Book 9

Tyson's Treasure: Heroes for Hire, Book 10

Jace's Jewel: Heroes for Hire, Book 11

Rory's Rose: Heroes for Hire, Book 12

Brandon's Bliss: Heroes for Hire, Book 13

Liam's Lily: Heroes for Hire, Book 14

North's Nikki: Heroes for Hire, Book 15

Anders's Angel: Heroes for Hire, Book 16

Reyes's Raina: Heroes for Hire, Book 17

Dezi's Diamond: Heroes for Hire, Book 18

Vince's Vixen: Heroes for Hire, Book 19

Ice's Icing: Heroes for Hire, Book 20

Johan's Joy: Heroes for Hire, Book 21

Galen's Gemma: Heroes for Hire, Book 22

Zack's Zest: Heroes for Hire, Book 23

Bonaparte's Belle: Heroes for Hire, Book 24

Noah's Nemesis: Heroes for Hire, Book 25

Tomas's Trials: Heroes for Hire, Book 26

Heroes for Hire, Books 1–3

Heroes for Hire, Books 4–6

Heroes for Hire, Books 7–9

Heroes for Hire, Books 10–12

Heroes for Hire, Books 13–15

Heroes for Hire, Books 16–18

Heroes for Hire, Books 19–21

Heroes for Hire, Books 22–24

SEALs of Steel

Badger: SEALs of Steel, Book 1

Erick: SEALs of Steel, Book 2

Cade: SEALs of Steel, Book 3

Talon: SEALs of Steel, Book 4

Laszlo: SEALs of Steel, Book 5

Geir: SEALs of Steel, Book 6

Jager: SEALs of Steel, Book 7

The Final Reveal: SEALs of Steel, Book 8

SEALs of Steel, Books 1–4

SEALs of Steel, Books 5–8

SEALs of Steel, Books 1–8

The Mavericks

Kerrick, Book 1

Griffin, Book 2

Jax, Book 3

Beau, Book 4

Asher, Book 5

Ryker, Book 6

Miles, Book 7

Nico, Book 8

Keane, Book 9

Lennox, Book 10

Gavin, Book 11

Shane, Book 12

Diesel, Book 13

Jerricho, Book 14

Killian, Book 15

Hatch, Book 16

Corbin, Book 17

The Mavericks, Books 1–2

The Mavericks, Books 3–4

The Mavericks, Books 5–6

The Mavericks, Books 7–8

The Mavericks, Books 9–10

The Mavericks, Books 11–12

Collections

Dare to Be You…

Dare to Love…

Dare to be Strong…

RomanceX3

Standalone Novellas

It's a Dog's Life

Riana's Revenge

Second Chances

Published Young Adult Books:

Family Blood Ties Series

Vampire in Denial

Vampire in Distress

Vampire in Design

Vampire in Deceit

Vampire in Defiance

Vampire in Conflict

Vampire in Chaos

Vampire in Crisis

Vampire in Control

Vampire in Charge

Family Blood Ties Set 1–3

Family Blood Ties Set 1–5

Family Blood Ties Set 4–6

Family Blood Ties Set 7–9

Sian's Solution, A Family Blood Ties Series Prequel
    Novelette

Design series

Dangerous Designs

Deadly Designs

Darkest Designs

Design Series Trilogy

Standalone

In Cassie's Corner

Gem Stone (a Gemma Stone Mystery)

Time Thieves

Published Non-Fiction Books:

Career Essentials

Career Essentials: The Résumé

Career Essentials: The Cover Letter

Career Essentials: The Interview

Career Essentials: 3 in 1